O Positive

Morgan M. Steele

Also by Morgan M. Steele:

L.O.S.T. and F.O.U.N.D.
Recensere: The Lost Queen
Doing Just Fine
The Averagers: a parody

Steele Bookcase Publishing

ISBN-10: 1732663025
ISBN-13: 978-1-7326630-2-2

For my roommate Daly,

thank you for many, many *Twilight*-filled days.

And nights.

Also, afternoons.

Chapter 1

Contrary to popular belief, being four hundred years old did not make losing people any easier. Elizabeth Bloodmere knew this better than most. Of course, she'd gotten better at it over the years, or so she'd like to think. The way things were, it would be in her best interest to not get attached, but what was life without making connections? No, it was meant to be this way, to happen like this, and she was doomed to feel every loss as it came, each just as real and painful as the last.

Today, it was Gladys Smith's funeral she'd attend. Elizabeth hadn't known Gladys for all that long, and admittedly, she didn't know her all that well. The old woman had been her roommate, too stubborn to let her children put her in a retirement home, and instead choosing to live with another old soul independently. Gladys had gone blind a few years before she'd moved in with Elizabeth, so she was unaware of her beautiful roommate's unusual schedule and her strange habits, and even *more* unaware that said roommate appeared to be approximately twenty-six years old despite the fact that she was much, much older.

Elizabeth's expert fingers manipulated the clasp of her favorite string of pearls until they sat in place resting against her collarbones. By now, she supposed, she should be used to dressing up for funerals, but it still wasn't something that came naturally to her. Yet, despite the emotional challenge, she managed to find a suitable black dress and a sensible pair of heels in her closet. It was vintage, although, it hadn't been when she bought it.

She took out her earrings, replacing them with a pair that matched her necklace, smeared another coat of red lipstick onto her lips, and gave her reflection one last once-over before standing from her vanity.

"You look *fine*, quit fussing."

"I know, I know...Thank you, Elijah," she replied, plucking her purse up from its spot on her bed. "I'll be back before dinner." She gave the cat's head an affectionate scratch before leaving him to nap in his little patch of sunlight.

Elizabeth's high heels clicked with every step down the stairs. She hadn't been down in the living room since Gladys had passed, choosing instead to take a few days to herself to let things settle. One look at the large, handmade blanket draped over the back of the couch was enough to make her heart sink. She'd sat beside Gladys on so many nights while the old woman knitted it little by little. She'd insisted that they needed one for their couch; she'd always had a blanket draped over the back of the couch in her previous house when her husband, Harold, was still alive. It made the place feel like home, she'd said, because even without her eyesight, she could still feel the soft yarn patterns of the blanket beneath her withered fingertips.

Letting out a long sigh, Elizabeth spritzed her plants with water before walking out the front door and locking it behind her.

It was sunnier than she expected it to be, she noted as she put on her favorite pair of sunglasses, large and dark, a special brand to protect her sensitive eyes from the harmful rays. She always thought a funeral was best done in the rain, or at the very least, under an overcast sky. It set the mood better.

Elizabeth's favorite black sun hat cast her face in harsh shadows, making her look darker and more mysterious than she'd like, but it effectively blocked out the bright sunlight. After all, people like her weren't known for their love of the sun.

Tucking a strand of raven hair behind a slightly pointed ear, she opened the door of her car and began the drive to the Great City Cemetery. It wasn't too terribly far from her townhouse, which was tucked into the city's historical district. She could have walked, if she was feeling up to it, but after the lonely pair of days she'd finished, she wasn't in any mood to. No, a drive would give her a good excuse to go somewhere after the funeral, pick up something for dinner, maybe, or just try to get her mind off of it.

Gladys hadn't been one for churches. She'd told Elizabeth that growing up, her father had been a pastor, and that was enough to keep her away from organized religion as soon as she was out from under his roof. She didn't like the things the churches preached these days, she'd told her. She didn't like the hate they taught when there should have only been love. She didn't like that her gay granddaughter felt uncomfortable when she was forced to attend a Christmas or Easter service with the rest of their family.

"I was never one for churches either," Elizabeth had reassured her with a sly smile, although she never quite gave Gladys a reason.

That was why instead of holding the service in a church or chapel, Gladys' family and friends had gathered under a pavilion in the cemetery, a wreath of roses mounted on the easel next to her casket. Elizabeth walked to the little podium at the back of the pavilion that was holding the guestbook and jotted down her latest alias. She was always Elizabeth Something, but never for very long. In fact, she had a feeling she'd be done being Elizabeth Simon in a year or two, and then she'd be on to whatever name felt right for the next decade.

Elizabeth found a seat in the last row of chairs, crossing her legs and propping her program open. She'd been through enough of these things to know the gist of them. There'd be some songs, some of Gladys' family would speak, and then they'd lower her into the ground at her little plot of land beside Harold. She doubted she'd stay for that; nor would she go to whatever secondary location they were using for the late afternoon luncheon after. She was simply here to pay her respects, and then she'd be out of their hair. Elizabeth figured she could find time to bring Gladys some flowers in a few days once all of the people were gone.

The service was nice and simple, the way she would have liked it. Gladys wasn't one for flashy things. Elizabeth made sure to say something to Gladys' granddaughter on her way out, the only member of the old woman's family she'd ever met before. Though Gladys had insisted she didn't have favorites, Elizabeth could tell her late roommate saw something special in Robin, and she made sure to pass that much along, giving the girl her condolences before complimenting her on the thin rainbow-colored bracelet she was always sporting around her wrist, one little burst of color, even in a place as bleak as this.

And then it was over. She'd been dreading it for days, and it was already over, as fleeting as mortal life in the sprawling city she'd called home for so long. She hit a drive-thru in the suburbs before heading home, parking in her spot in front of her colonial townhouse. It was just her now. Her and the cat.

When she opened the door, he was sitting on the floor looking up at her with those big green eyes. They were the only sliver of his humanity his curse allowed him to keep.

"How was the service?" The gray cat's tail waved curiously. He was fairly certain the limb had a mind of its own.

"She would have liked it," Elizabeth answered plainly, setting the grease-stained fast food bag on the table. "It was simple and meaningful. Not preachy, not tacky. I'm bringing her flowers later on, if you'd like to accompany."

"I just might." Elijah tilted his head, his back leg raising to scratch behind his ear. He stared at the paw, watching it. Even after all of these years, he still wasn't used to his own cattish behavior. "I hope you brought me French fries."

"How could I forget?" Elizabeth's porcelain fingers retrieved the cardboard carrier from the bag. She held it out for the cat, who gripped it between his teeth before scampering off into the next room, leaving her to follow him shortly after. In all reality, she didn't *need* to eat anything. Her body was satisfied by...other things, but she was hoping an old-fashioned burger would help get rid of the ache in her chest. And it did. A little. But that was better than nothing, she supposed.

Things would get better, she knew. Time would heal the wound, as it always did.

Once they were both finished, Elizabeth got rid of the trash, prying the salt-covered fry box from Elijah, who was desperately lapping at the inside of it. He looked up at her apologetically, but she only chuckled and shook her head at him. When she returned to the living room, she stared at the blanket on the couch for a long time before she reached out for it, pulling it from its spot and draping it across her legs as she sat.

Elijah looked at her, eventually deciding to climb into her lap. With both of his little paws, he secured her hand in his grasp and pulled it right on top of his head, a rare invitation, to say the very least. Gently, Elizabeth began to scratch him between the ears. She did feel a little better. She'd miss Gladys, sure, but there were a lot of people in her life, one being her adorable gray cat who hated being a cat.

It would get better. Maybe not right away, but it would. She just had to hang in there.

Chapter 2

"Liz, open up." Jack's fist rapped against the door. He'd given up on her brass knocker about three minutes prior. "It's hot out here, come on—"

The door swung open, leaving the tawny-haired man standing there wide-eyed, his fist in the air. Elizabeth's long, raven hair was up in a towel, her porcelain skin freshly moisturized. She tilted her head, grinning as she opened the door a little further and let him slip past her.

"I heard you when you knocked the first time, I was just in the shower. I'm sorry."

"I thought you might be huddled in a blanket cocoon, eating ice cream by the gallon, so I much prefer the alternative," he teased, setting his portable cooler on the floor before pulling his oldest and dearest friend into a tight hug. Jack hadn't seen her since he'd gotten the news about Gladys, too preoccupied with his job at the hospital to find time to go to the service or visit Elizabeth. So, to make up for it, he'd asked for some extra time off to spend with her. God knew she needed it.

"I've been...pulling through, thank you."

"That's not to say she *didn't* sit in a blanket cocoon and eat ice cream for a good while there, though." Elijah stretched and then stalked into the room. He knew he'd heard a voice outside, and yet, he hadn't been bothered enough to wake from his nap in his warm patch of sunlight to investigate.

"Thank you for that." She looked at the cat pointedly, chuckling to herself. "I lost track of time, Jack. I'm sorry. I'll go dry my hair, and then I'll be ready."

"I'll go ahead and...put your *groceries* away." Jack picked up the cooler he'd brought and started walking towards the kitchen. While Elizabeth wandered back up the stairs to finish getting ready, he popped the top off of the cooler and started transferring the bags of blood inside it onto the thin metal rod mounted to the back of the fridge, hanging bag after bag until Elizabeth was restocked. It would get her through the week, at least.

He straightened up and looked around the rest of the room. There was a red number one blinking on the ancient answering machine that still sat on her kitchen counter underneath the landline she refused to get rid of. There were only a few people that had the number for it, but some of them were her older friends, and so in case any of them needed to call her after all of this time, she kept it. Curious, he pressed the round blue button, letting the little white box announce its message.

"Hey, Elizabeth, it's Joelle. Just checking that we're still on for Thursday night. Call me back when you get the chance!"

Ah, Joelle Hunter. Jack had met her and her husband, Jordan, a handful of times over the years. Elizabeth had been friends with the Hunter clan for at least half a century. They were monster hunters by trade, usually tracking down people like Elizabeth and Jack, the things that go bump in the night, but they were good people, and they knew the difference between true monsters and supernatural individuals who were just trying to live a normal-ish day to day life. They had five kids, the beginnings of a strong pack. Elizabeth often babysat for them on date night or when Joelle and Jordan went bowling.

"Who called?" Elizabeth asked, her fingers buried in her dark strands as she pulled them up into a high ponytail. Her hair was still a bit damp, but it was manageable.

"Joelle."

"I'll call her later. I forgot they have their anniversary dinner this week."

Jack gasped and held a hand over his heart. "*My* Elizabeth forgetting one of her engagements? Where's this incredible planner you boast endlessly?"

"Oh please, can you blame me for being a little behind?" She grinned and bumped into him playfully.

"That, I cannot." Jack looped his arm through Elizabeth's before starting towards the door.

It was another sunny day, which meant both Elizabeth and Jack had to wear their special sunglasses if they didn't want to burn their retinas. It was the only disadvantage to her physical state that Elizabeth could think of, but even then, it wasn't that bad. As a pureblood, she didn't experience much discomfort from things that her formerly human friend did.

The two of them walked a few blocks, down the winding streets of Great City's historical district. Elizabeth had been in town longer than some of the buildings there had. She'd seen them through generations of owners and centuries of new paint jobs and broken windows. Jack didn't remember those times, of course. When Elizabeth had first moved to Great City, Jack hadn't been more than a glimmer in his great-great-grandparents' eyes.

There were a lot of stores there, in the little neighborhood by the sea. Most of them were tourist traps, little shops filled with overpriced T-shirts and keychains and snow globes, little plastic toys that wouldn't work for very long. And then there was Castor's Hall of Magick, which, although it looked like it was just another hoax, was very much not.

Dianne Castor, one of the youngest members of the Castor line, ran the place with her girlfriend, Nadia. She'd inherited it from her mom, who had inherited it from her grandmother, and so on and so forth. The Castors had been in town since a time when both witches and lesbians had been treated a lot worse. It meant a lot to Elizabeth to see the girl thriving, a rainbow flag hanging proudly in their front window.

When Jack and Elizabeth walked through the front door, the bell overhead jingled, and the witch in question looked up from whatever large leather book she had sitting open on the counter.

"Elizabeth!" Dianne sprang up from her stool and ran over, enveloping her in a tight hug. "Did you like the casserole?"

"I did, thank you. It was very sweet of you. You and Nadia are spoiling me."

"You've always taken care of us, we're just returning the favor." As soon as she was mentioned, Nadia pushed open the curtains dividing the rest of the store from their divination room and walked out into the shop. Somehow, she always seemed to know when people were talking about her. Perhaps it was some kind of witchy intuition. "It's good to see you. You too, Jack."

"Elizabeth's here?!" Max, Dianne's kid brother and ward, ran out from the back of the store, his youthful smile missing a few teeth as of late.

"There he is!" Elizabeth embraced the child as he raced into her arms. "Staying out of trouble, I hope."

"No!"

"Good." Jack grinned, chuckling at the young sorcerer. He reached over and ruffled the boy's hair, sending it into further disarray.

"Don't encourage him." Nadia shook her head, smiling. "Just this morning he tried to clone Binx."

"Cloning? Isn't that a little advanced for a Level 1?" Elizabeth rested her hands on her hips, tilting her head.

Max sneered. "I'm Level *2* now."

"My mistake."

Nadia turned to Elizabeth as Jack and Max wandered further into the store, leaving the three women up by the register. "Is everything alright? You know we're always next door if you need anything."

"Thank you. I...I'm doing fine. Should be used to it by now, I suppose." Elizabeth shrugged, a small frown settling onto her ruby red lips only to be replaced by a friendly smile again. "I'll just do what I always do. Find a new roommate. Take on a new name. Start over."

"Change can be good." Dianne nodded, a supportive look in her magic-filled violet eyes. She wrapped an arm around Nadia as she said it, pulling the girl closer to her. "Though, I'm sure you know that better than most."

Elizabeth stared at the witches for a few long moments. She remembered a handful of years ago when the two of them had gone to prom together. She remembered when Dianne had been only a child, standing at her mother's hips in the front of that very store. So, so much had changed, and yet, it seemed like only yesterday she'd been holding little baby Dianne in her arms while Dianne's mother dealt with a customer.

"I do, yeah."

"Ready?" Jack emerged from the back of the store, a small stack of books in his arms. He set them on the counter so Dianne could ring them up.

"I'm ready." Elizabeth nodded. She looked around the store, taking a long whiff of the sharp cinnamon scent that clung to the rugs and curtains throughout it. There were jars of herbs and spices on a shelf on the furthest wall, a table with a crystal ball (covered, for safety reasons) sitting on it tucked away into the back corner. It was for show, mostly, but Dianne did readings for tourists on occasion. There were so many stories, so many memories kept in this place. It helped her to go there when things were happening, talk to whichever members of the Castor line happened to be running it.

When it was all said and done, Jack had some new books, and Dianne had sent Elizabeth out with a bag of vanilla scented candles and some rose quartz "on the house." With all the money Elizabeth had saved up over the years, she hardly needed it, but the witch's act of kindness made her chest warm all the same.

She and Jack visited a few thrift stores, each of them finding a few knick-knacks, campy mugs, pairs of shoes, old board games, funny shot glasses, and other small but meaningful additions to their ever-growing collections of things. They wouldn't replace Gladys, and Elizabeth knew that, but a distraction was nice, even if it was only temporary.

When the sun was low and tickling the horizon, Jack walked Elizabeth back to her cozy little townhouse tucked into the historical district.

"You're going to be okay," he stated, giving a little shrug as the pair walked up the stairs, stopping in front of the door. "You are."

"I am." Elizabeth exhaled a breath, soaking in the orange rays that bounced off of her best friend's face. "I always am, aren't I?"

"You have to be. Because if you're not, how the hell am I supposed to be?" Jack's grin was lopsided, but sincere. He pulled her into a tight hug. "Hang in there, Liz."

"Of course. Besides, we're still on for coffee tomorrow, right?"

"Wouldn't miss it." Jack pulled away from her and studied her calm expression. Elizabeth had always been hard to read, but now she was even more so. "I'll see you tomorrow. Have a good night."

And then he was gone, leaving Elizabeth standing alone in the twilight.

Chapter 3

"Let me guess...a large, iced chai with coconut milk and a shot of vanilla?" The barista, Cody, according to his nametag, was already punching the order into the computer.

"Exactly right." Elizabeth handed him her card with a smile. "You're getting good at this."

"I'm trying." He chuckled and shook his head. The pink-haired, baby-faced boy hadn't been working there for all that long. In fact, he'd picked up the job a few months earlier to help pay for college, like so many After Hours baristas before him had. "You two are in here just about every day, so that makes it a little bit easier to remember."

"Isn't everyone in this neighborhood in here every day?"

"That's a good point." He handed her card back. "But you're usually in during my shift."

"Of course we are. You're the best barista here." Jack winked, stepping forward in Elizabeth's absence. "Got mine down yet?"

"Oh, of course! Caramel macchiato, whipped cream, extra chocolate drizzle, and a blueberry muffin," Cody recited. Jack's order wasn't as difficult to remember, given that he visited the coffee shop even *more* frequently than Elizabeth did, almost exclusively on his favorite barista's shift.

"Impressive." Jack handed him a ten and winked. "Keep the change."

"T-thank you!" A bright grin spread across his face as Elizabeth and a smug-looking Jack retreated to their favorite booth, tucked into the corner of the shop underneath a vintage *Dracula* poster.

"Could you be any more obvious?" Elizabeth laughed. She rested her laptop bag against the side of her seat and slid the device out, along with her wireless mouse and mousepad. This year, she was hell-bent on crossing yet another activity off of her infinite bucket list: writing a novel. It was harder than people made it look.

"Whatever do you mean, my dearest Elizabeth?"

"Don't you 'my dearest Elizabeth' me." She rolled her eyes. "How long have we known each other? A *hundred* years now? You think I don't know what it looks like when you flirt?"

"You wanna see flirting? I'll show you flirting." Jack smirked. He heard the footsteps of none other than his favorite barista approaching their booth from behind him. Once Cody reached the table with their drinks and Jack's muffin, Jack turned. "Thank you. I like your hair, by the way. The pink suits you."

"T-thanks! Just, uh, trying something new." Cody shrugged, his cheeks burning red while he set the cups and plate on the table.

"Life's short. May as well."

"Yeah, for sure." Cody nodded and shuffled in place, obviously flustered. He murmured a quiet "I...like your hair too..." before walking back to the counter.

Once he was well out of earshot again, Jack turned to Elizabeth, a confident grin plastered on his face. He puffed out his chest. "I've still got it."

"Of course you do." Elizabeth chuckled, fingers flying across her keyboard. In the days since Gladys had died, she'd been holding in a cluster of new ideas, something to get her out of the hole she'd written herself into, and now, she finally had the time to get it all out. She was glad she'd picked up her new hobby now, when writing and editing was physically so easy to do. As much as she admired the technology of the past, it sure did make it difficult to reliably write and store something as lengthy as she wanted her book to be.

"Did you bring the—"

"Flyer! I almost forgot!" Elizabeth bent over and reached into her bag to pull out the advertisement she'd made in search of a new roommate. As much as she'd love to live with Jack, as they had once many years before, his job at the hospital required an apartment that was much closer to downtown, and unfortunately, further from the older side of town. Therefore, she was on the hunt for yet another roommate, hopefully one who wouldn't die on her too soon.

Reading it over one last time for any typos, Elizabeth stood up and walked across the coffee shop, her high heels clicking with every step. She pinned it to the community bulletin board and stared at it for a few more seconds before spinning around, only to get a blouse-full of steaming hot coffee all down her front.

"Oh my God, I am so, so sorry!"

Elizabeth half-expected her assailant to be Cody, but instead, it was a frazzled young man, mid-twenties, thick brown hair, glowing tan skin, and thin black glasses resting on the bridge of his nose. They'd never spoken; she didn't know his name, but she could have sworn she'd seen him there before, dressed as he always was in a gray college tee, his long legs wrapped in faded black sweatpants.

"Don't...worry about it." Elizabeth, entirely unscathed by the hot drink, watched as he scrambled to get a handful of napkins in a vain attempt to save her soiled blouse. He was still panicked, so she blotted at the dark stain calmly before looking up at him. "Really, it's alright."

"No, it's not. I totally ruined your shirt. It's my fault. I didn't see you until—"

"Listen, I'm not hurt. This blouse is old anyway, and I don't live too far from here, so I can just—"

"No, no, I have a hoodie in my backpack. Just give me one second. You can keep it. I definitely owe you." The guy hurried back to his table and retrieved the sweatshirt in question, a large, dark gray one with the logo of the Great City Historical University. He handed it to her, shrinking away sheepishly as he did. He reached up to rub the back of his neck.

Elizabeth wished there was something she could do to make him look less like a kicked puppy. Smiling, she held up the sweater and motioned back towards the bathroom in the back of the store. "I'm just gonna go...change. But thank you. For the sweatshirt."

"Again, sorry!"

"It's really fine," Elizabeth called over her shoulder as her heels click-click-clicked all the way back to the bathroom. It didn't take her long to change out of the soiled blouse and into the soft fabric of the man's sweatshirt. It smelled fresh, like he'd washed it pretty recently, and it was warm against her chilled skin.

Once she finally emerged from the dimly-lit bathroom, she found Jack chatting with the guy who had spilled coffee on her in the first place.

"Trust me, she's not mad. I've seen her mad. She's not mad." Jack smirked when he saw Elizabeth, her stained white blouse wadded up in her hand. "Speak of the devil and she shall appear." He tilted his head towards the flustered, butterfingered college student. "Tell him you're not mad."

Laughing, she did. "Really, I'm not mad. Believe me, this is hardly the worst thing to happen to me in this very shop." She carefully tucked the blouse into her bag, folding it so the stain was on the inside. "I'm Elizabeth. You are...?"

"Benjamin Kim." He paused before amending, "Ben is fine. Nice to meet you. Again, I'm so sorry—"

"Don't be. Life is far too short to waste time crying over spilled coffee."

Ben smiled softly, chuckling and nodding. "Thanks. Well, uh, I'll be over there. This paper isn't going to write itself."

"Good luck."

As Elizabeth slid back into the booth, Ben retreated to his table on the opposite side of the cozy little coffee shop, burying his nose in his books. Jack looked at her pointedly.

"What?" She grinned coyly. "What's that look for?"

"Seems you've still got it too."

"Oh hush." Elizabeth shook her head. Silly. The whole matter was silly. "You know I don't date anymore."

"Mmhmm. Sure." Jack took a sip of his drink, a muffin crumb clinging to the corner of his pink lips. "That's what you said last time, too."

"Yeah, yeah, whatever." Elizabeth blew him off and went back to typing. She doubted there was any sliver of truth in what he had insinuated, but...she couldn't deny that her new sweatshirt was warm.

Chapter 4

"Why do you never consult the cat?" Elijah lamented upon being broken the news that Elizabeth had posted an inquiry for a new, assumedly human, roommate. "You *have* a roommate! Me!"

"Of course, of course. But we have an empty bedroom, an empty office, and I'm the one that pays for your vet appointments. And your toys. And your scratching post. And your—"

"I get the point." He scowled, squinting his green eyes up at Elizabeth, his tail hovering back and forth in frustration. "But don't you think maybe you should have asked me first?"

"We've had this same argument a million times. *Gladys* was human!"

"Gladys was BLIND! *Literally* blind!" Elijah hissed, and then shuddered, stopping himself. "Sorry. Reflex. My point still stands."

"We don't even know that anyone will call; it's just a possibility. Thought I'd let you know." Elizabeth zipped up her black boots, double-checking her bag for everything she needed for the night. Cards, check. Phone charger, check. Child-appropriate movies, check. "I'm headed out. Do you need anything?"

"I'm perfectly content. Thank you for asking." Elijah pounced up onto the couch and curled into an angry little ball, glaring at her.

"You'll forgive me." She shrugged.

"Give me a few centuries to think about it."

Elizabeth chuckled and stepped out the door, locking it behind her. The drive to the Hunters' cozy little cabin/house was admittedly a little long, but it was understandable. Their occupation and all it entailed usually involved separation from society in some capacity. The last thing they wanted were their secrets to fall into the wrong hands.

So, to pass the time, Elizabeth hummed along to her CDs. After so many years, she knew the drive like the back of her hand; winding down the tree-lined roads, her headlights illuminating the rapidly darkening forests until, finally, the driveway came up on the right. She turned in and drove, her tires crunching on the gravel, following the faint lights in the distance until she was finally in front of the large house, tucked far away from civilization.

"Elizabeth! Elizabeth!" The door whipped open and out came the twins, Thomas and Brayden, followed by the youngest of the Hunters' children, Andy, an adorable, curly-haired menace.

"It's just me! Why's everyone so excited?" Elizabeth smiled and laughed, getting out of the car.

"Will you play with us? Sage says she's busy!" said Thomas, who for the third time that year had tape wrapped around the bridge of his glasses.

"Please? We're soooooooooOOOOOOOooooo bored!" Brayden clasped his hands together and dropped to his knees in the grass.

"Well, that's my job, isn't it?" Elizabeth raised an eyebrow, plucking Andy off of the ground and resting him on her hip. "I'm the fun committee."

"Yaaaaaaaay!" the twins cheered, racing back inside.

"And what's my Andy up to?" Elizabeth asked, poking his nose, which caused the small boy to giggle.

"I read a book all by myself today!"

"All by yourself?" Elizabeth gasped, walking up the front steps slowly. "Just yesterday you were learning to walk!"

"No, you're just old!" the child protested, luring a smile out of his ancient babysitter.

"By the next time I come here, you'll already be doing algebra and driving the car."

"I can already drive the car!" he insisted, huffing. He squirmed, so she set him down, only to be tackled by the large, fluffy Husky-something mix fondly referred to as Wolf.

A large, warm tongue trailed up Elizabeth's face from her chin all the way to her forehead. She laughed, slowly sitting up as the giant dog eased off of her. Giggling, she reached up to scratch him between the ears, just the way he liked. Wolf's tail thumped loudly against the hardwood floor, and he couldn't seem to decide which paws stand on, constantly shifting from one to the other.

"I missed you too, Wolf."

"And we missed *you*."

When Elizabeth looked up, she saw Joelle standing there wearing a short, formal black dress. This was one of the rare days that her hair was down. Her profession was often pretty active, all things considered. Having her hair down while hunting down some rabid werewolf or feral demon wasn't an option unless she wanted it chopped and/or burned off in some freak supernatural accident.

"You look beautiful, Joelle."

"Thank you." She offered Elizabeth a hand and pulled her off of the floor. "And thank you for coming tonight. The kids really missed you."

"Too busy for bowling night these days, huh?"

She exhaled an exasperated sigh, nodding. "We're just lucky it's been quiet today, or we wouldn't have been able to go out at all. There's just so many creatures out there lately. I don't know why..."

"Well, let's just thank the gods the humans have people like you to protect them from the things that go bump in the night." Elizabeth smirked. "And I'll be grateful you haven't given *me* the stake after all of these years."

"Oh, Elizabeth, if we staked you, who would watch the kids on date nights?" Jordan, a tall, muscular man with long, raven hair, walked into the living room next, wearing a sharp suit that matched his wife's dress. He pulled their old family friend in for a hug. When he was a child, Elizabeth had babysat him, and his father before him. She had a long history with the Hunters, which was smart. After all, there were people out there who weren't above killing well-meaning vampires like herself.

"Well, I guess you'd just have to get Jack to do it."

"I prefer you," said the only daughter of the Hunter clan, Sage, from her spot sitting on the couch. She didn't get up to greet Elizabeth, as her little siblings had, instead choosing to stay planted in front of the TV, some inaccurate teen vampire drama playing as background noise for whatever she was doing on her laptop.

That left all of the Hunter children accounted for aside from one: Connor, the oldest.

"Is Connor...?"

"Out for the night with a friend who happens to be a girl." Joelle smiled knowingly. "He should be back sometime before you leave, I assume. He knows curfew."

"I'll keep an eye out for him." Elizabeth saluted, nodding.

"Aside from that, you know the house better than we do, probably. There's some lasagna in the fridge when the kids get hungry." Jordan jabbed a thumb back towards the kitchen. "We'll be back kind of late."

"Stay out as late as you want. You two deserve it."

"Thank you so much, again. Really, Elizabeth, I don't know what we'd do without you."

"Yeah, yeah." She shook her head and shooed them towards the door. "Go, have fun. The night is young."

So, without much more fuss, Joelle and Jordan left, the door clicking closed behind them. Elizabeth set her purse on a chair at the dining room table before walking over towards where Sage was settled and sitting down beside her.

"What grade are you in again?"

"I'm a sophomore this year," Sage replied, her fingers not pausing for even a moment as they flew across her keyboard.

"God, time flies."

"When you're four hundred and something, I'm sure it does." Sage bit back a smile, and Elizabeth chuckled.

"You're the second Hunter child that's called me old tonight!"

"It's only mean if it isn't true."

"You've got me there," Elizabeth said, grinning at the girl before looking up at the TV for a split second, just in time to catch sight of an adult man cast as a teenager biting into some girl's neck. "That's not realistic. I'm speaking from experience."

"Yeah?" Sage's eyebrow quirked up with interest, and she glanced up from the soft glow of her laptop.

"Oh yeah. With that biting technique, he'd get blood *everywhere*, and at that point, it's just inconvenient, it really is. Not that I've had blood from anyone's neck in a long time, but I drank that way for long enough to know how it's done."

"You should give the producers a call. I'm sure they'd love some pointers because this is season seven, and they obviously still don't know what they're doing."

"You know what, someday I just might. It's not like I don't have all the free time in the world."

"Must be nice." Sage tucked a piece of dark brown hair behind her ear, staring at her laptop with wide eyes, scanning lines of text intensely. "I've been writing this paragraph for three hours, and it still doesn't sound right."

"Paper for class?"

"Yeah, for my Lit class."

"Let me check it out." Elizabeth held out her hands, and Sage handed over her laptop. She read over the paragraph Sage had written.

"One common theory about the meaning of Romeo and Juliet is that the story is a satire. This is a modern notion, as readers nowadays understand that it takes longer than three days for someone to fall in love. Also, the dramatic context of Romeo and Juliet's deaths..."

"Change 'theory about' to 'interpretation of.'" Elizabeth continued scanning the paper until she reached the end of what Sage had written. "Wow, *Romeo and Juliet*, huh? Would it make me old if I said it came out the year before I was born?"

"Yes. Yes it would." Sage's jaw dropped, and she took the laptop back from Elizabeth. "Are you kidding?"

"Wish I was." She shrugged. "My father took my sister and I to see *Macbeth*. I was around..." Elizabeth ran the numbers in her head. "I think I was twelve or thirteen. Still living in Europe at the time."

"Jesus Christ. You need to write a book or something, good God."

Elizabeth chuckled. "I'm finally working on that one."

"You have more experience in your pinky finger than I ever will in my entire life."

"I wouldn't say that, Sage. I think you have quite a bright future ahead of you. This is the twenty-first century, after all. Things are much different than they were when I was growing up. So, so much different. Sure, it's...well, it's not always great, to be frank, but your generation has the power to fix things. You're angry and young, and both of those are powerful things. *Anyway*..." Elizabeth glanced over her shoulder to find Thomas and Brayden wrestling on the carpet behind the couch. "I'm gonna go stop your brothers from killing each other. Let me know if you need more help."

"Will do." By the time Elizabeth stood up from the couch, Sage was already typing away again.

"Alright, you little monsters, no biting!"

At the sound of Elizabeth's voice, both of the twins sat upright on the floor, mischief gleaming in their eyes.

"Let's play vampire hunter!" Thomas declared, his grin missing a few teeth.

"Yeah!" Brayden agreed, springing up off of the floor and running out of the room to fetch the foam stakes their parents had made for training purposes. When Elizabeth was over, however, they served as the equivalent of a monster hunter's Nerf gun. There was never any real harm done, but it helped teach the Hunters how to take out threats to humankind from a young age.

"I wanna play! I wanna play!" Andy ran to Elizabeth and tugged on her pantleg, tapping his hand against her thigh.

"Oh, of course you get to play." She hoisted the youngest Hunter off of the floor. "You'll be my little bat. My fledgling."

"Yeah! I get to be a vampire!" He held his hands near his mouth and mimicked fangs with his pointer fingers, causing Elizabeth to laugh.

"The scariest vampire I've ever seen." She squished his cheeks, making him scowl.

"I *am* scary!" he insisted, his little eyebrows turned downwards, lip settled into a pout.

"Of course you are," Elizabeth agreed, nodding. "Any knowledgeable monster hunter would quake in their boots at the sight of you."

Andy nodded proudly. "Damn right."

Elizabeth's eyes widened. "Hey! Where'd you learn that?!"

"Better run, vampires!" Brayden returned just in time, holding a foam stake in each hand, a pair of his father's oversized sunglasses slipping steadily down the bridge of his nose. "I'm gonna get you!"

So, Elizabeth ran, laughing and smiling a fang-bearing grin. These children, yes, they were Hunters, and knew more about the world around them than their human counterparts, but they hadn't yet experienced the terrifying side of the supernatural world their parents had brought them into. It was her hope that she would be able to protect their innocence, even if it was only for a little longer.

Chapter 5

It was a particularly cloudy autumn afternoon when the bell above the Turning Page's front door jingled. In swept a crisp breeze, accompanied by a few stray leaves and a familiar stranger.

Elizabeth was restocking the shelves with the store's latest shipment, perched precariously on the middle rungs of the wheeled ladder. Among other things, her state of being had gifted her with incredible balance and the willingness to stock the higher shelves that the store's owners, a pair of little elderly women, couldn't. They liked Elizabeth's "old soul and new spunk," as they said, and they planned to keep her around as long as they could. Little did they know, their favorite employee didn't have plans to skip town anytime in the next century or two.

At the sound of the bell, Elizabeth glanced up. She smiled politely. "I'll be with you in a second."

"No rush," he replied, walking through the store to get to the non-fiction section, tucked away into the back.

Elizabeth pushed the last few books into their spots on the shelf before climbing down and wandering back to help him. Once she had a better look at him, she grinned and chuckled to herself. If Jack ever found out about this, she'd never hear the end of it.

When the man turned around, he almost bumped into her. Taking a step back, he got a good look at her, and a sheepish smile overtook his features, a dimple digging into his tan cheek. He rubbed the back of his neck. "It's Elizabeth, right?"

"That's my name." She motioned to the nametag pinned to her knitted red sweater. "Don't wear it out. Can I help you find anything specific? Ben, was it?"

"Yep. Ben. Hi." He paused to process the question she'd asked before that. "Oh! Yeah, actually, I was wondering if you had anything on the Battle of Bloodborne? I need it for my thesis."

"Battle of Bloodborne, huh?" She hummed, reminiscing. Elizabeth drummed her crimson fingernails on the wood of the shelf. "I think we have a few, yeah."

Ben sighed in relief. "Oh, thank God. I've been to, like, four bookstores in the past week and haven't had any luck. I have online sources, but I'd like to get some physical ones too."

"Right, the more the better for that kind of thing." Elizabeth led him a few rows down from where he had been looking previously. She ran a slender finger along the spines of the books until she found the ones she wanted. "There's, like, five or six here. What's your thesis about? Maybe we could narrow it down to two or three."

"I'm researching women of the American Revolution, so anything about Elizabeth or Katherine Bloodborne would be great."

Elizabeth blessed her lucky stars that she was bent down to get the books from the bottom shelf so he hadn't seen the face she'd just pulled. Dianne was always telling her that things happened for a reason...

"I'm getting my Masters in history, and it's about driving me insane. But I really like the topic for my thesis. I feel like a lot of the really great women got overshadowed by the men of their time..." He chuckled to himself, shaking his head. "Sorry, I tend to ramble a lot."

"Ramble away." She laughed. "You know, you're in luck. This one is about the midwife that helped deliver Katherine, this one is about Elizabeth's life before the battle, and this one is the memoir of the innkeeper." Elizabeth straightened up with the small stack of books. "The rest are about the actual battle itself."

"Those three are exactly what I needed." Ben took them from her and turned the top one over to read the back of it. "Thank you so much."

"Is there anything else I can help you with?"

"No, I think that was it. I'm gonna look around for a little while longer, though."

"Alright. Holler if you need anything," Elizabeth said. She smiled and turned from him, walking towards the register to see if there was another box of new books stowed away back there, but there wasn't. So, seeing as Barb and Jean were still out to lunch, she started running numbers in the lined spiral notebook they used to keep track of sales until Ben finally approached, setting the three books and a few bookmarks on the counter.

"Thanks for helping me, and I'm sorry, again, for ruining your shirt."

"You didn't ruin my shirt. I got it out with some vinegar and stuff." Elizabeth grinned, jotting down the book titles and the prices on them. If there was anything she knew from her four hundred years of drinking blood, it was how to get out stains. "I can get your sweatshirt back to you, though, if you want."

"Nah, that's okay." Ben shook his head. "It was an old one, anyway."

"Well, sometimes older things hold the best memories."

"That's true," he replied, considering it. "I'm really alright, though. But thanks for asking."

"Of course." She put the books in a paper bag and slid it across the counter to him, and he handed her his card, which she slid into the chip reader. When the little machine was done, she handed it back. "There you are. Have a nice day, and be sure to stop in if you need anything. I'm…" she grinned her blood red lips, "well, I'm a bit of a history buff myself."

"In that case, I'll be sure to stop in if something else comes up." Ben took a business card from the little holder on the counter and slipped it into his bag before he walked out the front door and back into the chilly autumn air.

Elizabeth smiled to herself in the silence he'd left her in. He was endearing. Clumsy, yes, but endearing no less. And she suspected that if she and Jack continued to frequent After Hours as often as they currently did, she'd be seeing a lot more of him in the near future.

When Elizabeth finally got home, she hung her purse on the back of the chair, shedding her light autumn coat and setting her sunglasses on the table. She didn't particularly mind working in the afternoons, what with her sleep schedule being so short, but she always felt like there was so much to do when she got home. Dinner to cook, laundry to fold, dishes to wash, and after all of it, a novel to write.

And there was something else Elizabeth had to do, too, she remembered, glancing at the calendar. So, once she'd exchanged her high heels for some comfortable slippers and collected herself, she walked to her office to fish through her stationery drawer for something suitable. Then, once she found it, she sat down and twisted the front half of her favorite pen into writing position.

Elizabeth opened the cream-colored card and pressed the tip to the paper.

"My dearest Katherine,

Happy birthday! I know you don't get many cards in the mail anymore, but I'm old-fashioned, what can I say? I hope you have a good day. Do something fun! Go get some bubble tea or hang out in a coffee shop or adopt a rescue dog. With lives like ours, it's easy to forget to enjoy the little things. Carve a pumpkin, make a Halloween costume, crunch some leaves beneath your boots.

This is the place I'd tell you everything that's happened since we last talked, but almost nothing has changed. I still work at the bookstore. Elijah is still a cat. Jack is still around, and we still digest copious amounts of caffeinated beverages. The only thing that's changed is Gladys, who passed on a few weeks ago. I'm looking for a new roommate to make the house feel less empty (though Elijah is not entirely keen on the idea), but I haven't gotten any calls about it yet.

I look forward to your reply. How are things? Have you heard from your brother? It's been a while since he's visited. I miss both of you so much. We should get together sometime soon. Maybe for Christmas or New Year's Eve.

Happy 241st. I hope there are many, many more happy birthdays in your future.

Sincerely,
Mom"

When she was satisfied with the sprawling cursive letters stretched across the page, she twisted her pen closed again. She looked up from the paper at the gray cat who had perched himself on her desk, his very green eyes peering down at her.

"Kids, eh? Never coming to visit."

"You didn't have any kids, did you?" Elizabeth's eyebrows furrowed. She supposed that in their handful of decades living together, the topic had never come up. It wasn't like she talked about her own children all that often, given that the prospect of her having grown children completely shattered the illusion that she was eternally twenty-six.

"I was seventeen when I was cursed, so no, I did not sire any children during my short years as a human." Elijah stretched all the way out, his tail curling up into the air behind him and his toes spreading out like little clawed fans. "Never really cared to. Back then, well, you know how it was, to an extent."

"Another person was just another mouth to feed." Elizabeth nodded. Though she hadn't struggled financially, like she knew Elijah had in his human life, she'd seen the poverty that was so prevalent in the colonies. "And children had trouble surviving winter."

"I lost three sisters by the time I turned thirteen." Elijah sighed, settling onto the surface of the desk. His adorable ears were almost begging to be scratched. "So did everyone else, though."

"I have too many siblings to count. I feel like any time my parents get bored, they just have another child. It's not like there's anything else to do when you're a thousand years old."

"So what's stopping *you* from having another child?" The gray cat rolled onto his back, curious green eyes studying Elizabeth's sharp amber ones. "If you're so keen on having another roommate, I mean."

Elizabeth rolled her eyes, laughing. "Would you really rather have a baby fledgling waddling around than a human roommate?"

"Yes. Undoubtedly."

"And what exactly would you have me do about my bookstore job, huh?"

"I could babysit it," Elijah insisted, rolling back onto his stomach. "I think I'm quite responsible for a cat, all things considered."

"I'm not having a baby, and I'm not backing down on the roommate thing." Elizabeth stood up from the table, giving Elijah a quick scratch between the ears.

Elijah shrugged. "Eh, it was worth a shot."

Chapter 6

All Hallows' Eve, of all of the holidays she'd celebrated, was among Elizabeth's favorites. The Great City weather was unusually kind to the trick or treaters, bringing them a cool breeze instead of the snow or rain showers of recent years. Elizabeth had a sneaking suspicion that the nice weather had something to do with her next-door neighbors, but Dianne claimed she was innocent and that the stars had merely aligned to bring them a nice Halloween after so long without one.

As she did every year, Elizabeth stocked up on the king size candy bars at the grocery store for a few weeks before the holiday in order to make sure she had enough for all of the trick-or-treaters that came by. In her years living there, she'd built up a reputation after all, and she had no intention of letting the kids down, especially the ones from other neighborhoods who flocked to the historical district to maximize their candy intake.

Before he'd started working at the hospital, it had been a tradition for Jack to come over and hand out candy with her, but since he'd gotten the habit of taking the graveyard shift so some poor college girl wouldn't have to, Elizabeth was on her own for most of the night, or at least until Max got sick of trick-or-treating and he came over with Dianne and Nadia to drink cider and watch *Hocus Pocus*, one of Elijah's least favorite movies, due to his shared trauma with Thackery Binx.

So, to fill the time before her witchy neighbors and their mischievous little sorcerer arrived, Elizabeth donned her favorite Halloween attire. This consisted of a long black glittering dress that was known to make some of the neighborhood kids think she was Morticia Addams, a pair of black stilettos, red lipstick, and a large pair of fake fangs over her real ones.

"You know, you could just, I don't know, use your real fangs for the one night of the year when that's not suspicious at all." Elijah tilted his head as he watched her jam the wax fangs onto her teeth.

"What's the fun in that?" Elizabeth grinned an especially fanged grin. "And besides, I don't like flashing my fangs unless it's necessary. Wouldn't want to scare the trick or treaters away. What else would I do with all of this candy?"

"Give it to the kid next door."

"That's fair." Elizabeth shrugged.

Interrupting her next thought, the doorbell rang, accompanied by a loud chorus of "TRICK OR TREAT!" So, she walked to the door, heels clicking against the hardwood floor, and pulled it open, revealing a variety of little faces, all dressed in different disguises. There was a pirate with a stuffed green parrot perched on his shoulder, a fairy with giant blue wings, a princess with a sword hooked to her dress, and a trio of little Draculas, each with a black and red cape and faces powdered white.

"What do we have here? Why, is it Halloween already?" She feigned confusion, causing the little fairy to giggle. "I suppose you've come here for blood—I mean candy—right?"

"Yes!" the kids replied.

One of the moms standing back on the sidewalk asked, "And what do we say?"

"Pleaseeeeee!" the trio of vampires asked, raising their bags up higher.

Elizabeth pulled her large silver platter piled high with king size candy bars into the doorway and held it out to the trick or treaters, who all gaped at the sight. "Take your pick."

A frenzy of little hands snatched their candy bar of choice off of the platter, and they all shouted their thank yous before running back down the stairs and on to the next house. Well, all aside from one.

The little red-haired fairy stayed behind, smiling up at Elizabeth for a moment before asking politely, "Could I have one for my sister too?" She pointed behind her to where one mom was standing on the sidewalk beside a little girl in a wheelchair, who was dressed as a mermaid with a sparkling purple tail.

"You know what, why don't we let her pick?" Elizabeth walked down the stairs beside the fairy until she was standing in front of the mermaid's chair with her tray of candy. "Which one would you like?"

The mermaid thought for a moment, her hand hovering over the tray before she finally picked one. Then, once she'd put it in her bag, she smiled up at Elizabeth. "Thank you!"

"Of course," Elizabeth handed each of the girls one more candy bar, pressing her finger to her lips, which made them giggle. "Have a happy Halloween!"

Once they turned to continue down the sidewalk, Elizabeth ventured back up the steps and into her house.

Elijah looked up at her from his spot sitting on the carpet, amused. His tail waved behind him. "You know, for a vampire, you're pretty nice. I thought you were supposed to be scary."

"Don't act like we don't make fun of *Twilight* at least once a month. Look me in the eyes and tell me Edward 'the hair' Cullen is supposed to be scary."

Elijah stretched out his back, walking closer before nuzzling against Elizabeth's leg, a rare plea for affection if there ever was one. She bent over and scratched between his ears, drawing out an even rarer purr from him. He looked up at Elizabeth, blurting, "Edward is scarier than you are."

"You take that back!"

"Never!" He ran off into the next room, probably to go get one of the mouse toys that he was so fond of. Figured.

Elizabeth chuckled as he zoomed away. As much as she knew he probably wasn't overly fond of the circumstances that had brought them together, she was glad to have him around. Every once in a while, he even seemed to like her.

She stood around for a little while longer, organizing the candy, restocking her tray, and then there was another knock on the door. She opened it, and in walked Max, Dianne, and Nadia. The youngest of the three, who was wrapped in a Slytherin scarf, pushed right past his godmother and flopped onto the couch dramatically.

"All done trick-or-treating?" Elizabeth laughed at his defeated form.

"I'll say." Nadia dropped the rather heavy-looking pillow case on the floor beside the front door. "Our little spellcaster tried his hand at a duplication spell."

"And it worked," Dianne added, setting down an identical pillowcase, just as stuffed with candy as the first one.

"Impressive for a Level 2," Elizabeth noted. "You've got the makings of a pretty powerful spellcaster, Max."

"I know." He mumbled into the couch. As he laid there, Elijah came back into the room, a fuzzy mouse toy caught in his mouth, and hopped up onto Max's back. "There's a cat on my back."

"There's a child on my couch," Elijah replied, curling his legs into himself and becoming a little gray ball of fur. "Hello, Max. How are you today?"

"I'm tired."

"Me too," Elijah agreed, laying down further. "I'm gonna take a nap on your back if you're not careful."

"Okay." Max pulled a throw pillow under his head and closed his eyes.

"Did you have fun?" Elizabeth turned to Dianne and Nadia, who, as they were every year, were dressed up as witches.

"It was really nice out there tonight." Dianne nodded. "And all of the neighborhood moms are really nice."

"They always are." Elizabeth smiled.

"But yes, we had fun. Well, aside from scolding our ambitious little spellcaster for using magic in public. Again." Nadia rested her hands on her hips, looking pointedly towards Max, who was pretending to be asleep.

"I said I was sorry," he mumbled.

"Enough chit chat, let's pop in the movie." Dianne wandered over to the Blu-Ray player and put in the disk. She waved her hand, conjuring a bowl of warm, buttery popcorn in Nadia's arms.

Nadia looked at her girlfriend with stars in her eyes. "I love it when you do that..."

"That's why I do it." Dianne straightened up and stole a piece of popcorn from the bowl. She leaned in and kissed Nadia.

Elizabeth watched the exchange with a warm, fanged grin.

"What?" Dianne asked.

"I just like seeing you happy, is all." Elizabeth shrugged. "You two deserve to be happy."

Nadia smiled, settling onto the couch with Dianne.

It was a bittersweet feeling that bloomed in her chest as Elizabeth watched them. Max wouldn't be a mischievous little spellcaster forever. And Dianne and Nadia wouldn't always be the young witches next door. Youth, like life, was fleeting, and she knew it, but she wouldn't trade her eternity for anything in the world, not when she got to watch hundreds of people grow up and fall in love.

Life was tough sometimes, it was true, but it could be happy and magical too. Those little moments were the reason she always found herself in friendships with mortals and witches and monster hunters and all varieties of supernatural beings she knew she'd outlive eventually. There was too much love in the world to spend it lonely because she was afraid of losing people.

The doorbell rang again, which meant more trick-or-treaters were waiting on the front steps. So, Elizabeth grabbed her candy tray and opened the door for the latest round. No matter how many Halloweens came and went, she'd always love the endless parade of costumed children, even if she knew that someday, they had to grow up.

Chapter 7

As October ended, November swept in quickly to take its place, the winds getting colder with each day that passed. There wasn't any snow yet, but Elizabeth could feel the spirit of it hovering there, waiting to drift down and cover her sleepy little neighborhood in a blanket of shimmering white.

It was in the afternoon on a rather normal November afternoon that the doorbell of the townhouse rang. Elijah shot straight upright, wide green eyes fixed on the front door. Eyebrows furrowing, Elizabeth set her laptop beside her and got up.

As she wasn't particularly expecting guests, she was wearing an old pair of black sweatpants and the sweatshirt she'd been given by Ben after he'd quite literally stumbled into her life. And it seemed his stumbling wasn't quite finished because, when she opened the front door, it was his face she saw on the other side of it.

He was holding a crinkled flyer in his hand, the one she'd put on the bulletin board, which advertised the empty space in her townhouse. When he finally looked up from the paper, his brown eyes widened, magnified slightly by his thick glasses.

She could only watch as his cheeks darkened to a flustered shade of red. *Cute*, she decided.

"Elizabeth? I...I didn't realize you were the one who'd posted the ad..." He rubbed the back of his neck, his glasses fogged up from his warm breath in the cold air. He had a knitted blue scarf wrapped around his neck.

"I did. Would you like to come in?" She motioned further into the townhouse.

Hesitating, he nodded, taking his boots off inside the door before Elizabeth could stop him. "So, uh, how long have you lived here, exactly?"

"At least six years now." Underestimation of the century. "I've had quite a few roommates come in and out of this place. You know how it is, but the place feels empty without someone else."

Elijah scoffed, rolling his eyes, but the noise he'd made drew Ben's attention.

He cooed. "Awwww, you have a cat?"

"Yep! This is Elijah. He's a rescue," Elizabeth explained, much to the gray cat's dismay. "He's a little grumpy sometimes, but he'll warm up to you eventually."

"Good to know." Ben, who'd looked like he was going to attempt to pet Elijah, cautiously lowered his hand, deciding he didn't want to get clawed today if he could avoid it. "So, I meant to ask, the rent that was on the flyer, is that legit?"

"Yeah, of course." Elizabeth nodded. She suspected this might come up. A nice townhouse like the one she owned in the historical district usually rented out for much, much more than she ever listed. But given that she didn't really need the money, she never asked for it, instead asking for a small, but reasonable sum in order to not seem suspicious. It wasn't like she could just rent out the room for free without raising some red flags.

"Seriously?"

"Yeah. Why?"

"Well, I've been looking for a place for...well, for a few months now, and all of them have been like twice the price and not nearly this...nice." He motioned around at Elizabeth's crimson-painted walls, which were covered with paintings and old portraits in an eclectic variety of frames.

It was vintage and contemporary all at once. The chandelier above the dining room table was old school, but the floors looked new, and the paint on the windowsill pretty fresh. From the little glimpse he had into the kitchen, it looked like the appliances were all new too.

"Well, things happen for a reason, I guess." Elizabeth shrugged, not really sure what else to say. After being around for so long, she believed there had to be at least a sliver of truth in the statement, especially given how many times she'd run into Ben in the past month or so alone. "Do you want to take a look around? The grand tour and all that?"

"Um, sure, lead the way." Ben motioned Elizabeth on, and she walked in front of him, into the kitchen.

It was larger than the kitchens in the other apartments he had looked at, the countertops all redone with black and white marble. There was a large island with a light overhead. The appliances were all stainless steel, and the fridge looked huge.

Ben grabbed the handle of the refrigerator door to take a look inside, but Elizabeth stopped him, her eyes wide. She still had some blood bags in there. What a close call. She'd have to be sure to move them to her mini fridge upstairs before Ben, or anyone else for that matter, moved in.

"It's...It's a mess in there. I'll have it cleaned out soon, don't worry," she explained, trying not to let the panic slip into her voice. "But, yeah, this is the kitchen. The bedrooms are upstairs."

Elizabeth led him up to the second floor and into the second bedroom, the one that Gladys had lived in. It was further from the stairs for obvious reasons. It was a good thing Elizabeth had exchanged the sheets a few days before. Most of her belongings had been picked up by her family before the funeral. All that was really left was one of the blankets she had knitted and the rug on the hardwood floor.

"This is the room."

"It's really big!" Ben marveled, walking inside. He opened up the closet and looked inside of it. It was roomy. He could picture his clothes hanging there, his sweatpants occupying the drawers of the dresser. "Are you *sure* the rent is right?"

"Positive." Elizabeth laughed. "There's a bathroom adjacent. The door's over here. There's no tub, though, sorry, just a shower."

"That's...perfect, actually. Not really much of a bath person." He walked across the room and opened the bathroom door. It was spotless, tile floors shiny and clean. "This is so nice."

"Glad you like it. There's actually one other thing." Elizabeth beckoned him with a finger, and they left the bedroom, walking further down the second floor hallway to another room. This one was an office with giant bookshelves filled with classics and a large desk. "I figured you could put this to more use than I could, given your studies and all."

"Oh my God, a whole office?" Ben padded across the soft carpeting to the giant mahogany desk. He didn't always like solitude while he was writing, but he figured it might be nice to shut himself away and focus every once in a while, especially with exams creeping around the corner. "This place is seriously amazing."

"It's had some work put into it over the years," Elizabeth agreed. She felt something against her leg and looked down to find Elijah, glaring up at her with his most unamused of looks. "There's my boy."

If looks could kill, Elizabeth figured she'd be about six feet under just from that one look alone. She smiled and reached down to pet him, but he hissed at her, walking to the cushy desk chair and curling up in it.

"So, how does this work, exactly? Are you interviewing other roommates, or...?"

"If you leave me your number, I'll call you later today to let you know. Does that work?"

"Absolutely, yeah." Ben took a piece of paper and a pen from the desk, eyeing Elijah nervously as he approached, and then jotted down his number, handing it to Elizabeth. "Thank you so much."

They walked back downstairs and Elizabeth saw him out, watching as he almost tripped down the front steps. There must be some reason he kept walking—er, *stumbling* into her life. For some reason, the fates kept bringing them together.

"This isn't happening, right?" Elijah padded down the stairs and looked up at Elizabeth. "That's why you didn't have him sign, right? You're gonna call him and tell him it's not gonna work out."

"Elijahhh," she sighed, "don't make this harder for me than it has to be."

"For *you*?! You're not the cat that's going to have to not talk ever for as long as it takes for him to move out!"

"Not *never*, just when he's here and awake."

Elijah sulked. "Still."

Elizabeth walked over to the couch and sat down, staring at his phone number for several seconds. Maybe she should call Jack and ask for an opinion, but she'd been friends with him for long enough to know what he'd say. He'd tell her to shoot her shot. She knew Dianne and Nadia would just give her some cryptic advice about fate, given the way everything had unfolded so far.

"He's a grad student. He's probably broke and looking for a cheaper place to live. He'll be writing papers for most of the time he's here anyway."

"You're not going to win me over." Elijah narrowed his eyes.

"You won't even notice he's here half the time, I promise."

"Ughhhh…" The cat groaned before hopping up on the couch, resigning his argument. "Fine. But if you slip up and blow your secret, I get to scare the shit out of him. Deal?"

"That's fair." Elizabeth nodded. "Deal. I'll call him."

Chapter 8

"Ooh, be careful, that one's—"

Elizabeth already had the box balanced on her hip, her other arm free. Ben's eyes widened and his jaw dropped.

"—heavy..."

"It's not too bad." She shook her head, chuckling. She grabbed his suitcase with her free hand and started hauling things up the stairs to Jack, who was standing in the doorway, keeping it propped open. Dianne and Nadia were inside, moving all of the boxes up to Ben's room with a little magic here and there when Elizabeth's new human roommate wasn't looking.

There were just a few boxes left, and then the truck was empty. Jay, one of Ben's friends, walked around the side of the truck and gave Ben a quick hug. He motioned his thumb towards Elizabeth and said, quietly enough that a human would be out of earshot but loud enough that Elizabeth could still hear it, "Dude, you definitely upgraded. She's so hot."

"I know, right?" Ben chuckled and shook his head. "And this place is so nice. So much nicer than my old place. And more affordable. Is it weird that it's more affordable?"

"Yeah, a little. But that's not really something to complain about." Jay laughed, nudging his friend.

Elizabeth walked back down the stairs, trying her best to hide the smirk that was slowly overtaking her features. "Anything else, or are we all set, fellas?"

"I think we're all good here, ma'am." Jay patted the side of his truck. "Thanks again for putting my best friend up. He'd be sleeping on a bench if it weren't for you."

"Yeah, of course. Thanks for helping my new roommate move in." She winked, shaking his hand.

"Ooh, strong grip," Jay noted. He turned to Ben, beaming brightly in a way that made his cheekbones pop. "I like her."

Elizabeth laughed, and Ben chuckled to himself, shaking his head. "Thanks for everything, Jay. See you around."

"Let me know if you need any help with anything." Jay gave Ben a nudge and then waved to each of them and hopped back into his truck, driving off towards the horizon.

"Well, come on in. Make yourself at home."

Ben followed Elizabeth up the stairs and into the townhouse, where a good chunk of his boxes were cluttering the living room. He looked around at the people who were there to help out. Two of them, he knew, were the next-door neighbors, and he recognized the other man, Jack, from the coffee shop the day he'd met his now roommate.

"You're Nadia, right?"

"Dianne." The violet-eyed witch offered her hand. She shook his and tilted her head towards Nadia. "My girlfriend is Nadia."

"Sorry. Dianne. I'll try to remember."

"Don't worry about it." Nadia laughed, walking over. "Welcome to the neighborhood. We better get going. Almost dinner time."

"We have a little monster to feed," Dianne agreed.

"A cat?" Ben asked.

"Worse. My brother." The witches laughed. "See you later Elizabeth, Jack, Ben."

And then they were gone, walking next door to make dinner for their little rascal.

"It's been fun, but I've gotta get to work," Jack, who was dressed in his scrubs, said. "I'll see you later, Elizabeth. Welcome to the family, Ben. I'm sure I'll see you around at some point." Jack walked over to Elizabeth and kissed her cheek, hugging her tightly before walking out the door after the others.

"We don't have to unpack everything today. Just probably like your clothes and the stuff you need. We can work on the rest later," Elizabeth, a professional unpacker, told him.

Ben nodded, already compartmentalizing things in his head. He walked up the stairs, followed by Elizabeth. After reading the labels on some of the boxes, he pushed a few into his bedroom. There were quite a few sitting there in the little landing at the top of the stairs. He didn't recall seeing Dianne and Nadia going up the stairs that much. He'd feel really bad if they had. He'd have to bake them some cookies or something to thank them.

"Do you need any help with anything?" Elizabeth tilted her head, her hands on her hips in the most mom-like pose she possessed. That was what Elijah always said, anyway. It was what was left from raising two kids on her own; sometimes, she just stood like a mom.

"I think I'm alright. I'm just going to try to unpack some of my bedroom and bathroom stuff today. Thank you, though."

"No prob. I'll go downstairs and start dinner."

"Oh, you don't have to—"

"No, it's okay. I love cooking." Elizabeth shook him off, smiling. The truth was, due to her subdued sense of taste, if she didn't do the cooking herself, she probably wouldn't be able to taste it at all. Of course, she would tone down the flavors in Ben's, as to not overwhelm his sensitive human taste buds, but at least hers would taste like *something* to her. "Do you like stuffed peppers?"

"Considering I've been living on instant noodles and frozen pizza for the past...six years? I'll eat anything you cook." Ben grinned, his dimples digging into his cheeks. "Thank you so much."

"No problem. I'll just be downstairs, then." Elizabeth walked back down to the first floor and into the kitchen, where Elijah was sitting on the island, his tail flicking from side to side and his eyes narrowed at her. She chuckled at him. "What?"

He hissed and then hopped up off of the island, stalking into the next room. So, it was the silent treatment, then. Two could play that game. Well, maybe not. No, she did understand why Elijah was mad, but on the other hand, Ben needed a place to stay, and if his friend's casual remark was any indication, it seemed he was almost kicked out of his last place.

Not paying her grumpy cat too much mind, Elizabeth set to work on the stuffed peppers, sautéing the meat in a pan on the stove and adding in diced peppers and seasoning as she cooked. Very quickly, the kitchen started to smell heavenly as she put all of the ingredients together in the pan, cooking thoroughly until it was finally time to put them in the hollowed-out green bell peppers. For someone who technically didn't need to eat to survive, she sure was good at cooking.

Once she'd finally put the peppers in the oven to cook the rest of the way, Ben wandered downstairs, following his nose to whatever incredible miracle Elizabeth had in the oven.

"That smells amazing." Ben sighed and sat down at the bar stool next to the island. "I haven't had a home cooked meal since...well, since I got my bachelor's degree, at least."

"Get used to it." She laughed, taking her oven mitts off. Technically, she didn't really need them, but she figured she'd at least try to look normal for as long as that illusion would last. "Make me a list of what you like, and I'll make it happen."

She reached for the blood smoothie she had sitting on the table. Since Ben was going to be living there now, she'd had to revert to her old habits and techniques for hiding blood in plain sight. The easiest way: a darkly colored smoothie in an opaque plastic cup with a straw.

"It's like you were sent down from roommate heaven."

Ben's comment almost made her choke on her drink. She couldn't even count all of the times she'd been called the exact *opposite* of an angel.

"Well, as our neighbors would say, everything happens for a reason." Elizabeth pointed to the wall, on the other side of which was Dianne and Nadia's townhouse.

"You know, I was picking up some weird vibes from them. Are they, like, into that whole thing? Tarot cards and star signs and destiny and stuff?" Ben asked innocently.

It twisted something inside of her that he was so close to the truth, and yet had no idea, nor ever would, just how 'into' destiny and fate and *magick* the next-door neighbors were. Elizabeth forgot what it was like to live with someone so young. Like, someone really, *truly* young, not just an old soul in a young person's body. It was easy to look at someone like Jack and forget just how many years he was hiding behind that boyish face of his.

"Yeah, they're into that sort of stuff. I don't know, I've never really bought into the whole destiny thing. I like to think we make life what we want it to be, that we kind of have a choice in things." Elizabeth shrugged.

"I never really did either, but I don't think I'd be in this kitchen right now without pretty heavy interference from fate or whatever." Ben rubbed the back of his neck, distracted when the gray cat with the big green eyes slinked back into the kitchen. "I found your flyer the day after I got an eviction notice. My old landlord bumped up the prices again a few months ago, and I thought I could make all the ends meet, but I couldn't. This place is a second chance."

"Well, if it *was* 'fate or whatever,'" Elizabeth chuckled, "I'm glad it brought you here."

"Me too." Ben smiled softly, his eyes following the cat as he hopped up onto the table and approached Ben. "Hi, Elijah," he cooed, wiggling his fingers in an attempt to earn his affection.

"Here, you can give him some pieces of pepper. It's his favorite thing." Elizabeth slid Ben a little bowl of chopped bell peppers. Then, to demonstrate, she took a medium-sized chunk and held it in her palm, letting Elijah eat it out of her hand. He crunched the sweet treat and nuzzled against Elizabeth's hand. She hoped that meant that all was forgiven.

"I had a dog that loved lettuce a while back." Ben smiled, taking a piece of pepper like Elizabeth had done and offering it as a peace offering to the cat. Though Elijah hesitated, after a few moments, he accepted the pepper and crunched it just as happily as he'd crunched the first. "Awwww, good kitty."

Elijah resisted every bone in his tiny feline body that was screaming at him to bite Ben's hand for the 'good kitty' comment. Elizabeth would *definitely* be pissed at him if he bit their new roommate. So, instead, he accepted the peppers and, against his will, purred.

The oven beeped, and Elizabeth pulled her oven mitts back over her hands and pulled the peppers out, setting the hot pan on top of the stove before turning the knob to turn the oven off.

"Those look really, really good." Ben sat up straighter, staring at the peppers. "Thank you so much for this, again. You really didn't have to—"

"Quit thanking me," Elizabeth said, using a pair of tongs to move the peppers onto plates and handing him one with a fork. "You can make it up to me by doing the dishes."

Ben smiled at her, chuckling a little as he moved the plate in front of him. "Deal."

Chapter 9

It was the fourth day after Ben moved in, and he was still almost too afraid to go downstairs to get a drink in the middle of the night, but he convinced himself that if he ever wanted to feel comfortable in the townhouse, he'd simply have to start venturing outside of his comfort zone. It was only awkward if he made it awkward, and since he'd spent a lot of time cooped up in his room, and by extension, the office, he felt like he was crossing some nonexistent line by leaving the confines of his little cave.

When he finally worked up the courage to go downstairs, he noticed that the lights in the living room were still on, even at whatever ungodly hour it was (4 o'clock, according to the thin white numbers on his cracked phone screen). So, being the tree-hugger he was, he decided to do the right thing and turn the light off. Except, when he walked into what he assumed was the empty living room, it was not empty.

Elizabeth was sitting at her laptop, wearing his sweatshirt and an old pair of black sweatpants, a steaming mug of something sitting on the side table next to the couch.

He jumped, shocked, and held a hand over his racing heart. "Holy shit, you scared me."

"Sorry. Up burning the midnight oils tonight." Elizabeth laughed, her lips red and her eyeliner sharp. She hadn't even taken off her makeup for the day. Odd.

"Yeah, I was just about to ask why you were up so late."

"I got really into a chapter I'm writing. I don't know if I told you I'm writing a book or not."

"Right, I think you did. The one with the time traveler, right?"

"Yep, that's the one." Elizabeth nodded. She raised her mug to her lips and blew on whatever hot drink was in it. "I'm finally getting to the really good stuff that I've been planning out for...well, what feels like centuries."

"Ah, I get that. Sorry to stop your creativity train," Ben apologized, his curious brown eyes wandering to the sleeping cat curled up in the corner of the couch. Elijah was really, really adorable, especially when he wasn't glaring daggers at whoever was attempting to give him affection. "I was thirsty, so..."

"No worries. It's your house, too, after all," she reminded him. "I won't be up much longer, probably. And don't worry. I'll turn the light off when I'm done."

"Sounds like a plan. Have a good night. Morning? I don't know. Anyway, good luck, uh, with your writing endeavors."

"Thanks! Goodnight!"

Ben turned and walked into the kitchen, pouring himself a glass of cold water from the filter on the fridge, and then he went back up the stairs and climbed in bed.

He laid there for a while, staring at the ceiling and thinking. It wasn't too weird that Elizabeth was up so late, he supposed. He'd pulled so many all-nighters while working for his Master's Degree, and even while he was still an undergraduate. It had been almost natural for him, back when he had finals.

For someone their age, an all-nighter was normal.

But how many in a row were healthy? The next few nights, seeing as they were both writing (Ben, his thesis, and Elizabeth, her novel), Ben decided to sit in the living room with her to keep her company. Without fail, every single night, she'd stay up well past midnight, and by the time he went to bed, exhausted, she wasn't even sleepy. And that shouldn't have been weird, if she was tired the next day, but he swore that every day she was up before he was, making breakfast on the stove, wide awake.

Maybe she had a caffeine addiction. Maybe that was how she always seemed to have energy. He looked around the house, but he couldn't find anything extremely caffeinated that wasn't his own. He knew that sometimes Jack came around with coffee, and Elizabeth would drink that, or some tea on occasion, but all he could find in the way of hot beverages was hot chocolate and chai, which was caffeinated, but he was well accustomed enough to tea and coffee to know it couldn't keep her awake forever. She didn't appear to drink any pop either, and his search for energy drinks was fruitless too. There was no secret stash of Red Bull or 5-Hour Energy.

After about a week and a half living with her, Ben was pretty convinced his roommate didn't sleep.

Weird. But not weird enough to raise any red flags. Maybe she was just one of the few people who didn't need sleep because of some genetic malfunction. Or maybe she had some form of extreme insomnia. There had to be some logical explanation for it.

So, he continued to spend his evenings writing on the couch next to her, plugging and plugging and plugging away at his thesis.

His laptop screen illuminated his features in the dim living room. The lights were down low, and it was dark outside. He scrunched his nose, trying to remember something. It was right there at the edge of his memory, something he *knew* he knew, but he couldn't remember the name of it.

"You alright over there?" Elizabeth laughed, sipping cocoa from her mug. Whipped cream clung to her lip. In his time with her so far, he'd noticed she had quite a sweet tooth. Every cocoa she made had at least one extra squirt of chocolate syrup, and they were always piled high with whipped cream and sprinkles, and as Christmas drew ever-nearer, candy canes.

"I'm trying to remember...the street that the Blackwood Inn was on. I know I know it, but..."

"Mahogany Lane," Elizabeth replied without skipping a beat. "It's, like, seven blocks from here, down by the river. It's the Bloodborne Bar now, though."

"Oh. Right. Of course." Ben nodded, his relief completely blocking out the fact that Elizabeth had just...*known* it. "Did you...study history?"

"A little." Elizabeth shrugged. "I mean, I'm a local, so I know my way pretty well around the historical district. It's hard to not be a bit of a history buff when it's so thick in this place."

"That's true." Ben chuckled, shaking his head. "You'll have to take me on a tour sometime. I still don't think I've seen it all yet."

"Maybe when it's not so dark outside," she teased.

"Right, for sure. Wouldn't want to get lost out there."

"Definitely." She hit a few keys on her laptop, clicked a few things, and then closed it, yawning. "Wow, I'm tired. I think I'm gonna get to bed."

"I don't think you've ever gone to bed before me. You're even more of a night owl than I am."

"Well, I am a night owl, that's for sure. Maybe not tonight, though." She laughed and slung her laptop case over her shoulder. "Well, goodnight, Ben. See you tomorrow."

"Yeah, see you." He waved, watching as Elijah uncurled himself from his fuzzy little ball and followed after Elizabeth, his little paws padding across the hardwood floors. And then Ben was alone in the quiet living room with nothing but his laptop, his notes, and his thoughts.

❧◈☙

"You think she doesn't sleep?" Jay asked. He and Ben had a history class together, so it wasn't uncommon for them to wander into whatever coffee shop was on their way to grab something warm to drink, especially with the weather getting colder by the day. "Like, at all?"

"Well, I assume she has to, right?" Ben shrugged, taking a sip of his mocha.

"That wasn't a no, though."

"Listen, I get it. I sound crazy. But you--"

"No, no, no, I'm on board. All aboard the crazy train. Plus, you said the hot neighbors are gay witches, right?"

Ben sputtered, coffee splattering on the table. He rolled his eyes and wiped up the mess with a napkin. "I never said they were witches, alright? All I said was that they were into tarot readings and astrology and stuff."

"They sound like witches to me." Jay thought for a moment, drumming his fingers on the side of his cup. "But you said she cooks a lot, right? Why would a vampire need to cook...? That doesn't make sense..."

"Woah, woah, woah. I think you're jumping the gun on this. I don't think she's a vampire, I just...think she has some weird energy deficiency thing and she doesn't need sleep? I don't know. But she goes to sleep super late every night and gets up earlier than I do to make breakfast, and she's never tired. Like, at all. And her cat? Super weird. It's almost like he knows what I'm saying, and he stares at me with these empty green eyes."

"Wait, she has a cat? Maybe she's a gay witch too." Jay was quiet for a second before gasping. "And maybe she cooks everything because she's putting a spell on you!"

"Dude, Halloween was like two weeks ago. I'm just saying, she's a little odd. Really nice, super sweet, but a little odd." Ben hadn't opened up to his friend to hear all of his conspiracy theories, he just wanted to know that what he was experiencing was at least somewhat normal. This conversation had convinced him the opposite was true.

"Maybe I'm getting a little ahead of myself but, Ben, that definitely sounds a little weird. Just keep your eyes peeled, alright? She's super hot, super nice, and that's how they get ya." Jay dragged his finger across his neck.

Ben laughed, shaking his head. He was being paranoid for sure. This was all silly. Just silly paranoia that had found its way into his brain because of everything else that was going on. Everything was normal, and Elizabeth was a nice, sweet, *normal* roommate.

Morgan M. Steele ∽

Right?

Chapter 10

"Were you ever into *Twilight?*"

The question caught Elizabeth a bit off-guard, if she was being honest. She laughed. "Uh, yeah, who wasn't? Team Carlisle all the way."

Ben chuckled and raised an eyebrow. "I thought his name was Edward, though."

"I said what I said."

It was the middle of the afternoon on a Saturday. Ben had curled up in the bay window at the front of the house with a book about fashion during the Revolutionary War, but his eyes were tired, so he was taking a break. Meanwhile, Elizabeth was knitting a scarf. She sure seemed to have a lot of hobbies: knitting, writing, cross-stitch, and he swore he'd seen a violin in her room the one time he'd gotten a glance through the door while it was cracked open.

"Real talk, though, *Twilight* is a guilty pleasure of mine. I only watch it when I need a good laugh without thinking too hard. It's like brain popcorn, you know? The real, superior vampire movie is *What We Do in the Shadows.*" Elizabeth mimicked a chef's kiss. "It's a masterpiece."

"Taika Waititi, right?"

"Yes." Elizabeth nodded. "He's the best."

"I've never seen it, but we'll have to watch it sometime."

"If you're done reading for now, I have the Blu-Ray over here." Elizabeth got up and walked toward the entertainment center to dig it out from her seemingly endless collection of movies, but was interrupted by the phone ringing. She redirected her attention. "I'll go get it."

Ben watched as she walked out of the living room. He couldn't help but overhear some of her conversation in the other room.

"Joelle! Hi, how are—? No, I'm free today, I can totally come over. Is everything—? Yeah, I can be there in...like, thirty minutes if traffic isn't too bad. Yep. No problem. Of *course*, of course. I'll see you in a bit."

"Is everything alright?" Ben asked once Elizabeth hung up.

She walked to the table in the dining room and picked up her purse from where it was hanging on the back of the chair. Next, she went to the coat hooks in the front room, pulling on her jacket and stepping into her boots. "Yeah, it's fine. It's this family I babysit for, the Hunters? They have a family emergency and need a babysitter for the three youngest. I'll probably be back pretty late tonight, so don't wait up."

"Oh, alright. Do you need me to do anything while you're gone? Laundry or anything?" Ben offered. He felt sort of useless, unable to do anything to help out. He hoped everything was alright.

"I actually have some clothes in the dryer, if you wouldn't mind taking those out for me and switching them out with the towels in the washing machine. I almost forgot about that; thank you. Um...Oh! There's lasagna in the fridge if you get hungry, and...there was something else..." Elizabeth squinted, tapping her temple with her index finger a few times until it came to her, but it didn't. "I don't remember. If I do, I'll shoot you a text. Anyway, have a nice day! See you tomorrow, probably."

"Right, uh, have a good time." Ben waved.

The door closed behind her, and she was gone, leaving him, once again, alone with the cat. He looked down to Elijah, who was staring back up at him with his empty green eyes.

"Just you and me, huh, buddy?" Ben asked.

It looked like Elijah considered his question for a moment before disregarding him completely and curling up in the spot Ben had been reading in. Figured. Ben was pretty sure that cat would disown his own mother if it meant sitting in a warm little patch of sunlight.

So, determined to get something out of the day, Ben picked up his book and sat in a different spot to get back to work, jotting down notes and marking pages as he went. When it was time to take a break, he switched Elizabeth's laundry like she asked, setting the basket of clothes outside her bedroom door before getting back to work. Time seemed to zip by while he was reading, as it usually did, and the next time he looked up, it was dark outside, his stomach was growling, and there was a knock at the door.

Ben stood up and walked to the front door, peering out of the intricate glass window set into the polished mahogany. Jack was standing there in his full scrubs with a mini cooler. What the hell was he doing fresh out of the hospital with a mini cooler?

He figured there was no way to find out without opening the door, so he did.

"Ben! Is Elizabeth home?"

"Nah, she's at the Hunters' place. Some family emergency or something. Do you want to come in?"

"Yeah, it'll be quick." Jack stepped over the threshold, hauling the cooler straight to the kitchen and setting it on the counter.

"Do you want to, uh, unload that into the fridge?" Ben asked. He was followed to the kitchen by Elijah, whose furry tail tickled Ben's ankle on his way by.

Elijah leapt up onto the counter, sniffing the cooler's lid. He watched Jack intently, and in return, Jack let him sniff his hand before he pet Elijah's little head.

"What?" Jack asked, looking at Ben and thinking for a second before he replied. "Oh, no, I'll just leave the cooler here for her to unpack later."

"What's...in it? I mean, if that's not too personal..."

"Uh…" Jack thought for a long moment. Too long. "It's just some…" Elijah looked up at Jack, staring at him expectantly. "My coworker makes this really complicated kind of pasta sauce, and it's really delicate, so I think it's best if Elizabeth handles it. No offense, but I've heard—and seen—that you can be pretty clumsy."

"Well, you're not wrong." Ben chuckled and rubbed at the back of his neck, heat gathering in his cheeks. "Is there anything else you needed?"

"Nope, I'm all set." Jack shook his head, walking back towards the front door.

As soon as Jack walked away from the island, Elijah hopped up and sat on top of the cooler, staring down at Ben, his green gaze sharp and intense. Intimidated, Ben turned and followed Jack to the door so he could close it behind him.

"Have a good night, Ben. And good luck on your thesis. Elizabeth said you've been working really hard on it lately."

"Thanks so much, dude! Have a good night!"

Once the door was closed again and Jack was gone, a sinking feeling settled deep into the pit of Ben's stomach. What was in that cooler, he was pretty sure, was either drugs or something…worse than drugs. His roommate being a drug dealer? He could handle that. His roommate having…what he was *pretty sure* was in that cooler? That was on an entirely different level of Absolutely Fucking Not.

So, feeling thoroughly unsettled, Ben sat on the couch and got back to working on his research as best as he could. That was to say, not very well.

There was something weird in that cooler, and the only thing stopping him from finding out was one very grumpy gray cat...

Chapter 11

"I fucked up, Liz. Like, majorly. Worse than majorly. I might have ruined everything. Ohhh fuckfuckfuck—"

"Jack, shut up, I'm sure it's fine. What happened?" Elizabeth had Andy up on the counter next to her in the kitchen. Given the language her best friend had just used, she was very glad she'd elected *not* to put "Uncle Jack" on speaker.

Only the three youngest Hunter children were home tonight. The older two had gone with Joelle and Jordan on a supernatural hunting trip of sorts, a "Siren Stakeout," as Jordan had so eloquently put it.

"I went to your place to drop off the blood, and Ben was there, and he already saw me with the cooler, so it would have been weird to just take it back to the car, right? So I took it inside and set it on the counter, and he asked what was in it, and I didn't know what to FUCKING SAY, so I said my coworker made some special complicated delicate sauce or something, I don't KNOW! I'm so sorry."

"No, you know what, I think it'll probably be okay. I've been pretending to sleep a decent amount recently because I think he's been suspicious. It should be fine. Plus, Elijah is there. He won't let anything happen. Take a few deep breaths, alright? It's fine."

"You're right. You're always right." Jack breathed for the first time since he'd gotten home to call her. "God, I'm glad I called you."

"Me too. It's been what, like ten years since your last panic attack?"

"Something like that..." Jack chuckled on the other end of the call, taking deep breaths. "I'll let you go now. Tell the kids Uncle Jack says hi."

"Uncle Jack says hi," Elizabeth parroted to Andy, whose face lit up like a Christmas tree despite the fact that he had only ever met Jack a handful of times.

"HI, UNCLE JACK!" Andy yelled, kicking his legs from his seat way up on the marble countertop.

"Bye, Jack, I'll see you soon, I'm sure." Elizabeth laughed warmly, one hand messing up Andy's already-messy curls.

"Later." The call went dead.

"Was everything okay?" Thomas asked, helping his twin brother stir one of the large pots, which was sitting on the stove filled with slowly-melting marshmallows and a hunk of liquidy butter.

"Yeah, he sounded worried," Brayden agreed.

Elizabeth supposed she'd forgotten that their Hunter blood granted them certain perks ordinary humans weren't given. Namely, advanced hearing, sight, and scent, the senses they used the most while tracking down whatever evil creature was terrorizing their assigned district at the moment. Well, they'd probably heard worse language from their older brother.

"He's fine. There was just a little mix-up with my roommate."

"You have a roommate?" Andy asked, tilting his head. "I thought Elijah was your roommate?"

"Elijah *is* my roommate, but I have a human roommate now, too. His name is Ben, and he wants to be a history professor." Elizabeth booped Andy's nose, making him giggle. "Now, my little bat, I need you to measure out six cups of cereal and pour it in this big bowl."

"Are we still stirring?" Thomas asked.

"Yep, keep stirring until it's all melted." Elizabeth looked back at them and checked on the pot briefly. It was *mostly* melted, but not quite all the way there yet.

"Does he know?" Brayden peeked back over his shoulder at his favorite babysitter while she supervised Andy's pouring of the Rice Krispies, keeping track because she knew he had a bad record of correctly counting but *insisted* on helping.

"Does he know what, sweetheart?"

"Does Ben know you're a vampire?"

Elizabeth laughed and shook her head. "No, I'm afraid not. I know you don't meet many humans, but...they don't exactly...Well, they don't *understand* people like me, people like you. The idea of me and Jack scares some people a lot."

Andy giggled. "But you're not scary!"

"That what I like to think too. But sometimes that's not how humans see it. They think my fangs are too sharp." She held her index fingers in front of her face, mimicking her fangs rather than actually unleashing them in front of the kids. "And they don't particularly care for my diet either."

"You drink blood! So what?! It's not like you're *killing anybody* to get it!" Thomas exclaimed, throwing his hands up in the air and letting his brother take a turn on the spoon.

"Maybe *you* should break the news to him, then." Elizabeth chuckled and grabbed the mixing bowl filled with cereal. She handed it to Thomas and motioned for Brayden to give her the spoon, as stirring was about to get difficult. "Because I still don't know when—or *if*—I'm going to."

"If he's a good guy, he'll understand. And if he doesn't, dump him," Brayden advised, rubbing his chin thoughtfully. "At least, that's what Sage would say, I think."

"Thank you, Brayden, that's good advice." Elizabeth knew that it was only inevitable, really. Someday, she'd slip up and Ben would find out, but that day wasn't today.

Once the Rice Krispies Treats were finished, cooled, sampled, and the boys were all long asleep, Joelle, Jordan, Connor, and Sage finally pulled into the driveway, their faces streaked in dirt and leaves and sand caught in their hair. Connor's clothes were fully soaked, and he didn't seem to be in great shape, his sopping black hair clinging to his forehead. Every step he took, he dripped water onto the floor, leaving little puddles behind him.

"Rough mission, bud?" Elizabeth asked.

Connor chuckled, ringing out his blue flannel in the sink. "You could say that again."

"He was siren bait," Sage explained, mud coating her boots and jeans up to her knees.

"Not intentionally," he interjected grimly.

Elizabeth shuddered. She'd had a few interactions with sirens in her many years, and she avoided them at all costs. Some creatures, like herself, fought really hard to get rid of the bad reputations their ancestors had left them. Sirens, 99% of the time, embraced their dark heritage, drowning sailors and college students and whoever or whatever else without so much as batting an eye.

"But we all made it in one piece." Joelle walked into the kitchen and hugged Elizabeth tightly. "Thank you so much for coming on such a short notice. You're a life saver."

"No, *you're* the life savers. But seriously, whenever you need me, I'm here. Just give me a call."

"Ooh, smells good in here!" Jordan walked in next, slowly taking all of the weapons out of his belt and setting them on the table to clean and put away later. "Do some cooking while we were gone?"

"Rice Krispies Treats are on the plate on the counter." Elizabeth jabbed her thumb behind her and crossed her arms. "The boys were a little nervous for you when I got here, so I decided to take their minds off of it."

"And if we know our Elizabeth, there's always some kind of cooking involved." Joelle smiled, her arm around Elizabeth's shoulders. "Thank you for the sweets. I'm sure we'll enjoy them for the next few days or so."

"In this house, I doubt they'll last that long." Elizabeth laughed. She glanced at her watch. "Well, I've got a cooler of blood waiting for me back home. I better get going."

"See you soon, I'm sure." Jordan laughed. "Thanks again."

"Don't mention it." Elizabeth said her final good-byes and then got in her car and drove back into the city. It was odd how quiet the place got at night. Orange street lamps illuminated empty streets, and stoplights blinked yellow, signaling ghost traffic. She could count the number of other cars on the road on one hand.

Finally, she pulled into her spot in front of her townhouse, and her heels clicked up the steps into the house. She took off her shoes and hung up her coat, hanging her purse on the chair before finally walking back into the kitchen, where Elijah was laying on top of the little red cooler sitting innocently on the countertop.

He looked up at her, annoyed. "Do you know how long I've been sitting on top of this cooler?"

"Probably a while. I'm sorry," Elizabeth whispered, mindful of her roommate sleeping upstairs. He was known to wander down to the kitchen at odd hours. "If it makes any difference, they caught the Siren."

"As expected." Elijah stretched out his back, a few of the joints in his spine popping as he did. "Have you ever known the Hunters to let their prey escape?"

"No, never." Once he was out of the way, Elizabeth popped the lid. Fourteen blood bags, as always. Two pints a day. Given that she didn't drink from the vein, like most vampires her age, and preferred instead to drink blood that no one was using at the moment, she required slightly more of it to keep her sustained. It wasn't an exact science, but she'd found through trial and error that around two pints was what she needed to operate efficiently. Glancing behind her, she pushed the lid back on.

Luckily, Elizabeth's mini fridge in her room was completely empty, so even if Ben did decide to snoop while she was gone, though she doubted he had, he wouldn't have found any incriminating evidence.

Well, in *there* at least. If he decided to read through her photo albums and scrapbooks dating back to *gods knew when*, then she might be in some trouble.

She turned to Elijah. "Thank you for guarding it. I suppose I owe you some peppers for that."

"I think you owe me more than peppers."

"You're right. I'll get you some new toys next time I'm out."

"That's fair," Elijah agreed, walking closer to her and butting his head against her shirt. "You know, I like Ben. I do. But the boy is not an idiot. He's going to figure out what's going on eventually, and when he does..."

"I know that, believe me. We can talk about it more when he's gone."

"Agreed."

Elizabeth sighed. She knew Elijah was right. She knew Jack was right. Everyone was right. She was four hundred years old; she wasn't naïve. She knew that rooming with a human wasn't her brightest idea, even under the best circumstances. But as Ben had said when he moved in, this place was his second chance, and she was pretty sure he'd rather live in a townhouse with a vampire than nowhere at all.

Chapter 12

It was Wednesday. Ben had just gotten home from the class he shared with Jay, who was more than delighted to discuss crackhead conspiracy theories with him before and after the class, with little spurts of it during. Ben laughed through most of it, but there was a piece of him that was just too scared something was happening right under his nose to really unwind and participate in the conversation; he was scared there was some sliver of truth in his friend's jokes.

So, when he got home, he decided to do some investigating of his own.

"Do you like Italian food?" he asked, jotting some numbers down in his Sudoku puzzle of the day.

Without skipping a beat, Elizabeth replied, "I *love* Italian food. I think I have a whole cookbook of recipes on the shelf in there." She looked up at him from her cross-stitch project. "Why, are you craving Italian?"

"Oh, no, I mean, well, maybe? I don't know. Maybe just some garlic bread or something?"

"You know, I think I do have a good recipe for that." Elizabeth carefully set down her work and walked out to the kitchen to investigate. It didn't take her all that long to find it. She had a pretty good memory for that sort of thing. "Yeah, here it is! I could whip up some pasta tonight, if you want, or later this week. Whenever."

"Whenever works for you." Ben shrugged, jotting down a quick note.

Not averse to garlic.

The next time he decided to test one of Jay's crack theories was a few days later while Elizabeth was home. He went into the downstairs bathroom, one of the only places where there was a mirror, and screamed bloody murder.

Elizabeth was there in a matter of seconds, panic strewn across her features. "Are you okay? What's wrong? Did something happen?"

Ben looked at her and then glanced at the mirror, noting that she did, indeed, appear in it, and then faltered when he remembered that he had to reply to her. "Oh, uh, I saw a spider. Sorry. I didn't mean t—"

"It's alright." She exhaled, her shoulders slumping with relief. "Where is it?"

"Oh...well, I don't see it now. Maybe it's because I'm not wearing my glasses."

"Right...I'll just, uh, be in the other room, then. Let me know if you need me to come kill it." Elizabeth jammed a thumb behind her before pivoting and exiting the bathroom.

Ben stared at himself in the mirror. Huh. Was *anything* he knew about vampires really right after all? Well, he figured there was only one way to find out.

Pausing for a long moment, he pulled out his pen and a little notebook from his pocket, adding to his list: *Has a reflection.*

❧ ◈ ❧

Over the course of the next week or so, Ben added more things to his list. On one particularly sunny day (not an easy feat in the middle of November), he invited Elizabeth to accompany him to a thrift shop down the street, and he was able to add a few things to his ever-growing list: *Likes antiques, Not averse to sunlight, Doesn't sparkle either.*

He added these beneath another note he had taken a few days before: *Doesn't need sleep.*

Elizabeth had a lot of skills too. In addition to the ones he'd already picked up on (knitting, writing, cross stitch, cooking, baking, handling spiders, the list went on...), it also seemed that she was good at painting and playing the piano and art in general, as well as sewing (with and without a machine), and playing the flute. It took time to get good at all of those things. Like, a lot of time. He wondered what kind of upbringing she'd had to pick up all of those talents.

That brought up another point: *Doesn't talk about family.* Then, thinking for a few moments, he tacked on, *Or childhood.*

After investigating her for the better part of a week, he met up with Jay again, this time in a different coffee shop. His conspiracy-obsessed friend had brought a whiteboard and a marker to organize the information Ben had gathered so far.

"Okay, so for evidence, we have the sleep thing, the childhood and family thing, the antique thing..." Jay listed, jotting them down in red marker.

"Don't forget all of her hobbies."

"Dude, some people are just insanely talented, that doesn't mean anything. Maybe she's just a Jack-of-all trades type."

"That's fair, that's fair." Ben nodded, accepting it. "I don't know. Something still doesn't feel right. I mean, she's so nice and—"

"I forgot the cooler! The cooler is definitely evidence." Jay jotted it down, ignoring whatever Ben was starting to say. Then, he looked up at his friend. "Vampires can be nice, but they're still vampires."

"That's...true, I guess."

They didn't stay at the coffee shop for much longer before getting up and parting ways. Ben was about halfway home when he realized that, in all reality, he didn't know what it really *meant* to be a vampire. He didn't know what was myth or fact or if they were ever even real at all. Weeks before, he'd have called himself a crazy person for believing that something like this could be possible, that his beautiful, kind roommate could be a bloodthirsty monster. And yet, there he was, switching routes so he could go to the GCHU library to do some research instead.

He was pretty familiar with the downtown campus' library, given that he had been there on quite a few occasions, particularly while he was an undergrad, but a lot as a grad student too. There was a nice little tea store tucked away there, so he ordered an Earl Grey with oatmilk and then set to work.

According to one of the computers downstairs, the only books the library had on vampires were all published as fiction, or, in some cases, as historical accounts of the vampire genre over time. He huffed. Was it weird that he was upset that there wasn't any non-fiction? Why was he expecting the library to have any actual information on vampires as though they actually existed? Jay was getting in his head.

"Need some help?" A cheery, chipper voice cut off his thought pattern.

Ben looked up. "Uh, no, I'm fine. But thanks."

"Oh, okay. Sorry for bothering you. You just looked frustrated, is all." The woman looked young, maybe twenty-three at the most. She had curled blonde hair that just tickled her shoulders, and she was wearing a vintage black dress with white polka dots, a string of pearls around her slender neck. Her nails were perfectly filed and painted red.

She looked like she'd stepped straight out of the 1950s.

"I'm just...looking for answers, but there aren't any." Ben shrugged. "Like every other research paper I've ever done."

"What's your paper about?" She tilted her head, her blood red lips curling into a soft, sympathetic smile. She offered her hand. "Oh, I'm Dottie, by the way."

"Ben," he introduced, shaking her hand, the icy temperature of which was excused by the cold weather outside. "I'm writing about...well, about supernatural findings over time. It seems like everything they have is listed as fiction, though."

"Ooh, supernatural findings? Sounds mysterious. Are we talking, like, the New Terrowin Witch Hunts or haunted mansions or..."

"Well, to be honest, vampires." Ben shrugged, laughing at just how ridiculous he sounded. "It's for a class, I swear. We had to—"

"No, no, I get it, yeah." Dottie nodded. "Don't worry, you don't strike me as some conspiracy theorist. Working in this place, I've seen them all."

"You work here?" Ben raised an eyebrow, looking for a nametag but not finding one.

"Off the clock, at the moment, but yeah. I usually work nights." She thought for a moment, touching her index finger to the corner of her ruby lips. "I think I know something that can help you, actually."

"Really?"

"Yeah, I think so. Follow me."

Ben logged off of his computer and got up, following Dottie to the elevator. They rode up a few floors to where it was quieter, all of the students there working in hushed whispers. This was meant to be a more focused studying sanctuary than the floors downstairs, where brighter colors and bigger tables invited and encouraged group work.

She led him down the aisles, balancing perfectly on her thin little high heels, until she turned and stopped. One of her slender fingers traced the spines of a few books until she finally found the title she was looking for and plucked the thick paperback from the row.

"One of the library's biggest secrets, I think, is that sometimes they hide the best information in the fiction section." Dottie handed him the book, and Ben studied the cover.

It was black with a swirling crimson design, the title spelled out in gothic white lettering.

"*The Death and Life of Count Bloodmere?*" Ben read, pushing his glasses up. "Interesting. I've never heard of him." He didn't think it was a lie, but it felt like one. In all of his studies, he couldn't recall ever hearing about a Count named Bloodmere. And yet, there was something about it that felt...familiar. He couldn't quite put a finger on it, though.

"It's an obscure tale, I won't lie," Dottie admitted. "Some people question the validity of the author's claims, hence its residence in the fiction section, but I promise you, just about everything you need to know about bloodsuckers is in those pages."

"Really…" Ben flipped through the yellowed book. It was old, that much was true, but based on the lack of dog-eared pages, he guessed it hadn't been read very much. He was pretty sure that because it was so well hidden on the shelves of his university's library, barely anyone had touched it. "Well, thank you so much! I'll be sure to give it a read."

"Of course." Dottie beamed. She took a few steps closer to him, her heels making her almost match his height. She continued, her tone becoming sickeningly sweet. "And while I've got you here, you don't mind if I ask for a teeny, itty bitty, little favor, do you?"

Her proximity made Ben nervous. He took a step back but found that there was nowhere left to go, a wall at his back and a tall wooden bookshelf on either side of him. She took another step forward, and he stood against the wall, helpless. He gulped. "And w-what would that be?"

"All of this talking has made me…a little…" Something dark flashed in Dottie's eyes before her irises were taken over by a bright red. Her canines sharpened into a pair of pearly white fangs, gleaming under the flickering fluorescent light above them. "Thirsty."

Ben didn't even have time to scream before she took him by the shoulders and plunged her fangs into his neck.

Chapter 13

To say Elizabeth was a little worried about Ben would be an understatement. Usually, on days when he had his Revolutionary War history class, he was home about half an hour later, depending on traffic and if he stopped in some coffee shop with Jay on the way home. Sometimes, he would push forty-five minutes or an hour or so, but it had been *three* hours, and he still wasn't home yet.

Trying not to be the overbearing mother of a roommate she always tended to be, she sent him one text, checking in, asking if he wanted mac and cheese or cauliflower pizza for dinner.

No response.

She waited a little while longer, trying not to get too concerned. She picked up her violin to distract herself, playing a few tunes before setting it down again.

"I'm sure he's fine. He's an adult." Elijah tried to set her at ease but had no such luck.

"I know he's alright, and I shouldn't be worried. But I am. I have this bad feeling in the pit of my stomach."

"Yeah, it's called anxiety. I'm sure he's okay. He'll be home any minute."

Ben was not, in fact, home any minute.

So, Elizabeth decided to call him, but it went straight to voicemail. "Hey Ben, it's Elizabeth. Just wanted to check in and make sure everything was okay. Don't rush to get home, just call me if you need a ride or anything. See you later! Bye!"

She hung up, sitting on the barstool in the kitchen with a huff. Was he mad at her? Had she done something? Worse, had he found her blood stash?

All of these fears subsided, however, when she heard the jingling of keys in the door and the sound of Ben's footsteps stepping over the threshold. She tried not to rush out to the living room too fast, but was glad she had by the time she got a good look at him.

There were dark bags beneath his eyes, his hair was messed up in the back, sticking up at odd angles, and his glasses were crooked on his nose. Ben's eyes were empty and glazed over, like he couldn't focus them on any one thing and instead just stared off into space. But the worst thing she noticed on him was the clean bite mark on the side of his neck.

There was only one kind of person that could have done that to him.

Elijah looked up at Elizabeth with a look that said, "*Okay, maybe YOU told ME so.*" His tail hovered behind him curiously as he studied their dazed roommate.

"Ben?" Elizabeth asked softly, taking a few steps closer to him. She waved a pale hand in front of his face. "You okay? Did...something happen?"

"Huh?" He mumbled and shook his head, blinking a few times. He looked at her and then at the book in his hands and then around the room. "How'd I...?"

"How'd you what?" she pressed, although she already knew the answer. "Everything alright?"

"Yeah, yeah, I just...Huh. Sorry for the concern. I'm fine. I'm pretty sure I'm fine."

"Did you get lost on the way home? You were out for like five hours."

"FIVE?! But it's only—" Ben glanced down at his watch. Sure enough, six o'clock. "Shit."

"Ben, you don't look so well. Why don't you sit down, drink some water. I'm...gonna run next door, alright? I have to talk to Dianne about something."

"Uh, yeah, sure. That sounds like a good idea..." Ben took a few steps forward, stumbling, but he regained his composure quickly, walking to the kitchen to get a drink. Elijah followed after him, silently promising Elizabeth he'd watch him while she was gone.

After hurrying out the front door, down the steps, and onto the porch of the townhouse next to hers, Elizabeth rapped the brass knocker against the door several times until, finally, Nadia opened it.

"Elizabeth, what's wrong?" she asked, picking up the negative vibes before Elizabeth even came into the house.

"Ben got bit, and it wasn't by me."

Nadia's eyes widened. "Oh, shit."

"Yeah. He's holding up, but he's really out of it. Is Dianne home? I want her to look him over."

"Yeah, she is. Let me go get her." Nadia hurried upstairs while Elizabeth stood in the front room.

Max was sitting on the couch, playing something on whatever video game console he was using currently. "Is Ben okay?" he asked, looking up from his game for a second.

"Yeah, I think so. Elijah's babysitting him for me right now. He's just a little dizzy and out of it. You know, how you get a little dizzy when the doctors take blood from you?"

"Oh yeah! But then Nadia and Dianne always take me out for ice cream after and I feel all better."

"Exactly. Except Ben didn't choose to get his blood drawn, so he's not feeling so well. I think he'll be alright, I just want your sister to check on him to be sure."

"Oh, gotcha. Tell him I said hi! I think we have ice cream if he wants some to make him feel better..."

Elizabeth smiled. "I'll be sure to let him know."

Dianne came down the stairs, followed by Nadia. She turned to Elizabeth. "I knew I was getting some bad vibes about today. Let me take a look at him."

The witch led Elizabeth back to her own town-house, and they walked inside to where Ben was sitting in the kitchen on a barstool, a glass of water in his hand. He was staring intensely at the wall. Elijah had perched himself on the kitchen counter, and he looked up at Elizabeth with wide, concerned eyes.

"Ben?"

"Mmm..." he hummed, looking over at his room-mate with his half-lidded eyes. He was in even worse shape than when she'd left.

"You okay, buddy?"

"I'm fine..." He yawned. "Just...sleepy..."

Dianne took a few steps forward and looked at him, studying his eyes and the mark on his neck. She reached out and very gently touched the wound. It was closed up, which was good. Some vampires, newer vampires especially, were messy and tended to leave the wounds open. This was a more experienced vampire, for sure. And his mental state was confusing too. Dianne had seen several vampire victims after they'd been through attacks, and none of them were quite this...dazed. Most of the time, they were in a panic about what had happened, that being because they remembered all of it.

Ben...didn't seem to remember *any* of it.

Aside from that, though, he wasn't showing any signs that any venom had entered his system, which was probably Elizabeth's main concern.

Dianne motioned for Elizabeth to follow her, and the two of them walked upstairs into Elizabeth's room, Elijah sliding in before they closed the door.

"Okay, so I don't think he has any venom in his system," Dianne told her.

Elizabeth nodded, her finger against her lip. "I didn't think so either; I would've smelled it on him."

"Right, right. We know it's an older vampire because the bite is clean. Definitely not a newborn. But I don't know any vampires that could have just...wiped his memory like that." Dianne shook her head.

Elizabeth felt what little heat was in her cheeks drain as her face went paler than it already was. Her stomach dropped, and she said very quietly, "*I do.*"

Chapter 14

It wasn't until the next day that Ben was back to his normal self. He woke up and hardly felt bad at all, aside from a crick in his neck. Huh. Weird. He must have slept on it wrong, he figured.

Once he was downstairs, he scooped himself some of the eggs Elizabeth had cooked and sat down at the island in the kitchen, using his fork with one hand while he propped open the book he'd gotten at the library with the other.

Elizabeth glanced at the cover of his book and chuckled. "Did you switch thesis topics or something?"

"Huh? Oh, no I didn't. Just a sudden interest of mine, I guess." Ben shrugged and took a sip of coffee from his favorite mug, which, unsurprisingly, had a *Hamilton* quote on it. "Interesting stuff, this Bloodmere guy."

"Oh yeah?" Elizabeth raised an eyebrow, amused.

"Yeah," he replied. "Says here he drowned when he fell through the ice as a young man and came out of it as an ice-cold, bloodsucking vampire."

"Jeez, wild stuff." She laughed and shook her head. She'd heard some insane tales about her father over the years, but that just about took the cake. But, deciding to play along with Ben's little game, she asked, "Did he turn into a bat too?"

Elijah, who was sitting on the island in front of Elizabeth, stopped licking his paw to look up at her. He rolled his eyes and hopped down onto the floor, stalking off towards the living room.

"No, I don't think so. Well, if he could, I haven't gotten to that part yet." Ben flipped the page. He glanced up at Elizabeth over the rim of his glasses, looking for some sort of reaction from her, but there wasn't one.

Instead, she just sat there, eating her eggs and scrolling through something on her phone. "You know," she said, setting her phone face down on the island and looking up at Ben, "since you're in a vampire mood today, we should finally watch *What We Do in the Shadows*."

"I'm so down." Ben laughed. He slid his bookmark into the book and closed it, following Elizabeth out to the living room to watch it with her.

What started with one movie quickly evolved into an all-day affair. When they'd finished watching *What We Do in the Shadows*, Elizabeth suggested (mostly as a joke) that they put in the *Twilight* movies so they could roast them together, and he had (surprisingly) agreed, under the condition that he could get some work done while they did it.

So, typing away on his laptop, Ben looked up at the screen just in time to catch Robert Pattinson's bare, sparkling chest. "Wow. That's just...why?"

"I don't know. I don't get it either. When I saw these in theaters, I was the only one laughing in a room full of teens, tweens, and vampire-obsessed moms. A few college girls thrown in for good measure."

"And you were...?"

She could feel his eyes on her now, testing not only her knowledge of the movies, specifically when they came out, but her math skills to be able to fudge a realistic age that matched her cover story of being twenty-six-ish years old.

She thought about it for a moment. "Oh gods, I think I was like..." *If it came out in 2008, and I'm 'twenty-six', then that was eleven years ago, so I was...* "Fifteen? Something like that." Then, to make the lie slightly more realistic, she tacked on, "I went with some friends from school. They were way more into it than I was."

Ben quit studying her and pushed his glasses up his nose, sitting back against the couch a little more. "Huh, I didn't realize it came out that long ago. I feel old."

Oh, he had no idea. Elizabeth laughed. "Right, though?"

"Did you read the books too?"

"I was at the midnight release of *Breaking Dawn*." She'd almost forgotten about that. As someone with all the free time in the world, of course she'd read the *Twilight* books. Everyone else was reading them, Jack included, so she had no reason not to. "I had just started working at Turning Page at that point, so I got the employee discount and everything."

"Wow, fancy."

"Very." Elizabeth shook the empty popcorn bowl. "Well, I'm gonna make some more. Do you want anything from the kitchen?"

"I'm all set, thanks." Ben smiled. When she got up, he asked, "Do you want me to pause it?"

"I've seen it a million times, I'll probably be okay missing the next five minutes," she said. "You enjoy it, though."

He laughed. "Oh believe me, I will."

❦◈❦

After the last movie, once the final credits had rolled, Ben was knocked out. When he felt himself drifting, he'd set his laptop aside and got into a comfier position, laying against a throw pillow. Elizabeth never really noticed how tall he was until she saw him sprawled out like that, his legs curled in so he could fit. She also didn't know he snored, but he did. *Cute*, she decided.

Although it was over, she didn't really want to wake him. He looked so peaceful, so *human*. It also meant he trusted her enough to be vulnerable in front of her. No, she wouldn't wake him. It did get pretty cold on the lower level, though, especially in the winter, so she took the blanket Gladys had made off of the back of the loveseat, unfolded it, and then gently draped it over his sleeping form. It didn't quite cover him all the way, but it was better than nothing.

She also noticed that his glasses were kind of crooked, squishing his face in a way that couldn't be comfortable. So, carefully, she took them off of him and set them on the side table, next to his phone. There. Much better.

Elizabeth left a lamp on for him so he wouldn't wake up in complete darkness, and then took the popcorn bowl back to the kitchen. Once she'd washed it out and put it on the drying rack, she walked up the stairs and into her room.

She bent down and opened her mini-fridge, only to find it empty. Huh. That never happened. Jack always came to give her fourteen-ish bags the day before she was going to run out so she'd...well, so she'd never run out. But there she was, crouched in front of an empty fridge, the fluorescent light shining bright against her pale skin. She'd just have to call him, she supposed.

"Fuck," she muttered, raking her fingers down her face and closing the door. It wasn't like a day or two without blood would kill her. She could actually last quite a while without it, due to her age. Younger vampires didn't last so long without giving into their thirst, but one that was four centuries and some odd years old? She'd manage.

"Something wrong?" Elijah sauntered into Elizabeth's room through the open door.

"Out of blood."

"Oh, yikes. Did you call Jack?" he asked, hopping up onto Elizabeth's bed and curling into a little ball on one of her pillows.

Elizabeth was already pulling up his contact. "About to." She clicked on his name and held the phone to her ear, listening as it rang a few times and then shot her to voicemail.

"Hey, this is Jack Ellis. If you're hearing this, I probably got called into work. Leave a message and I'll get back to you as soon as I can."

When it beeped, she replied. "Hey Jack, it's Elizabeth. My fridge is empty, so I was wondering if maybe you forgot to stop by. I'm alright, so don't worry about me. Just call me whenever you're on break. Bye."

"Voicemail?" Elijah raised his head, and Elizabeth nodded. "That's cold."

"He probably has work. I'm sure he'll get back to me."

"Maybe text him just in case? He said service in the hospital is no bueno."

"That's a good idea." Elizabeth sat on the bed and reached out, scratching gently between Elijah's ears. Then, she typed out a quick message and sent it to Jack.

His tail flicked due to the sudden unexpected contact, but eventually settled back into a steady slithering pattern across her comforter. "So, what are you going to do?"

"About?"

"The blood, Ben getting bitten, you know, everything?"

"The blood, nothing yet. I'll be fine. Ben, I don't know..." Elizabeth ran her fingers through her hair and sighed. "I...well, I certainly wasn't expecting to have to deal with this for another decade or two."

"Yeah, but I think we both knew you couldn't avoid her forever." Elijah rolled into an upright position and then took a few steps closer, curling up in Elizabeth's lap instead of on her pillow. "I *am* sorry it had to happen right now, though."

"I doubt she knows that he's connected to me. I'm not too worried about that. She just wanted a quick drink; she doesn't care about anything else. Never has."

"You would know, wouldn't you?" Elijah chuckled darkly. "You never did tell me why the two of you broke up."

"Dottie..." she sighed, thinking about it.

It had been decades since she'd seen her ex-girlfriend. Great City was big enough that they never crossed paths. They had different habits, was all. Elizabeth and Jack spent loads of time in coffee shops while Dottie detested the bitter drink. Elizabeth worked in a bookstore, Dottie worked in a funeral home. They didn't really have much reason to see each other, and so, as far as Elizabeth knew, she hadn't seen the blonde-haired demon since they'd broken up in 1954.

"She likes using people. She takes and takes and takes and never gives anyone anything unless it benefits her in some way. Her family...they have some dark gifts. Namely, the memory scrambling thing, and they use it to their advantage, always have. As soon as I found out the kind of business she was *really* involved in, I didn't want anything to do with her. And I've been a lot happier ever since. She only really wanted me for my bloodline anyway..."

"You're too good for her. Ben is much more your pace." Elijah grinned to himself, smug.

"Ben and I are not—!"

"It's a matter of time and you know it." He rolled onto his back to look at her. "You think I don't see the way he looks at you? Or the way you cook anything his little human heart desires? Or the way—"

"I get it, I get it. But I don't think it'll happen. I don't date. Especially not humans and *double*-especially not my roommates."

"Mmhmm. Sure." The cat did not seem convinced, rolling his green eyes at her. He crawled out of her lap. "Whatever you say, vampire. I'll be downstairs staring at him until he wakes up." Before she could ask why, he added, "I like to creep him out."

"Have fun with that." Elizabeth's eyes trailed after him as he left her alone in her room with only her thoughts for company.

Chapter 15

In downtown Great City, about seven blocks from the hospital, was a place called the Rock n' Roller Diner. The floors were checkered black and white, and the leather booths were a surprisingly bright shade of red, given their age. The waitresses all wore poodle skirts, and the waiters wore aprons and paper hats.

The jukebox in the corner played 1950s rock all day, and for just a nickel, you could request a song, even in the year 2019. The burgers were always fresh, the fries were always hot, and the milkshakes were always piled with whipped cream, chocolate sauce, and a few extra cherries if you asked nicely. These were the things that made the diner one of Dottie Edwards' favorite places to arrange meetings with clients, or in this case, potential business partners.

Her hair was perfectly curled for the occasion, fingernails freshly manicured. The bell above the door jingled as she stepped through, and her heels clicked against the tile floor. She had a black designer bag over her shoulder, and in her other hand, she was effortlessly carrying a baby bucket and a black diaper bag.

"How many?" the hostess asked, distracted.

The waitress beside her bumped her, and she looked up, her eyes widening at the sight of Dottie, who only smiled, showing off her perfect white teeth.

"Miss Edwards, right this way." The waitress grabbed two menus and skated in the direction of Dottie's preferred booth, tucked into the corner by the window. She set down the menus, and another waitress brought out a high chair and pulled it up to the end of the table.

Once Dottie had set down her purse and the large plastic baby carrier, she unbuckled the little boy inside of it, pulled him out, and lowered his squirming little body into the high chair. Then, when he was settled, Dottie slid into her seat and started looking over the menu, perusing carefully even though she had every word memorized.

The bell over the front door jingled again, and Dottie didn't even look up, merely listening as the crisp footsteps travelled closer and closer to her until, finally, her companion slid into the seat opposite her.

"Sorry I'm late, Miss Edwards," his silky voice apologized. "Lost track of time."

"Don't fret. I was running a bit late myself," Dottie admitted, setting the menu down to look up at him.

Arthur Valentine was everything she'd expected him to be. Tall, handsome, complete with a charming face and the siren-like voice he was so well-known for. She'd never seen him face-to-face before, only from afar at the occasional formal event, but his reputation preceded him. Every vampire of influence knew who he was and what he was capable of. He was one of the oldest vampires in the states, and he had the Lakeshore underground under his complete control. Those that crossed him weren't often heard from again, and if they lived to tell the tale, they were often very…different afterwards.

"Thank you for joining me."

"Well, your message was quite irresistible. I'm afraid I couldn't keep myself away." He picked up the menu and scanned the pages. "What's good here?"

"Their burgers are spectacular. The chef bends some rules for me and makes mine extra rare." Something twinkled in her *slightly* red eyes. "I'm also a fan of their milkshakes."

"It's quaint." He looked around, impressed. "Old-fashioned like me. I can see why you've stuck around."

"Great City is a good place to put down roots." Dottie reached into her diaper bag and pulled out a canister of Gerber Puffs. She twisted the lid off and sprinkled a bunch of them into the tray of her son's high chair. Immediately, his chubby little hand scooped up two or three of them, and he put them in his mouth. "A good place, but not always a safe place."

"And that's where I come in, then." He grinned and set the menu down.

Just before he could continue and put his offer on the table, the waitress, who was wearing a red poodle skirt and a matching scrunchie in her long brown hair, skated up to their table. "Are we all set, or do we need some more time?"

"I'll have my usual." Dottie folded her menu and handed it to the waitress with a wink.

She nodded and jotted it down on her notepad and then turned to Arthur.

"I'll have what she's having," Arthur answered confidently, turning over his menu right after.

The waitress skated away and left them alone once more, the quiet filled by chatter from other tables, the traffic on the streets, and the sound of the rain dripping from the gutter. It was probably the last rainy day before snow started falling.

"Where were we? Ah, yes. Protection." Arthur looked at Dottie's son, who was content in his high chair. It had been a while since he'd seen a child up close, let alone one like the one in front of him, with his little red eyes and hair so blond it was white. If he didn't have them already, his baby fangs would be coming in soon. That process was never fun. Human babies experienced pain while their teeth were coming in, but their teeth weren't sharp enough to pierce skin. For the children of vampires, the process was much more painful. "What's his name?"

"Nicholas," Dottie answered. Her expression was unreadable. "His father is out of the picture. He's not my concern."

"Then what *is* your concern, if I may ask."

"I've made enemies in this town. People that would hurt him. Or me. I have my men, but all it takes is one mole among my ranks for the unimaginable to happen," Dottie said. "There are people who know too much. They must be disposed of if I want to raise my son here without worrying about our safety."

"I can handle that for you. In exchange, I'm looking for someone, and I know you have the connections to help me find her. Well, that and a slice of your profits, of course."

"Deal," she agreed. "Money is no object. My resources are your resources. My connections are yours to exploit in any way you choose."

"Perfect. I'll have my men write up a contract." He paused, smiling devilishly. "And perhaps if our collaboration is successful, we could both benefit from further business in the future. Strength in numbers and all that."

"I like the way you think," she said.

Nicholas whined, out of Puffs and starting to fuss. But before he started crying, Dottie reached into her bag and pulled out a multicolored plastic bat that rattled when she shook it. Instantly, the baby's eyes widened, and he stared at the toy, reaching out for it until finally his tiny fingers fastened around it.

Arthur and Dottie chatted for a while longer about less consequential things until the waitress returned with their orders, burgers so rare they bled on the grilled sesame buns with mayo, ketchup, mustard, and extra pickles, plenty of perfect golden fries, and vanilla milkshakes decorated with strawberry syrup and extra maraschino cherries.

"Do you need anything else?" the waitress asked, her hands shaking.

"We're all set, thanks."

The waitress rolled back into the kitchen. Dottie took a long sip from her milkshake and hummed.

"Nothing quite like a good, old-fashioned milkshake."

"I can't help but agree." Arthur raised his glass and clinked it against Dottie's. "I have a feeling this is the start of a beautiful relationship, Miss Edwards."

∻ ◈ ∽

"I'll take care of this whenever you're ready." The waiter set the bill on the table, but it was handed back to him immediately, a credit card tucked inside of it.

"I'm ready," replied the man. He was seated at the table furthest from the front window, tucked away next to the bathrooms. He was partially hidden behind a newspaper. It was an old trick, but one that worked, especially while discreetly watching two of the most notorious members of the vampire mafia. The two of them in one place couldn't be good news.

"I'll be right back with your receipt."

The waiter left. The man narrowed his eyes, pretending to read the top of an article, but actually studying the baby in the high chair, sipping what he assumed was blood from his sippy cup. Definitely not a human baby, and Dottie Edwards was not stupid enough to turn an infant, so that meant the child had to belong to her.

Interesting...

He took a mental note of it and watched as Arthur took Dottie's hand, kissing the back of it before he walked out of the diner and into a black car that was undoubtedly driven by one of Arthur's many loyal vampires. Not long after, Dottie packed her things and left with her child.

Finally, the waiter returned with the man's card and receipt. He set a few crumpled twenties on the table as a tip and then stepped outside into the rainy, late November afternoon.

Chapter 16

"Hey, um, Elizabeth? Are you...okay?" Ben tentatively nudged the door of her room open a little further. He knocked his fist against the door as he did, and as soon as the door drifted the teeniest bit further, Elijah pushed past Ben's ankle to get inside. The room was mostly dark, her blackout curtains blocking out the sunlight and casting her bed and the rest of the room in shadow. "Are you...like sick or something?"

"Ughhhhhhh," she groaned, forcing herself away from her plush pillows when she felt Elijah's weight land beside her. "Yeah, I'm alright. I pulled an all-nighter last night, and I'm really feeling it. But I'm okay. I'll be downstairs in a bit. Why, is everything alright?"

"Oh, yeah, everything's fine. I was just worried about you. I hadn't seen you all day, so I was wondering if you'd gone out or something."

"Nah, I'm right here. I'm—really, I'm fine. But thanks for the concern." Elizabeth flashed him an exhausted thumbs-up, and he smiled softly, glad that she was alive, at the very least.

"I'll let you be, then. Let me, uh, know if you need anything." Ben closed the door with a quiet click.

Elijah looked up at Elizabeth, studying the dark bags beneath her eyes. She...didn't look so good. Her brown irises had a reddish tint to them, something that only happened when she'd gone a few days without blood. Her skin was paler than normal, that was to say, it was almost completely white. Her long, raven hair looked dried out, and her hands were shaking ever so slightly.

"You don't look so good."

"I'm okay," she rasped, coughing.

"No, you're not. Should I get Dianne?"

"No. Elijah, I'm four hundred years old. I'll pull through a few days without blood. I'm going to call Jack again, though." Elizabeth swung her legs over the side of the bed and let her cold feet dangle over the edge. She groaned. Her body ached, soreness reaching deep into her limbs. She hadn't been this sore in...decades, she was sure. Maybe a few centuries.

Yet, despite all of the pain she was in, she still managed to be worried about Jack. He'd been working at the hospital for a while, and even during his busiest weeks, he'd *always* managed to bring Elizabeth her blood. There had to be something that was stopping him from doing so.

So, she unplugged her phone from its charger, dialed his number, and listened to it ring. This time, it rang a little longer before booting her to his voicemail. Huh.

"Hey, this is Jack Ellis. If you're hearing this, I probably got called into work. Leave a message and I'll get back to you as soon as I can."

There was a long *beep,* and Elizabeth sat there, processing for a few moments before she said, "Hey, Jack. It's Elizabeth. Is everything alright? I'm worried about you. Call me back when you can, okay?"

And then she hung up.

"Liz, that's not good." Elijah spoke quietly, walking closer to her and curling up in her lap. He rubbed his cheek against her stomach. "You need to drink something or you'll—"

"I know that. I'll figure it out. I'll just...put a bit of concealer on and get some caffeine. That should at least help perk me up a little bit."

"Elizabeth—"

"Elijah," she cut him off, petting his little head between his ears, "I know my limits. I won't push it, I promise. But I'm not...drinking anyone's blood today if I can help it."

"Okay..." He was skeptical, but he let it go nonetheless. He was concerned, yes, but he knew how stubborn she was, and he wasn't likely to win an argument with her, even in her much weaker state.

Once the cat was out of her lap, Elizabeth stood and walked to her vanity, putting on some concealer and eyeliner to make her look a little more alive, as well as some blush and her favorite red matte liquid lipstick to disguise her chapped, dry lips. There. Now, at least she *looked* a little bit better. If she could fake it, she was sure she would make it. Or, she hoped so.

She got downstairs about twenty minutes later to find Ben sitting on the couch, reading something new for his thesis. It was about a woman who'd given birth on a ship on her way to the new world, and how she'd barely survived the ordeal. As soon as he saw Elizabeth, he closed the book, looking up at her with curious, concerned brown eyes, enlarged endearingly behind his glasses.

"I, uh, made eggs. They're not as good as yours, but I tried. They're on the stove." Ben pointed back towards the kitchen.

Elizabeth smiled. "Thank you. That's really sweet." She walked into the kitchen and scooped some eggs onto her plate, sprinkling salt and pepper over them before joining him out in the living room. They were a little burned, but it was sweet that he'd tried to keep the house running while she was out of commission.

"These are good, Ben, I don't know what you're talking about." She chuckled, shaking her head. "What time is it anyway?"

"Like, three. I was feeling breakfast for lunch, you know? Or would it be linner? Dunch? I'm not sure. Also, eggs are kind of all I know how to make." He scratched the back of his neck. "Maybe you could give me some pointers?"

"I'll teach you how to make anything you want to know. Cooking isn't hard, it just takes practice is all." She took a few bites of eggs, sitting cross-legged on the couch.

Elijah walked into the living room, looked at Elizabeth, looked at Ben, looked back at Elizabeth, and then turned and walked out the cat door.

"Probably going to hunt birds." Elizabeth chuckled. "He's only ever caught a few, but it's always gross when he comes back with one."

"Ew, I bet." Ben grimaced. "Gross."

She nodded. She took a few more bites of egg and then said, "I think I'm gonna head over to After Hours once I'm done eating, if you'd like to join me. I need some caffeine."

"I'm down. I'll grab my laptop, we can do some writing together."

She smiled. "Yeah, I'd like that."

So, once she was done eating and had rinsed out her plate to put it in the dishwasher, she got her purse, put on her coat, and slipped a cozy knitted cowl over her head, and then she and Ben walked a few blocks over until they finally reached After Hours Cafe. The bell over their heads rang, announcing their arrival, and the cute, baby-faced barista looked up at them, smiling. His roots were coming in dark, his hair a lot fluffier and longer than when she'd last seen him. The pink had faded a bit, but it was still hanging on. Ah, the miracle of modern hair dye.

"You're back! It's been a while. I thought you and Jack had switched coffee shops or something." Cody laughed as they approached the counter.

"And cheat on our favorite barista? Of course not." Elizabeth chuckled. "Sorry it's been so long. Still remember my usual?"

"Let me think, um..." He thought deeply, staring at the register before it finally clicked. "Large, iced chai...coconut milk, extra shot of vanilla?"

"Perfect, Cody." Elizabeth gave a thumbs-up, fishing her wallet out of her purse. "I'm sure that memory of yours is helpful during exam week."

"Yeah, it is. Definitely comes in handy." He chuckled and then glanced towards the front door. If Elizabeth wasn't mistaken, the barista looked a little disappointed. "And, uh, do you want Jack's usual too?"

Elizabeth looked up at him, raising an eyebrow. "Um, no, I haven't actually heard from him in a few days."

"Oh, alright. I...thought," Cody chuckled and shook his head, his cheeks going pink, "well, I thought he might be meeting you here. So just the chai, then?"

"And whatever he wants." Elizabeth motioned to Ben, who shook his head.

"You don't have to pay for mine."

"Yeah, but I am, so order your drink." She grinned and stepped slightly out of his way.

Ben rolled his eyes, chuckling to himself before looking up at the barista. "I'll just have an Americano, thanks."

"Of course. One chai and one Americano coming right up."

Elizabeth paid for the drinks while Ben went ahead and found a table for them, setting up his laptop and plugging his phone into the wall. She joined him a few moments later, sitting across from him in the booth at the back. Her face was grim, jaw set on edge, and an odd look was settled into her brownish-reddish eyes.

"You okay?"

"Yeah, I'm just worried about Jack, is all." She bit her red lip. "He's not usually like this, even when he's busy at work."

"Hmm, I hope everything's alright." Ben offered a supportive smile.

"Me too..." Elizabeth sighed.

Cody came out a few minutes later with their drinks, and they set to work, fingers flying across their keyboards as they periodically sipped from their cups. Elizabeth wrote mindlessly for about an hour, tuning everything else out. She was glad she had her little fictional world to escape into, especially when everything in her real world felt so... *wrong*. She typed paragraph after paragraph, each more intense than the last, and then after a little while, she stopped.

She stared at her last page or so of writing and read it over again. Huh. Good stuff.

It wasn't all that often she felt that way about her own work. She'd found, writing a novel for the first time, that reading what a previous version of herself had written was somewhat like watching a video of yourself. It wasn't always a good feeling. But this wasn't so bad. Maybe she wouldn't feel that way about it in a few days, but she felt good about it in the moment. It was the little things sometimes.

After analyzing her words for a long while, she finally reached for her cup and put the straw in her mouth only to find that it was empty, the ice cubes knocking against each other. For a brief time there, the sweet taste of cinnamon and vanilla had distracted her from the real, scorching, underlying thirst that was slowly killing her from the inside out.

"You sure you're okay?" Ben asked again, catching the empty look in her eyes.

Elizabeth made eye contact, looking up at him, suddenly hyper aware of that vein in his neck.

"Yeah, just...I," she blinked a few times to stop herself from staring at it, "I think I have a headache."

"Oh, alright. Do you think we should head out, then? I got a lot done, so I'm ready if you are," Ben offered, already slowly sliding his notebook into his laptop bag.

"Yeah, I think that would be a good idea…" Elizabeth nodded and closed her laptop, packing everything away. "It's just been a rough day, you know?"

"I feel that." Ben stood up beside her, and once she'd straightened up, he put a large, warm hand on her shoulder. "Let's get you home, alright?"

Elizabeth nodded, almost in a daze due to Ben's warmth, or maybe due to her lack thereof. Was it just her, or did he smell…better today? Like coffee beans and rain and his laundry detergent and old library books with yellowed pages…

She clenched her fist, digging her nails into her palm. It had been so long since she'd been thirsty like this, she'd almost forgotten the way the thirst warped her mind, making her a puppet to its monstrous hunger. Without blood, it would only get worse.

She needed to find Jack, and fast.

So, when they got home, Elizabeth went up to her room and grabbed her blessed wooden stake, which had been a gift from Dianne and Nadia a few years back. It did come in handy on occasion, mostly when she was babysitting for a family full of monster hunters on particularly strange and supernatural nights.

She closed its case, slipping it into her bag.

"Where are you going?" Elijah asked, stirring from his cat nap on her bed. "And why are you taking *that?*"

"I'm going to find Jack, and I doubt it will end well."

"Please be careful. Our idiot roommate has been known to forget to feed me unless I yell at him."

"If I die, you have my full permission to yell at him with words as opposed to meows." She saluted, swaying a little on her feet. Was she in the best condition to fight another vampire? No, probably not. But if it came down to it, she doubted she'd have a choice.

"Oh, believe me, I will." Elijah hopped up, jumped off of the couch, and rubbed against her leg. "I know I don't say it a lot, but I'm really glad I found you all of those years ago, Elizabeth."

"Don't go all mushy on me now." She bent over and petted his little head affectionately. Then she straightened back up, a serious look in her eyes, which were even redder than they had been a few hours before. "Besides, I'll be back in an hour or two."

Elijah nodded before following Elizabeth back down the stairs, to where Ben was sitting, watching *What We Do in the Shadows* for what must have been the third time that week.

"I'll be back in a bit. I'm going to Jack's place to check on him. I'm gonna make sure he's alright."

"Oh, okay. Uh, call me if you need anything." Ben adjusted his glasses. He had a warm bowl of popcorn sitting in his lap, and she could smell the delicious salt and butter from where she was standing.

She could think of a few things that would be *more* delicious...

No! She stiffened up, hand clenching into a fist. The sooner she got out of the house, the better. For Ben's sake and hers.

"I will, don't worry. See you later."

"See you." He waved tentatively.

Sighing, she opened the door and stepped back out into the cold, only to find Dianne standing on the sidewalk. Elizabeth raised an eyebrow.

"What, you thought I'd let you go on your own?" Dianne tilted her head. "What kind of friend would I be?"

"Elijah..."

"Told me about Jack. Let's go check on him." She motioned towards Elizabeth's car. "Back-up wouldn't hurt, right? All things considered?"

"It'd definitely be appreciated. Thank you. But I have to warn you, I don't know what we're walking into."

"Has that ever been a problem before?"

"You know what, not really, now that you mention it." Elizabeth chuckled, unlocking her car. They both got in and buckled up. She slid the key into place, turning the car on with a satisfying purr. Elizabeth gulped.

Being what she was, there was always some risk involved when she went out, but she had a sinking feeling that the night was long from over...

Chapter 17

With Elizabeth out of the house, Ben didn't really have any other choice than to call Jay over to keep him company. He'd also invited one of their friends named Karter, but he had a night class and an exam the following day, so he couldn't make it, but promised that they'd hang out soon.

"Do you think vampires can get sick?" Ben asked, taking a sip of his Pepsi between Mario Kart matches. The two of them had ordered pizza and were waiting for it to arrive, so what better was there for them to do to pass the time than race go-karts as Mario characters?

"Why?"

"Well, she was sick today, and a little bit yesterday, I think. Like, really sick."

"Define sick?" Jay pressed, listening as he picked the next course for them to race on. "Like runny nose, sneezy sick or throwing up, fever sick?"

"Neither? I'm not really sure, but she was really, *really* pale. I mean, you've seen her. She's pale, but she was like...paler than usual, and her eyes were bloodshot, and she said she had a really bad headache. She looked pretty dizzy. I'm starting to think I shouldn't have let her leave the house in that condition. She...really didn't look good."

"You said her friend is a nurse or something? If she really is that fucked up, I'm sure he'll make sure she's alright."

It was always Jay that looked on the bright side of things. In their friendship, even back in high school, Ben had *always* been the worrier of the two. That was why he needed people like Jay and Elizabeth around, to pull him back from the brink of a panic attack.

Jay was quiet for a bit, and then chuckled. "So you still think she's a vampire, huh?"

"I...don't even know anymore. Maybe? Probably not. I'm just...well, you know how worked up I get about things." Ben shook his head. "She made some pasta with that 'special sauce' Jack brought over, and let me tell you, it was insanely good. I definitely over-reacted."

"Yeah, but didn't you say Jack was acting weird about it, too?" As crazy as the theory sounded, Jay wasn't willing to let the case close just yet. "I don't know, something's off. But maybe she's just, like, a drug dealer or something. I mean, it'd be lame compared to the other option, but, like, that kind of makes sense, right? The bloodshot eyes, the cooler full of mystery stuff..."

"She's not on drugs." Ben rolled his eyes. "Believe me, if you knew her, you'd know. She's not the drug type."

"Pfft, the '*drug type*.' What's that supposed to mean?" Jay laughed and finally settled on Rainbow Road.

Ben laughed too, shaking his head. "I don't know, but you remember the druggies from high school. They all have that vibe. She doesn't."

"Yeah, the *stoners* all had a vibe. Maybe she does crack."

"She's not on crack. I can't even believe we're having this conversation."

Jay burst into laughter, consequently falling off of the edge of the brightly-colored course. "She's *probably* not on crack. But that's a solid probably."

"Noted." Ben turned the wheel, drifting around the corner until he heard a very urgent beeping sound and then spun out a few seconds later. "DID YOU JUST FUCKING BLUE-SHELL ME?!"

"Heheheheheheh..." Jay cackled, pulling ahead of Ben a few seconds later and speeding across the finish line.

Just as they finished, the doorbell rang. Ben got up. "Must be the pizza. I'll go get it."

❧◈❧

When Elizabeth and Dianne got to Jack's apartment building downtown, they buzzed up to the room, but didn't receive a response. There was a possibility that he was at the hospital, but Elizabeth had a sinking feeling that that wasn't the case.

"Here, let me try." Dianne twiddled her pointer and middle finger, murmuring something softly before pressing the button again. Immediately, the door popped open, and they walked in, taking the elevator up to the seventh floor in silence.

It was a pretty nice building, Elizabeth noted. She'd been inside a handful of times, but she didn't visit him there that often. Jack much preferred the privacy of Elizabeth's little townhouse to the nosy neighbors and thin walls of his place. Hell, he'd live with her if it wasn't so far from the hospital. If there was anything he hated in his years of living in Great City, it was commuting on public transportation. He'd rather die *again* than ride the subway to work every morning.

When the doors opened, they walked down the long, starkly lit hallway to Jack's apartment, 7-12B.

Elizabeth knocked a few times, her knuckles rapping sharply against the wood. There was no response from the other side. She knocked again, a little harder this time, and called, "Jack? It's Liz! You home?"

Silence.

"Do you...want me to...?" Dianne held up her sparkling fingers, wiggling them slightly.

Elizabeth considered it for a few moments. Obviously, if he ever thought she was in danger, Jack would do the same for her. Without a doubt, he would. "Yeah, go ahead."

Without hesitation, Dianne spelled the door open, and the two stepped inside.

"Oh shit." Elizabeth surveyed the room, flicking on the light as they walked through the littered space. A chair was overturned, Jack's cooler laying on its side on the floor, a cluster of blood bags spilling out of it. Well, there went her food for the week.

There was a thick, black substance smeared on the wall. Vampire blood, no doubt. Probably Jack's. And sitting in the middle of the table, all too neat, was a business card for Edwards' Funeral Home.

"Edwards'...as in—?"

"Dottie Edwards, yeah." Elizabeth exhaled a long sigh. At the very least, now they knew where he was. "Fuck. I mean, when Ben came home all messed up, I *knew* that she...but *this...*"

"We're not gonna let her get away with it, though." Dianne had sparks fizzling from her fingertips. She pulled out her phone with her other hand. "I'll call Joelle."

Elizabeth nodded grimly. She let her eyes wander to the sacks of blood littering the floor. She scowled. It wouldn't do her any good now. This had been Dottie's plan all along, she realized, piecing things together: 1) Mess with Ben to get in her head, 2) take Jack to cut her off, 3) use her bloodlust to finish her. It made sense. Elizabeth wondered how long she'd been watched without knowing, but she knew Dottie had connections all over town. It had been well over half a century since their breakup, couldn't her ex get over her? Or did she have some motive other than jealousy that Elizabeth was finally moving on?

And then she realized with a gasp, "Shit, Ben!"

When Ben started walking towards the door, Elijah sniffed the air a few times, hopped off of the couch, and zipped in front of him, blocking him from opening it.

"Elijah, come on..." Ben sighed. He thought the cat had finally made amends with him. Just the other day, he had snuggled in Ben's lap, albeit hesitantly, and mostly because Elizabeth had been cooped up all day. He was even planning on giving him some of the peppers from the pizza he ordered.

Elijah hissed at him, stepping back into the door and planting himself there, raising a clawed paw as a threat.

"I've got him," Jay offered, getting up and walking towards Elijah to scoop him up, but the cat snapped his jaw, threatening to bite him, so he jumped back. "Oh, *fuck* no!"

In the brief second Elijah was distracted, Ben managed to pull the door open to find the pizza guy standing on the porch, two rectangular pizza boxes balanced in one arm.

"Sorry about the cat, come on in." Ben stepped out of the way.

That was the first mistake.

As soon as he'd been welcomed inside, the pizza guy lunged at Ben, ditching the pizzas on the porch as he hurried into the house.

"Woah, man, what the—!" Before he knew it, Ben had his back slammed against the wall, his shoulders pinned in place, and a pair of fangs dangerously close to his carotid artery. Elijah lunged, sinking his teeth into the pizza guy's leg, but he didn't budge no matter how hard Elijah pulled, the rancid taste of vampire blood filling his feline mouth.

"Get off of him!" Jay grabbed a dining room chair and raised it above his head, ready to whack some sense into the guy, but before he could, the pizza guy was wrenched off of Ben by a pair of pale hands.

Elizabeth was in full attack mode, her eyes completely red and her fangs fully elongated, gleaming and sharp.

"Oh...shit..." Jay passed out with a harmonious thud.

She threw the pizza guy into the wall, leaving a large dent in the paint. While he was slightly dazed, she rushed towards him, grabbing him by the collar of his shirt and hoisting him up so his feet didn't quite touch the floor. He kicked her shins and tried to get one of his hands around her neck, but she didn't budge.

"Don't. Touch. Him." She said each word slowly, her voice deep and dangerous, and her fangs ever so sharp. Elizabeth was a lot older than she looked and, therefore, a lot stronger. Fortunately for her, the young vampires that often got hired and/or turned for this kind of job seldom knew that.

"Liz!" Dianne called, tossing Elizabeth her stake, and she caught it, plunging it deep into the pizza guy's chest.

From the spot where she stabbed him, he broke apart slowly, cracks stretching out from the wound until all at once, he disintegrated into a pile of ash.

Elizabeth stood there, huffing deep breaths. She looked up at Ben, who was watching her with wide, brown eyes. He gulped, his hands shaking, and he looked between Elizabeth and Dianne for some sort of answer, but surprisingly, it came from the cat.

"Well, now that the cat's out of the bag, I suppose there's no reason to pretend I'm your pet anymore," Elijah said, stepping over Jay's limp body.

"What the fuck!" Ben pointed at the (*talking?!*) cat. Then, he pointed at Elizabeth, whose pointy fangs were still jutting from her line of straight teeth and whose bright red eyes had not faded in the slightest. "What the fuck?!"

"I will explain *everything* to you, I promise. But right now, you have to go to Dianne's house. Until we get a proper protection spell, it's not safe for you to stay here."

"Elizabeth, what's going on?" Ben's face was serious, and his tone stable despite his racing heart and twisting stomach.

"You were right, is what's going on." Elijah rolled his eyes.

"Right about...?" Dianne asked, looking at Ben, who shrugged.

"Well, everything, I guess..." He fiddled with his hands, unable to make eye contact with his roommate while her irises were so...*red*.

Dianne wandered over to Jay and checked on him. She took his pulse. "He's okay. Passed out from the shock, I think. Let's get to my place." She waved her hand over his unconscious body, and he rose into the air, floating out the door. She followed him, leaving Elizabeth, Elijah, and Ben in the townhouse.

"Listen, if I wanted you dead—if that's what you're worried about..."

"I'm—no, I know you'd never—I just..." Ben finally dared to look up at her, at the concerned expression in her red eyes. Something in him buckled. He didn't want to be right. "We should get next door."

"Yeah..." She nodded. "Yeah, we should."

Elijah walked out the door first, his collar jingling with every step. Once they were outside, Ben spotted the dead body on the front lawn, shirtless in the cold November air, his blood pooling in the frost-coated grass. That must be the *real* pizza guy, he deduced, sizing him up. A chill ran up his spine and he started walking a little faster.

Once they were finally inside Dianne and Nadia's townhouse, Elizabeth closed the door behind her, exhaling a long breath. Her knees buckled. As if she wasn't already weak enough, the fight with the fanged pizza guy had taken its toll on her, and now she was paying for it.

"Elizabeth, are you...okay?" Max asked, his voice small and tentative. He couldn't remember a single time he'd ever seen his godmother looking so rough.

"I'm fine, Max. Don't worry about me." She forced a fanged smile, stumbling over to the couch.

"No, you're not." Nadia walked over and lifted Elizabeth's chin, studying just how far the bloodlust had gone. *Too* far was the answer. "There's no way you're going to the funeral home looking like that."

"I don't really have a choice, though. Jack—"

"Doesn't want you to die trying to save him." Dianne crossed her arms. "We're going to get him, but not while you're so weak."

"It's not like blood bags grow on trees." Elijah hopped up into Max's lap, letting the child pet him.

Ben was quiet, sitting on the sectional with his hands in his lap, absorbing the conversation unfolding around him. He looked at Elizabeth, whose glassy, red eyes were locked on a succulent sitting on the entertainment center beside Max's Xbox. Something in him pulled. He didn't understand what it was or why he was feeling the way he was feeling, but seeing her like that...hurt. It hurt more than he imagined her fangs possibly could...

If his past self from the week before heard what he was about to say, he doubted he'd believe himself, yet despite the dread settled in the pit of his stomach, he offered quietly, "She can...have some of mine."

"What?" Nadia looked at Ben.

"Ben, no—"

"You look like you're going to die, and it sounds like Jack *will* if you don't do something about it. So, if it'd help...you can, uh, drink from me."

Elizabeth was quiet about it for a long time, thinking. On one hand, if she didn't drink from Ben, Jack might very well die. Again. And if she did...there really wouldn't be any chance of going back to the way things were before.

"*Ben...*" she whispered, daring to meet his eyes. "I can't."

"You can. And you have to," Elijah asserted. "We can figure out boundaries tomorrow when everything is...well, it'll never be *normal*, but you get what I mean."

"It's fine. Really," he tried, and when she didn't look convinced, he continued softly, "*I trust you.*"

It took her another long moment, silently wrestling with herself in her mind, but she finally relented with a soft, "Okay, fine." She took a breath, looking at

Ben with a forlorn look in her hungry, red eyes. "Let's do it, then."

Chapter 18

"So how does this work, exactly?" Ben tried his hardest to hide his sweaty palms, the slight shaking in his fingers. "Do you need me to do anything, or...?"

Elizabeth looked to Nadia, who turned to the others in the room.

"Let's give them some privacy." Nadia nudged Max's shoulder towards the kitchen. Dianne and Elijah followed after, leaving Elizabeth and Ben alone with Jay's unconscious body.

"It's kind of, uh, well, do you want me to drink from your wrist or your neck?" she asked, inching closer to him.

"What's easier for you?"

She laughed. "I'm about to drink your blood, and you ask *me* what's easier? Either is fine, Ben, just whatever you're comfortable with."

His face went red, and he locked his gaze on the rip in his jeans. Now was not the time to act on his silly crush on his beautiful vampire roommate, but the day was already weird enough, so why not make it just a little more awkward? "I'm fine with you, uh, drinking from my neck..."

"Okay." She nodded. If she was physically capable of blushing, she was sure her face would be beet red.

"It's been a while since I've done this, but..." Elizabeth stood and took a few wobbly steps towards him until she was standing over him.

He looked up at her, wide-eyed, and swallowed thickly. It had seemed like a good idea a few seconds ago, but now he wasn't so confident in his decision. Well, it was too late to back out now.

"I'm gonna need to get close, if that's alright."

"That's fine." He scooted backwards until his back was flush against the couch and pulled his legs together. "Get as close as you need."

Elizabeth took one more step forward and lowered herself onto his lap, straddling his legs. Sitting there, face to face with him, she failed to remember a time the two had ever physically been that close. In fact, she couldn't even remember a time they had hugged.

It was wild how fast things moved when the circumstances were dire.

Being without blood for so long had taken a toll on her. She was dizzy, pressure built up right in the front of her head. She ached everywhere, her limbs weak and heavy, and yet, sitting in front of him, she felt more alive than she'd felt in days, electricity crackling through every inch of her at the realization that it was finally happening. In minutes, she'd be back to normal, and the past few days would just feel like some twisted dream.

Elizabeth was quiet, listening to Ben's pulse as it raced, his heart pounding against her chest and the vein in his neck calling to her as though it belonged to her. Maybe it was the bloodlust that was making her feel that way, but every miniscule movement he made registered with her, the way his breath hitched when she leaned a little further in, the bead of sweat clinging to his temple, the stray thread on the collar of his shirt.

"I'm gonna tilt your head a little, okay?" Elizabeth asked gently.

He nodded. "Will it hurt?"

"Only a little. It's like a shot at the dentist," she tried to explain, taking his chin with one cold hand and carefully tilting his head to the left so she could get a clean bite. "I'll try to make it quick. If you get light-headed at all, tap out, okay? I haven't...well, I haven't had blood straight from the source in a very long time. You have to let me know if I'm taking too much."

"I will," he promised.

Elizabeth sighed, leaning a little further in. His warmth called to her like a siren, drawing her closer. She let her nose touch the crook of his neck, and she tugged the collar of his shirt further down and out of the way. "Do you want me to count?" she whispered. She felt him jolt at the sound of her voice, goosebumps pricking up all down his arms.

"No, just do it," he said, squeezing his eyes shut.

Elizabeth inhaled, and once the breath entered her lungs, she drew her fangs, sinking them immediately into Ben's neck. He didn't scream or yell, but he gasped at the excruciating pinch of his skin breaking. His hands snapped up, wrapping around her back and hugging her body closer to his as she drained his blood, her jaw making gentle movements and her lips latched onto his skin.

As soon as the blood hit her tongue, her body jolted, and an unfamiliar *zing* zipped through her all at once, her toes tingling. She stopped for a second, shocked, before resuming. Her mind was racing. One taste of his blood had set off something in her so ancient, so buried by four centuries of her endless life, that she'd all but forgotten it was even there. She'd given up on it, figuring that it would never happen, that she'd never find what was promised to her so long ago. And yet, there was only one explanation for the way her heart was burning.

Ben was her mate.

It was so obvious now that she *knew*. Everything about it made sense, from the way he was continuously thrust into her life to the fact that she was sitting in his lap, her fangs plunged into his neck. Even once he finally found out what she was, he'd been quick to offer his own blood for her instead of running away or passing out like Jay had. It was Ben. It had always been Ben. *Of course* it had always been Ben.

Meanwhile, Ben was in absolute bliss. His limbs were tingly, his heart was racing, and he was intoxicated by the scent of her vanilla perfume. She was right, it didn't hurt. He figured there must be some chemical in her saliva that was preventing him from feeling pain, because the area around her fangs was numb and had been since she pierced his skin. It actually felt...good? Was it weird that it felt good despite the fact that he was very rapidly losing blood? If it was, he didn't care. Now, he got the vampire hype. He understood. He took back everything he'd ever said about the *Twilight* girls in middle school.

Was she taking too much blood? Maybe. Did he care? Absolutely not.

Finally, Elizabeth stopped herself, perking up. She dotted her tongue on the small, round indents where her fangs had entered his neck, quickly sealing them up, and then she looked at him, guiding his face towards hers so she could get a good look at him and make sure he was okay.

He blinked a few times, smiling at her softly with those stupidly plush lips of his, dimples on full display. "All done?"

"All done," she confirmed. She took a deep breath, centering herself. The difference was recognizable immediately. She no longer felt like she was dying, breathing was easier, and her headache had disappeared, replaced instead with her usual sharp awareness and enhanced senses. "Thank you, Ben."

"O-of course," he stuttered, coughing. "I think after everything you've done for me, I definitely owe you."

"Not anymore." She chuckled, shaking her head. She was amazed by how easy it was for them to slip back into their usual banter after something like that. "You just did more for me than I could ever do for you. I'll cook you whatever you want tomorrow. And any day after that into the unforeseeable future."

He laughed. "Is that a promise?"

"On my life."

It was quiet between them for a second, their chests pressed up against each other, Ben's arms still hanging loosely around Elizabeth's hips. She considered telling him then and there what she now knew, but decided against it. Maybe she'd never tell him. She didn't know. She'd need to take some time to figure out what this meant for her before she got Ben involved. The last thing she wanted was to make things even *weirder* between them.

But before she could do anything, he leaned forward, ever so slightly, his chin tilting up until he was dangerously close to her blood-stained lips, and she lowered her face, letting her eyelids flutter shut until finally—

There was a knock at the door, immediately splitting them apart.

"I'll get it." Elizabeth stood up quickly, walking over to the door.

Ben attempted to stand up after her, but Nadia walked swiftly into the room and pushed him back down onto the couch, forcing a cup of *something* into his hand. It was purple and steaming and smelled like raspberries.

"Drink that. It'll help replenish your blood supply a little faster. Old family recipe," Nadia explained. "I'd suggest not getting up for a while. It's different than donating blood because it all came out of you so fast."

"Oh. Right. Thank you."

While Ben gulped the strange, sweet, burning substance down, Elizabeth opened the door for Joelle. Her belt was lined with stakes, and she had her fancy leather monster hunting gloves on, tailored specifically to help her hands better grip her weapons.

"Well, I take it he knows, then." Joelle motioned to Ben, who was sitting on the couch with his hands folded innocently in his lap, an empty potion cup on the coffee table in front of him.

"It's a new development, believe me." Elizabeth moved out of the way so Joelle could come in. "Ben, this is Joelle, the mother of the family I babysit for."

"Pleasure to meet you, ma'am." He waved, remaining planted in his seat, as Nadia had requested. He didn't know much about witches, all things considered, but he was pretty sure he shouldn't go out of his way to piss one off.

Dianne, Max, and Elijah wandered back into the room next. Dianne had changed into one of her spell-casting tops, which was black with protective sigils all up and down the sleeves. Her fingers were covered in rings and metal bracelets that jangled against each other, each of them spelled with a very specific enchantment that served her well in times like these. Around her neck was a choker, a purple stone, polished amethyst, dangling in the middle of it.

"Be careful. Please." Nadia approached her girlfriend and took her face in her hands, kissing her deeply. "Come home to me."

"I will." Dianne chuckled, pulling her in for another kiss. And then another. And then one last kiss for the road. "I always do."

"We'll be back in two hours tops. And if we're not, call Jordan." Joelle did her best to reassure the others. She frowned a little when she saw the look on Max's face. He was young. Living with two witches had made him many things, but naïve was not one of them. "I won't let anything happen to your sister, okay?"

"Okay." He nodded, but didn't look all that convinced.

"We've gotta go get Jack back." Elizabeth booped his little freckled nose. "And tell you what, how about I bring over some cookies tomorrow?"

"That might make me feel a *little* better." Max laughed, hugging Elizabeth and then Dianne.

"Go out there and get him already, would you?" Elijah said. He was right, though. If they wanted their friend back at all, they'd better get going before Dottie got impatient.

But as they finally walked out the door, Elizabeth began to wonder if they were already too late...

Chapter 19

The parking lot of the Edwards' Funeral Home was eerily quiet, the streetlamps casting the few cars that were scattered across it in harsh shadows. A peek through one of the small rectangular windows on the garage doors told them that there were two hearses inside, and the door to the elevator entrance was locked. Thanks to her knowledge of the place from her handful of years dating Dottie, Elizabeth knew that this door would also grant them access to the employee entrance, through which all of the flowers were carried into the building.

But that wasn't where they needed to go. Elizabeth was almost completely certain Dottie would be keeping Jack in the morgue, the most secure place in the entire funeral home. She shivered at the thought. Dottie was many things, but she wasn't stupid.

Dianne murmured something, wiggling her fingers. The golden sparkles that so often accompanied her magic floated around her hands, and a few seconds later, the door clicked, unlocking itself. Joelle tugged on the handle and escorted the other two inside quickly and quietly. Elizabeth was expecting guards, Dottie's bouncers, to be there, but there wasn't anyone. Weird.

Elizabeth followed her memory trail as far as it would lead her, trying to remember where to go, which way to get down to the morgue. She knew there was a way to get there through the garage, but the quickest way was through the basement.

There was a door to their right marked "Florists Only." Elizabeth pushed through it, opening the door slowly. She cringed as the hinge squeaked. Past the door was a little room with a bulletin board. Straight ahead was the garage, but to their left was the door to the basement. The stairs were old and steep, and creaked precariously as they walked down them. They passed a bathroom and a refrigerator and a folding table with a few chairs pulled up to it.

The carpet was old and a musty shade of green. Elizabeth was certain it had to be from at least the '70s. A mouse scurried past her foot, and she jumped, but managed to stay quiet despite the scare.

"This way," Dianne whispered. When Elizabeth looked over at her, the witch's purple irises were glowing, as was the amethyst hanging from the choker around her neck. She led them further, to a metal door, and pressed her hand against its shiny steel surface. A few seconds later, it drifted open, revealing a set of narrow stairs illuminated by a single swinging light. Ominous.

With no choice, and nowhere to go but down, the three walked down the stairs and passed through the final door into the morgue.

As soon as the door swung open, Elizabeth locked eyes with one of Dottie's men, a giant muscled vampire with a shaved head and glowing red eyes. Immediately, Dianne pinched her index finger and thumb together and pulled them across her lips, staring at the guard, and his lips sealed together. The guard charged with incredible speed, faster than Elizabeth had ever seen a vampire run before, and shoved Elizabeth into a wall, pinning her there by the shoulders. He was unbelievably strong, and Elizabeth had a tough time struggling against him. Joelle did her best to pull him off of her, but her human strength was no match for his, and he reached behind him, shoving Joelle into a metal stretcher, which rolled and clashed against the wall.

In a calculated move, Elizabeth reached between the vampire's arms, shoved them apart, and in the second it took for him to adjust, she slipped under him and through his legs, allowing Dianne to come in with the killing blow, a stake to the heart.

A few moments later, their attacker was no more than a pile of ash on the floor.

With the immediate danger out of the way, they could focus on what they'd come for. Jack's limp body was lying on the slab on the other end of the room, a stake poised directly above his heart and a blood bag hanging above his head.

So their plan was to bleed him out, then. No doubt as soon as he reached for the blood bag, the stake would plunge straight into his chest. A genius plan. An evil one, sure, but Elizabeth couldn't deny Dottie was clever. It scared her that someone so smart had bad blood with her.

"Jack?" Elizabeth asked softly, approaching him slowly.

He didn't reply, his breaths coming out in rasps, quiet and frail. She was glad he was breathing at all.

Dianne cast a quick charm and drew the stake that was suspended over Jack into her hand instead. With the stake over his heart finally out of the way, Jack turned his head slowly, looking up towards Elizabeth, but not really registering that she was actually standing there.

"Jack, I'm here. It's okay." Elizabeth walked up to the table and reached overhead, taking the blood bag off of the hook and uncapping it, slipping the tube into Jack's mouth. She tilted his head forward, and he drank greedily, gulping it down as fast as he could until the bag was completely empty.

He sat up, sputtering. He coughed a few times, and Elizabeth watched as the red faded from his bloodthirsty irises. Some of his color returned to his pale cheeks.

"I've been here for three days," he told her, his breaths heavy while Elizabeth pulled him into an upright position. "I thought I was gonna die on this table...Well," he chuckled, shaking his head, "I thought I was gonna die *again* on this table."

"You alright?"

"I will be." He nodded, looking up at Elizabeth. He smirked. "Thanks for the save."

She tilted his head towards the door. "Let's just get you out of here, okay?"

"Yeah, that sounds good."

Elizabeth pulled one of his arms around her shoulders, and Dianne took his other side, leaving her casting hand free. Joelle led them out of the morgue and back up the stairs, through the mouse-infested basement, and out into the parking lot.

Elizabeth was on edge the entire time, nervous that there would be more guards. There was no way she'd go so easy on them when she'd gone to the lengths of starving out Elizabeth's blood supply. Although, with Jack out of the way and Elizabeth without a source of cruelty-free blood, Dottie probably thought she was too dead to do any rescuing. The pizza man that tried to kill Ben must have been sent to finish the job.

They hauled Jack into the back seat of the car with Joelle, and then Elizabeth and Dianne climbed into the driver and passenger seats. Glancing back at the door for a few seconds to make sure they weren't being trailed, Elizabeth shifted the car into drive. Had she looked a little higher, at the second floor window, she would have seen the red-lipped blonde standing behind the curtains.

∾◆∽

When they finally got back, Dianne and Nadia cast a protective barrier over Elizabeth's townhouse, and Elizabeth and Ben went inside. Jack followed after, choosing to stay with them rather than risk a night in his apartment. Ben went off to get ready for bed while Elizabeth got Jack set up in the guest room and closed the door behind them.

Jack motioned to the wall that was connected to Ben's room. "Does he...?"

"He knows everything now. He...well, he's the reason we're both here. He let me drink his blood."

"Is he holding up okay?"

"I think he...well, I think we both knew that he knew, a little. He took it better than I thought, though." Elizabeth shrugged. "I guess we'll see tomorrow if he still wants to stay."

"And his other friend? The loud one with the red hair?"

"Jay will be okay too, I think. With time." Elizabeth shook her head. If someone had told her that morning what would unfold that night, she wouldn't have believed them in the slightest. And yet, this was her life now. Her human roommate knew that she was a vampire, and that was that. So far, it seemed like he was fine with it. And then there was then other thing... "Jack?"

"What?"

"I..." She didn't even know how to say it. "When we, uh, when I drank his blood...I felt..."

"It really is him, huh?" Jack laughed softly, a warm smile lighting up his soft, boyish features. He ran a hand through his tawny hair, shaking his head. "I thought so. I just—wow, I never thought I'd see the day."

"Me either, honestly."

"Did you tell him?"

"No."

Jack paused. "Are you going to?"

"I don't know. I just...that would be a lot to lay on him all at once. I don't think he'd be adamantly opposed, but I don't know if I'm really ready to take that chance with everything else that's going on."

"That's fair. It's your decision at the end of the day. Just try to keep me in the loop so I don't slip up."

"Will do. It's a mess, but I'm sure we'll get it figured out tomorrow."

"We'll get it figured out tomorrow," Jack repeated. He opened his arms, and Elizabeth hugged him tightly, burying her face in the crook of his neck. "You've been through a lot today, Liz. Get some sleep. You need it, for once."

"Yeah. I'm sure you do too." She laughed into his ear. "Goodnight."

"Night."

Elizabeth walked out of the guest room and into the hallway, where Ben was standing in the doorway of his room, his toothbrush hanging out of his mouth. He waved awkwardly. She waved back. They were both quiet for a long time, until finally Elizabeth said, "Are you okay? I didn't take too much, did I?"

"No, you didn't. I'm okay." Ben mumbled through toothpaste. He held up a finger. "One second." He retreated back into his bathroom, the water ran, and then he returned, toothbrush free. "I'm fine. I'm not even light-headed or anything. I think the, uh, potion Nadia made for me helped a lot."

"Good. Good. Well, goodnight, Ben."

"Aren't we gonna, you know, talk about it?" He fiddled with his large fingers, eyes locked on them. Elizabeth couldn't remember the last time she'd seen those curious brown eyes without his glasses shielding them from her. He looked so different, like his face was naked, almost. "I mean, if you want to. We don't..." he scratched the back of his neck, "We don't *have* to."

"We will. Of course we will. Tomorrow, though, once we've both slept it off." She exhaled, shaking her head. "It's been a long day."

"Yeah, it has been." He nodded, smiling softly so his dimples poked into his tan cheeks. "Goodnight."

"Night." Elizabeth smiled and turned, walking to her own room. She tried not to be, but she was the tiniest bit afraid that when she woke up, he'd already be gone.

Chapter 20

The next morning, Elizabeth woke up expecting to find the house empty aside from Jack and herself, but much to her surprise, Jack, Elijah, and Ben were all awake when she finally emerged from her hibernation, chatting over hash browns and bacon in the kitchen.

"There she is." Jack motioned to Elizabeth with a spatula, her favorite apron tied around his hips. "We thought you were *never* going to come out."

"Good morning, everyone." She waved to her three boys, and Elijah looked up at her with a smug look in his green eyes. "You can say 'I told you so.'"

"I was going to, believe me, I was, but honestly, I'm surprised you kept the act up as long as you did." Elijah tilted his head, his tail waving behind him. It appeared he was very excited to be able to actually talk out loud again. "And I'm sorry for being an asshole."

"Yeah, I'm never gonna get used to that." Ben sipped from his coffee, his voice caught in the ceramic mug.

"Oh come on, Ben. Vampires and witches are cool, but talking cats is where you draw the line?" Jack laughed, plating up some food for Elizabeth. "Just the way you like it."

"Thanks." She grabbed a fork and sat down next to Ben, who was watching her carefully, his mug cradled in his large hands. When she looked up at him, his eyes flicked away.

"I didn't tell him anything," Jack explained. "Told him you should get to do the honors."

"Well, thank you for that." Elizabeth laughed. "What do you want to know?"

"Everything, I guess." Ben shrugged, tentatively letting his eyes wander to Elizabeth's. He chuckled nervously. "How old are you? Where are you from? How did you...well, you know, *turn*?"

"I'm...Oh gods, four...twenty...?"

"Four twenty-six. Why are you so bad at that?" Jack finished for her, smirking.

"Not all of us are young, you know." She nudged him. "Give it a few more centuries, it'll get harder to care about keeping track, believe me."

Ben's eyes widened as he watched their exchange. He'd known since the previous night that things were weird, that nothing he knew was true anymore and the world had been hiding things from him, but listening to them talk about specifics was different.

"I'm from Europe, a tiny little country that isn't on the map. My parents are still there, cooped up in their giant castle, upset that I never visit. Well, that's what my sister says, anyway. And I didn't turn. I'm a pureblood, meaning my parents are both pureblood vampires and they had me the natural way."

"Her family is *old* money, and her parents are a count and countess. Don't let her be modest." Elijah walked closer to Ben, looking up at him. "You're reading a book about her dad, actually."

"Wait," Ben said. "What?" He thought about it for a second until it clicked. "Wait, Count Bloodmere?"

"That's the guy." Jack laughed. "Like he said, old money."

"And is any of the stuff in the book...true?"

Elizabeth burst out laughing. "No, none of it. He wasn't cursed, he didn't fall through the ice or get bitten by a snake or any of the other ridiculous stories I've heard. It's just a bunch of old legends from the village, hearsay that some desperate researcher collected and wrote down. My father's a pureblood like me and the rest of our family tree. Humans always need some explanation for things they can't understand."

"Makes sense," Ben said, his thoughts wandering to Jay. Yeah, that checked out.

Elijah sat down in front of Elizabeth, his tail waving behind him, his big green eyes looking up at her innocently. "Aren't you going to tell him your name?"

"Your name?" Ben raised an eyebrow.

"You mean Elizabeth Bloodmere? I thought that was implied."

"No, not *that* one! The other one!"

"*Which* one? There have been quite a few."

"Maybe the one he's writing his thesis on, then."

"Oh, *that*. I'd almost forgotten. Thanks for bringing it up, Elijah," Elizabeth said, mostly sarcastically. It wasn't like she thought about it every single time Ben pulled out his laptop or a book about the Blackwood Inn or the Battle of Bloodborne.

"What is he talking about?" Ben was hooked, but he didn't want to jump to conclusions.

"You know what, let me go get something from upstairs. I'll be right back." Elizabeth rushed up to the second floor, into her room, and scanned her shelf of scrapbooks for one very particular collection of memories. There. The 1770s. Perfect. She plucked the thick book off of the shelf and hugged it to her chest, carrying it back down the stairs until she finally set it in front of Ben. She flipped through a few pages until she came across the print of the painting she was looking for.

"HOLY SHIT!" He jumped off of the barstool he was on, his hands slapped over his mouth. He stared at the image and then looked at his roommate and then down at the picture and then back up at his roommate. "YOU'RE ELIZABETH BLOODBORNE!"

"I *was*. It was a long time ago..." Elizabeth laughed softly. "It figures that you'd be writing about me, all things considered."

"Wait, you mean to tell me I've been slaving over these books and websites and newspaper clippings and anything I could get my hands on to find out what happened to her—to *you*—and Katherine and you've just been *sitting there*?!" Ben stewed on it for a moment, and then asked, "Wait, doesn't that mean you have a daughter?"

"Like I said, I'm older than I look." She chuckled a little.

"Wow. That's...that's wild. I don't think I can get over that. Holy shit..."

"Any other questions?" Jack crossed his arms and leaned against the island.

"So you don't sparkle?" Ben checked.

Laughing, Elizabeth replied. "No."

"You don't burn in the sun?"

"No, but we do have sensitive eyes."

"And you're not allergic to garlic."

"Right."

"I...how often do you need to drink blood?"

"I drink two pints a day, but it's different if it's live blood. Then I only need about one every few days. Depends on the vampire."

"I need more than she does because I'm not a pureblood," Jack interjected. "But, the hospital gets rid of a lot of blood every week, so we get by. Hence the, uh, cooler full of 'special sauce.'"

"I thought so, yeah." Ben nodded, thinking. "So witches, vampires, is anything else real that I thought was just a bedtime story?"

"A ton of things, I'm sure," Elizabeth said. "For starters, the family I babysit for is a bunch of monster hunters. Sirens are real, so are faeries and merfolk, werewolves, shapeshifters, and every once in a while, a Starchild or two."

"What about Bigfoot?" Ben was mostly joking when he asked, but Jack looked to Elizabeth quizzically and she shrugged.

"Unconfirmed, but I've had my suspicions."

"Aliens?"

"Not that I know of, but who knows? Space is a big place." Elizabeth shrugged. "I've been around the block, but even *I* don't know everything about everyone."

"So, do you, uh, age then?"

"I used to. Way, way back when I was still living with my parents. I think I stopped around twenty-five or so, but it's hard to tell once you hit a certain point. Purebloods freeze sometime in their early to mid-twenties. Vampires that are turned—"

"End up like me, with a baby face forever," Jack deadpanned and pointed to his face. "I was turned at the tender age of nineteen, and I've been carded in every club and bar and pub for the past hundred or so years because of it."

"Holy shit, nineteen?! What...what happened, if you don't mind me asking?"

"It's a tale for another day. I don't mind talking about it, but it's a long story." Jack reached up and scratched behind his ear. "Mistakes were made, but I mean, things happen for a reason or else I wouldn't be here."

"Very true." Elizabeth looked at Ben, waiting for another onslaught of questions, but he wasn't looking at her anymore. Instead, his gaze was fixed on Elijah, who rolled his eyes.

"Alright, go ahead. Ask what I know you're gonna ask." Elijah sat down in front of Ben.

"Yeah, so what's your deal?"

"Well, for starters, don't cheat on a witch." He looked up at Jack, and then said, "Mistakes were made."

"Have you ever seen *Hocus Pocus?*" Jack asked Ben.

"Yeah, I have—"

"For the last time, I am *NOT* Thackery Binx!" Elijah hissed, his tail flicking back and forth in irritation. "Yes, we're cats. Yes, we talk. That does not mean we're the same. Besides, he's a black cat, and I, as you can see, am very much *not.*"

"Of course, of course." Ben nodded. "Not to pry, but are you...you know, trying to change that?"

"Dianne and Nadia have been working on a counter curse for years and still haven't had any luck. It can be done, I'm sure, but whatever Agatha used on me is way outdated by now. It's hard to find a lot of those older spells, especially considering that the witches who cast them are all long-dead."

Ben was quiet for a long moment, absorbing all of the information the three immortals in front of him had given him. They'd seen so much, it was almost impossible for him to comprehend. Someone like him had to be a mere blip on the radar of their immeasurable lives. By the time they blinked, his grandchildren would be dying of old age. Being immortal must suck, he decided. The three of them put together had probably lost so many people. Jack especially, because he worked in a hospital of all places.

"Well, thank you, I guess, for taking me in. I'm sure it probably couldn't be easy. I'm like walking dinner for you."

"It's not as hard as Edward Cullen might make you think." Elizabeth laughed and shook her head. "The only time that's ever actually a problem is if we haven't fed in a few days."

"Bloodlust." Jack nodded, flashing back to the previous night and the rather torturous few days leading up to it. "Not fun. Other than that, we're just like normal people who drink Capri Suns full of blood."

"And live forever."

"And have talking cats," Elijah added. "On occasion, that is. Not all vampires are quite as lucky as Elizabeth, I'm afraid." He walked over to the vampire in question, nuzzling against her hand. Then, he stretched, yawning. "Well, it's been nice, but the patch of sunlight in the front window is calling my name." And with that, he hopped off of the counter and slinked out of the kitchen.

Elizabeth was surprised by how quickly things shifted back to a normal-ish state. But it still took her a few days before she felt comfortable enough to drink blood in front of him. Ben's eyes were locked on her blood bag, and she looked up at him as she stopped drinking.

"If this bothers you, I can go into the other room."

"No, no, it's fine." Ben shook his head and looked back at the TV. "I'm sorry for staring. I'm just intrigued is all."

"Okay, good."

"Does it…" Ben started, but then quickly let it die off. "Nevermind."

"No, go ahead."

"Does it taste good?"

She laughed. "Why, do you want a sip?"

"Oh! N-no thanks. Uh, that's okay—"

"I'm kidding." Elizabeth smirked. It was fun to watch him squirm, she decided. "It tastes good to me, but I've heard blood tastes kind of metallic to humans."

"What does it taste like to *you*?"

"Depends on the blood type, but they all kind of taste like mixed berry smoothies, if that makes any sense. Thick and sweet, but not really any distinct flavor." She took another long sip, pondering. "You're O Positive, by the way. You said you didn't know a few weeks ago. You're O Positive."

"You could tell?"

"Yep. I've been at this a while, remember?"

"Right, right." Ben nodded. It was easy to forget, looking at her, just how many years she was hiding behind her youthful brown eyes. "Do you ever...miss it?"

"Miss what?"

"You said your parents are still around, right? Do you miss, like, living with them, I guess? Or your siblings? Do you have siblings? You mentioned a sister."

"I do. I'm not sure how many I have, but I do have siblings. I don't really...miss it, per se. I miss growing up with them. I still hear from some of them every once in a while, but not nearly as often as I'd like. We're all grown up now. We have lives, we've all gone down different paths. We used to be really close." She sighed. "I don't know, things were just different then. But my parents made some interesting choices, and they impacted me especially. I'm sure if I went back to visit, it would be different than it was, but part of me is still afraid they're mad at me for running away."

"Mmm. Yeah, that's tough." Ben nodded. "But I'm sure if they're anything like you, they'll forgive you if they haven't already. Maybe you should send them a letter or something. They probably miss you."

"I will one of these days." Elizabeth finished off the rest of her blood bag and set the empty pouch on the table beside her. "Just not today."

"Fair enough."

Elizabeth opened her mouth to say something else, but the doorbell rang, so she stood up to go see who it was. She wasn't expecting anyone, and she didn't think Ben was either. When she got to the door, she looked through the window to find a very familiar figure standing on the other side of it. She pulled the doorknob and looked up at him.

"Long time, no see." Elizabeth had tears clouding up her vision.

He went to take a step forward, but was stopped by the protective barrier the witches next door had put in place after the bloodsucking pizza delivery boy had visited.

"Oh, sorry. Come in." She motioned him inside, and suddenly, he was able to step through. His black hair just brushed his shoulders. She always seemed to forget just how tall he was, and his face was dusted with more stubble than she remembered. His brown eyes looked tired.

Ben got up from the couch and walked over to where Elizabeth and the stranger were standing.

"This must be the roommate Kate told me about. Ben, right?"

The man held out his hand and Ben shook it. His hand was cold, he noticed, and he didn't look any older than his late twenties at the most. It was entirely possible that he was a vampire too.

"Right. Nice to meet you." Ben replied, looking to Elizabeth for some sort of an explanation, but the stranger answered for her.

"I'm Will, Elizabeth's...brother."

"Son. He's my son," Elizabeth interjected, looking up at him with warmth in her eyes. "He knows."

"Wasn't sure. Kate didn't get that far."

"That's because Kate doesn't know that yet." She shrugged. "Somewhat of a new development. We haven't talked in a little while."

"And Kate is...Katherine?" Ben asked, trying to put the pieces together. "Wait, do you have *another* daughter?"

"No, I just have the two. Will and Kate."

Will chuckled to himself, taking his shoes off by the door and hanging his jacket on a hook. "Well, Mom, I'm afraid I didn't come with *good* news."

"Do you ever?"

"These days, not really." Will took a seat at the dining room table, and Elizabeth joined him. Ben hovered near the doorway, unsure of whether he should follow her or not.

"You can come listen, Ben," she told him, motioning him over, and as she did, Elijah came down the stairs and hopped up onto the table.

"I thought I heard trouble." He smirked at the sight of William. It had been years since he'd seen him.

"Elijah, still a cat?"

"William, still annoying?" He walked up to him and nuzzled against his large, outstretched hand. "I missed you, you know. You never come visit me anymore."

"Busy hunting monsters, I'm afraid. It's a job that never really has an off season." Will scratched gently between Elijah's ears until, finally, the cat walked closer and sat down right in front of him. "Speaking of, that's what I needed to talk to you about. And it's been a while since I visited, so…"

"What did you find?" Elizabeth asked, serious and quiet. The resurfacing of Dottie set her on edge. As they said, bad things came in threes, and with Ben being bitten and Jack being kidnapped, that left room for one more thing.

"Arthur Valentine is in town."

She felt physically sick. "Arthur Valentine?"

He sighed and raked a hand through his dark, shaggy hair. "I tracked him to an underground in Lakeshore, but the trail led here. I caught him having lunch in a diner by the hospital."

"That's not good." She let out a long breath, eyes locked on the table. "Does your sister know?"

"Yeah, I told her when I figured it out."

"Good. I don't want him anywhere near her. I can't believe this is happening."

"The situation is definitely not ideal."

"I'm sorry, I don't mean to interrupt, but who's Arthur Valentine?" Ben asked, his hands folded neatly on the table.

Elizabeth thought about it for a moment. "You remember how you had that theory that Elizabeth Bloodborne was running away from someone when she sailed to the new world?"

"Yes...?"

"He's who she was running away from," she replied darkly.

"Oh. Got it."

"He's Katherine's father, and the guy is bad news. Runs the vampire mafia down in Lakeshore. He came up here to negotiate with—"

"Dottie, yeah. We had a little issue with her the other day. I thought she might be involved."

"And Dottie is...?" Ben asked. He wasn't sure why, but he swore that name sounded familiar.

"My other ex. She's the one that kidnapped Jack."

"Oh. Her. They sound like quite the pair."

"It's bad. Arthur and his thugs plus whoever Dottie has...It's a catastrophe waiting to happen. I didn't hear their entire conversation; the diner was noisy. I do know that Dottie had a kid with her, and Arthur is looking for someone, and he wants to use Dottie's network to find them."

"He's probably looking for Katherine," Elizabeth realized, biting her red lip.

"That's what I thought too," said Will, a grim look on his face. "I told her to be extra careful. She's been laying low, but Arthur has a way of getting what he wants."

"Believe me, I know." She paused. "I have a bad feeling about those two in cahoots. Sure, it starts out with something like this, but I don't have any doubt the threat will escalate. Arthur is power-hungry. Always has been. He's been out in Lakeshore for a while, but if he could figure out how to expand and rule Great City too..."

"No one would be safe." Will pulled out his thick, leather journal and flipped through the yellowed pages. "Mom, who can you call if things get worse?"

"Well, I've always got the Hunters on speed dial. Dianne and Nadia are next door. I'm sure I can pull some strings if I need to." Elizabeth thought about her seemingly endless list of contacts. The only problem was, she'd lost touch with a bunch of them.

"Okay, good. I'll keep you posted. There's not much we can do right now. No reason to start a war with them if we can avoid it."

"Right. Thank you for bringing it to my attention. I knew there was something going on, but this..."

"We'll figure it out together. We always do." Will stood up. "Well, it was nice to meet you, Ben. Welcome to the wonderful hidden world of crazy magical things. I'm sure this last week or so has been eye-opening for you."

"More than you could know." Ben chuckled. "Nice to meet you too."

"Be careful out there." Elizabeth hugged her son tightly and kissed his cheek. "And call your mother every once in a while, would you?"

"Of course. I love you, Mom."

"I love you too."

Will slipped on his coat and boots and walked out the door. As soon as he was gone, Elizabeth sighed deeply. One ex in town was bad enough, but two of them? Fate couldn't have picked a worse time to let her finally find her mate.

Chapter 21

The end of November passed and swiftly after, snow fell, covering Great City in a sheet of sparkling white. As she did every year, Elizabeth put up her Christmas decorations with the help of Jack, who was too busy to put up (and subsequently take down) his own lights every year, but loved helping Liz with hers.

Three steaming mugs of hot cocoa sat on the coffee table as Jack began the tedious process of wrapping the lights around the tree. Somehow it seemed that every time he set them down, even for a few seconds, they managed to get tangled into a giant knot again. Elijah was on the carpet, playing with a stray bit of tinsel Ben had given him, and Ben and Elizabeth were hanging the stockings on the mantle. She'd spent the week before embroidering Ben's, which impressed him to no end.

"Jack, you're coming over for Christmas, right?"

"Would it be Christmas if I *didn't* come over?"

"It would not." Elizabeth pulled out Jack's stocking and hung it next to Elijah's. She stood back and admired her handiwork. They were perfectly spaced, hanging from the Command Hooks she and Ben had put up. "There. All done."

"Need some help with those lights?" Ben walked over towards Jack, who handed him a strand, his hand sticking out from behind the Christmas tree.

"Yes, please."

"Hey, uh, Jack, should I make an extra Christmas stocking for Cody?" Elizabeth teased, smirking.

"Oh shut up." Jack rolled his eyes, stepping over Elijah to get to the power socket. He lit up the tree. "I don't think it's gonna go anywhere. I don't think he's that into me."

"Did you ask him out?" Ben asked.

"Well, no, but..."

"Then how do you know?" Elizabeth started pulling ornaments out of another box, laying the tree topper carefully on the couch. "I'm sure he'd like to go out with you. He's in college, you *look* like you could be in college. Plus, you can't deny that there has been an *incredible* amount of flirting done by both parties. I don't know, it sounds perfect to me."

"Well, you know how difficult it is to date. It's not like there's Vampire Tinder or anything."

"Cody is a vampire?" Ben asked.

"No. That's the other problem." Jack shrugged. "I don't think it'll work out."

"Shoot your shot, dude." Ben gave Jack a thumbs-up. "What's the worst that could happen?"

"He could pass out like your loud, red-haired friend," Elijah pointed out.

"Oh, sheesh, I didn't even think of that." Jack ran his hand through his hair. "That would be a disaster."

"Jack," Elizabeth deadpanned and looked at him. "You're a trained medical professional. If something goes wrong, it is literally your job to fix it."

"I still don't know. We'll put him down as a solid maybe."

"I'll start his stocking tomorrow. And Ben, is Jay coming? You mentioned he might."

"Yeah, I think so. His parents are going on vacation for Christmas, so he doesn't really have anyone to celebrate with."

"Tell him to bring a dish to pass. We don't let freeloaders into the Bloodmere Christmas Extravaganza," said Elijah, who was finally done playing with tinsel and instead hopped up onto the arm of the couch to get a good look at everything. He stretched a big, long stretch, his toe beans extending to their fullest before he settled down.

Ben laughed. "I'll be sure to let him know. I think he's taking the vampire thing pretty well, all things considered."

"That's good to hear. I was worried about him for a little while there."

"So was I." Ben chuckled and shook his head. "It probably helps that once when we were undergrads, he went hunting for Bigfoot. He's always been *that guy*, you know? The one with the alien posters on his walls and a million theories about the moon landing."

"*Those* guys always seem to take stuff like this easier." Jack mimicked fangs with his two pointer fingers. "It also probably helped that he woke up to a pretty witch baking him cookies."

Ben laughed. "It definitely didn't hurt."

Once they had the majority of the ornaments on the tree, Elizabeth fished the tree topper out of the box. It was vintage. She'd had it since at least the '50s and had taken good care of it every year since. Although, the cherub's little face did need a new paint job. Maybe this was the year to retire it, with all of the other change already in motion.

"I brought these." Ben pulled her out of her memories, carrying a small cardboard box into the room labeled 'ornaments' in messy Sharpie. "Just some stuff from my childhood. Crafts from elementary school and whatnot. My mom pawned them off on me when she and Dad moved down to Florida."

"Well, we *definitely* have to put them up." Elizabeth made room for the box on the couch, scooching over a pile of lights.

He set it down and pulled the cardboard flaps apart, fishing the ornaments out one by one. There were popsicle stick snowflakes covered in sparkles, foam reindeer with pipe cleaner antlers and red poofball noses, fake candles made from toilet paper rolls and tissue paper, and finally, an angel topper made from a paper plate that was absolutely *doused* in glitter.

"We have to put *that* on top of the tree." Elijah stared at it and then looked up at Elizabeth. "Liz, face it: it's time to replace Creepy Angela."

"Creepy Angela has had a good run," Jack agreed mournfully, nodding. He pointed to Ben's childhood masterpiece. "But Plate Angel *belongs* on top of the tree."

Ben was laughing, his face getting redder by the second. "Well, I don't know about *that...*"

"Since when have we been calling my angel 'Creepy Angela?' Is she really that creepy?" Elizabeth looked over the angel's porcelain face. Maybe the boys were right... "You know what? I think you're right. It's time." She set Creepy Angela down, and Ben handed her his angel instead. Elizabeth approached the tree, but the one Jack had found this year was so tall, she couldn't reach the top of it, even on her toes.

Ben walked over and took the angel from her, reaching above her to perch it on the top branch of the tree. "There. Now it's a Christmas tree."

She looked up at him through her eyelashes. Ben was...taller than she'd noticed before. Maybe it was because she wore heels all the time. Huh. She smiled and repeated the sentiment, "*Now* it's a Christmas tree."

Chapter 22

"I think I'm having an identity crisis," Elizabeth blurted, staring at her reflection in the mirror and evaluating her blood red lips, her pristine white blouse, her pressed black slacks and her shiny black pumps.

"Oh yeah?" Ben didn't glance up from his Sudoku, pushing his glasses further up his nose.

"Yeah..." She bit her lip, looking herself over. Something wasn't right. It was like the feeling of staring at a word until it doesn't look like a word anymore, a familiar feeling to someone who had been around as long as she had.

"And how many times a century does *that* happen?"

"A few." She tilted her head, turning to the side a bit to see if that helped. "I just...don't feel like *me* anymore, does that make any sense?"

"Like a mid-life crisis?"

"Kind of. Yeah, actually. I think they build up over time if you don't spend them."

"So...what do you do about it, usually?"

"Depends on the decade." Elizabeth shrugged. "In 1912, I ended up taking a cruise, but I met Jack, so hey."

"Wild."

"Very." She nodded.

Ben, who'd just fully processed what she'd said, looked up with wide, brown eyes. "Wait, are you talking about the Ti—"

"No, the Carpathia, actually. *Jack* was on the Titanic. That's also the reason he won't watch the movie."

"Gotcha. Makes sense." Ben nodded, still caught off guard by the information that had been thrown in his lap. "You know, you're a history major's dream."

"I have been told that, yes."

"Are there any other historic moments you've, uh, witnessed over the years?"

"Well, I gave birth and stopped the Battle of Bloodborne, so that's gotta count for something, right?"

"That's so weird."

"Wanna know a fun fact?" Elizabeth took off her heels and pulled the pearl earrings out of her piercings.

Ben perked up. "Always."

"The gunshots from the battle blew out the medic's hearing. He asked me for my name, and I said I was Elizabeth Bloodmere. He was just half deaf by the time I went into labor. He thought I said Bloodborne, and I decided that was a good name to hide under for a while, lay low with Katherine. So I ended up going by Elizabeth Bloodborne until the turn of the century when I decided to be Elizabeth Bloodstone. And then just Elizabeth Stone and so on and so forth."

"So, you're Elizabeth Simon until when?"

She shrugged, laughing. "Until I get bored of it, I guess." She glanced up the stairs and then looked at Ben. "I'll be right back." And then she left him, walking up to her room to rummage through her closet.

Even as someone who had been so many people, she always had trouble figuring out who she should be next. And then she spotted it, the familiar gray hoodie that still smelled faintly of the coffee shop. She smiled softly before plucking it out of her closet and finding a comfortable pair of jeans to match. She was done putting so much effort into standing out. Maybe it was time to look just like everyone else, to blend in for the time being.

In fact, with two of her most dangerous exes running around, camouflage might be her greatest weapon.

So, much more comfortable than she had been before, she walked down the stairs, only to find Ben on the landline, a panicked look on his face.

"Uh, yeah, I can go get her—never mind, she's here." He handed the phone to Elizabeth. "It's Joelle."

"Hey, Joelle, is everything—"

"Rogue werewolf. Maybe two. It's pretty bad. Can you—?"

"I will be there in less than thirty. Go get 'em."

"Thank you so much." The call went dead.

"She didn't sound good," Ben said, staring at the sweatshirt she'd changed into. He didn't know why, but his cheeks were warm. Maybe Elijah had messed with the heat.

"Yeah, she needs a babysitter pronto." Elizabeth was already stalking across the apartment to grab her purse and lace up some winter boots. As a vampire, she may have been immune to the cold, but she definitely was not immune to slipping and falling on her ass.

"Do you want someone to go with you?" he offered softly.

She looked up at him, her hands stopping for a second before she resumed weaving the laces up her boots. "Do you... *want* to come with me?"

"I think I'd like to, yeah." He nodded, his thumbs jammed in the pockets of his joggers and his eyes locked anywhere but hers. "I mean, if you want me to. I don't want to be in the way."

"Sure, you may as well. I bet Andy could teach you a thing or two about the supernatural world, and he's, like, five."

Ben chuckled, putting on his own winter boots. "I could probably use the lessons."

❧ ◈ ❧

The drive to the Hunters' house became a little more dangerous in the winter time, snow and ice making the roads slippery and the thick coat of white all but obscuring the entrance to their private property. It took a while, but Elizabeth found it, pulling into the long driveway and parking the car.

Her usual welcoming committee wasn't outside like they usually were when she got there, which meant that they were either really busy playing games inside or the threat was close enough that Joelle and Jordan had told them to stay inside. The latter was probably true, as Andy was standing in the window with his hand on the glass, his little face lighting up when he saw Elizabeth standing there, leading a stranger up to the front door.

Thomas pulled the door open once she was up on the porch, stomping the heavy snow out of her boots. Ben followed her inside, and the two of them set their wet boots in the massive pile of shoes heaped beneath the coat hooks.

"Who's the guy?" Brayden asked, crossing his arms and looking Ben up and down with his critical Hunter eyes. "He doesn't look like a vampire."

"He doesn't smell like a vampire either," Andy chimed, trotting into the room just as Elizabeth closed and locked the door.

"This is my roommate, Ben. He's human. He decided to tag along today, and given the circumstances, it might be nice to have a little back-up, huh?" she asked, looking over the three boys. "Just the three of you tonight?"

"Connor and Sage went with Mom and Dad," Thomas told her, fiddling with his fingers. "They said not to go outside. I guess it's pretty close."

"Are we on lockdown, then?"

"We probably should be." Brayden nodded, biting his lip. He looked close to tears. As brave as these kids were, and after everything they'd lived through so far, they had every right to be scared, especially when there was a threat so close to home.

"Thomas, take Ben and Andy and go unlock the safe room. Brayden, we're gonna put up the protective ward. I'm sticking with you, alright?"

"O-okay." Brayden nodded. He held his hand out for Elizabeth's and she took it, giving his hand a tight squeeze.

Elizabeth leaned over slightly so she was closer to his eye level and locked onto his gaze. "I'm not gonna let anything to happen to you, okay? You know that. That's why I'm here."

"Right." He nodded, taking a few deep breaths.

"Um, Elizabeth—" Ben looked at her with wide eyes. What the hell had he gotten himself into?

Andy reached up for Ben, his little hands latching onto Ben's cozy knitted sweater and pulling until he finally picked the child up. Thomas took Ben's free hand.

"Go with Thomas. He knows what to do. Brayden and I will be down there in a second, alright?"

Ben nodded before following Thomas down the hall to the basement's secret entrance. Meanwhile, Elizabeth and Brayden headed the opposite way. In the middle of the den, there was a giant flat screen TV mounted on the wall. In times like this, it doubled as a monitor to the activity outside. There were four purple dots on the screen, one that represented each of the Hunters that were outside the house. While Elizabeth and Brayden were watching, one of the purple dots began flashing red.

Brayden gasped, squeezing Elizabeth's hand tighter.

"It's okay, it's gonna be okay. Your parents have been doing this their whole lives, remember?"

"B-but..." Tears welled up in his little eyes. "Connor and Sage haven't..."

"They'll be okay too. I promise. But we have to put up the ward to protect Thomas and Andy, right?"

"Right." Brayden nodded, wiping the tears from his cheeks.

"You're gonna be strong for me, right?"

"Right." He inhaled a breath and pivoted one of the coasters on the coffee table about forty-five degrees. A panel of wood slid aside, revealing a little touchscreen about the size of a tablet. Brayden pressed his hand against the glass, and the screen blinked a few times before a circular panel rose in the center of the coffee table. From that panel rose a smaller circular panel, and in the center of that was a smaller circular panel, making the center of the table resemble a short, layered wedding cake. The smallest panel at the very top, which was no larger than the inner ring of a CD, had a short, sharp needle sticking out from the center of it.

Brayden reached, wincing as he struck the spike with his pointer finger. "Ouch," he mumbled, pulling his finger away to look at the blossoming bead of crimson slowly growing from his fingertip.

Once the system registered his blood, an automated voice announced, "Activating Ward...Activating Ward...Please report to the safe room as soon as possible."

"You heard her. Let's go." Elizabeth and Brayden rushed back through the house, down the secret stairs, and into the basement.

Ben was standing at the door to the safe room, and he let out the breath he was holding once he caught sight of Elizabeth. She pushed Brayden into the room first and walked in after him, and then Ben closed the thick, metal door behind them.

Elizabeth took a head count. Andy, Thomas, Brayden, Ben. All of her boys accounted for. She exhaled, letting the tension out of her shoulders.

"You okay?" Ben asked quietly, taking a step closer to her.

She nodded and then remembered the tiny wound on Brayden's fingertip.

The safe room was meant to be a comfortable place, complete with a TV, video games, cushy recliners, a fridge and cabinet stocked with snacks, several board games on a shelf in the wall, an immense movie library, and a private bathroom tucked away into the back corner.

One of the walls was covered in metal panels, which hid away extra shelving storage. Elizabeth walked to the second and slid the door aside, pulling a bright red first aid kit off of the shelf. She took it over to the center of the room and set it on the coffee table, rummaging through it until she found what she was looking for: Band-Aids.

She took a *Spongebob* Band-Aid out of the kit and walked to Brayden. He held out his finger to her, and she applied triple antibiotic ointment before wrapping it around the punctured spot.

"There." She smiled at him. "All better."

"Thank you." He sniffled.

"Of course." Elizabeth ruffled through his hair, and he walked over to where Thomas was sitting, Andy curled up against his side. She couldn't even count how many nights she'd spent down in that safe room. A few decades earlier, she'd been hunkered down there with Jordan and his siblings, and now, she was protecting his kids. It was funny how quickly the years went by, just how fast one generation rolled into the next.

"So what do we do now?" Ben asked, his heart pounding so loud she could hear it.

"We stay down here until the threat passes. There are snacks over there, bathroom through that door. We'll be fine."

"Okay. You've...done this before, right?"

"Tons of times." Elizabeth took a moment to study him, his quickened pulse, his reddened cheeks, his jittery shaking fingers. She reached out and took his hand, warmth radiating from her chest, and his eyes darted up to hers. "You'll be alright."

Ben nodded, intertwining his fingers with hers. He opened his mouth to reply, but he was cut off by one of the kids.

"Ben! Do you want to play *Monopoly?*" Andy asked, springing over towards him with the box in his hands.

"Sure. I'll play." Ben slowly let go of Elizabeth's hand and walked over, taking a seat in one of the chairs around the coffee table, helping the boys set up the board and distribute the colorful paper bills.

Elizabeth stood off to the side of room, watching them. She crossed her arms. As much as she'd like to join them, she was on high alert. Should anything go wrong, she was the only defense standing between her boys and whatever snarling monsters were roaming around outside.

"No fair! I want to be the top hat!" Brayden whined as Andy took the shiny piece, smiling.

"Youngest goes first," he reminded his brother smugly.

She listened to them bicker and start their game for a handful of minutes. And then the alarm went off, red lights flashing. Ben sat at attention, his back stiff.

"*Perimeter breached. Prepare to defend...Perimeter breached. Prepare to defend...*"

"What do we do?"

"Take the kids. Get in the bathroom. Close the door and *do not open it* until I come back, alright?" Elizabeth instructed, red flashing in her irises, her fangs sliding into place as she switched into attack mode.

"Got it." Ben stood up and grabbed Andy, hauling him off of the floor and back into the bathroom. The twins followed quickly behind him, the door closing and locking with a click. Elizabeth stood beside the heavy bookshelf next to the bathroom door and pushed it across the door until it was effectively covering it.

Once she was sure they were safe and out of sight, she opened the door of the safe room and closed it behind her, punching in the code to lock it again. She walked up the stairs and opened the door of the hidden staircase, swinging the faux bookshelf out of the way and then pushing it shut. She looked both ways through the red-drenched house. The red lights flashed, and she heard something pound against the front door.

In one swift move, she was there, looking out the window. Sage, whose face was covered in mud, was fiddling with the code to unlock the front door, her fingers too shaky to punch in the right numbers.

Elizabeth rushed to get it open, pulling the girl inside and slamming the door behind her. There was a bleeding gash on her bicep, and one of her knees was scraped, the fabric of her jeans ripped away to show the wound.

"Are you okay?" Elizabeth sized her up, struck by the scent of her blood.

"I'm fine..." She swayed on her feet. "The wolves are...stuck at the...ward. My parents..." She pointed a weak finger, out of breath.

"We're gonna get you down to the safe room, okay?"

Sage nodded, but didn't say anything, her eyelids drifting half shut.

Elizabeth didn't hesitate to pick her up, carrying her effortlessly and bypassing all of the security measures as quickly as she could. She re-entered the safe room and set Sage on one of the loveseats so she could push the bookshelf back out of the way, the heavy piece of furniture *screeching* against the metal floor. She knocked on the door.

"Ben! Open up!"

A few seconds later, Ben opened the door, three little heads peeking out behind him. "Is everything...? Oh my God."

Elizabeth walked back across the room and picked up Sage's limp form. She tilted her head towards the first aid kit, and Ben took the hint to grab it.

"Brayden, Thomas, grab some pillows and blankets," she instructed urgently, carrying Sage into the bathroom. The boys rushed back with the supplies, making a makeshift nest to set Sage in. Once everything was in place, Elizabeth laid her down carefully. She popped open the first aid kit. "You two know what to do, right?"

"Yeah, I think so."

"Keep her awake. Do not under *any* circumstances let her sleep. Stop the bleeding. I can give her some of my blood if it gets too bad, but I have to go help your parents and brother. I'll be back soon, I promise. Don't leave this bathroom."

"Okay." Thomas nodded, his expression hardened and determined.

Elizabeth held the power button on her phone down and when it blinked, she said, "Call Jack Ellis."

"*Calling Jack Ellis,*" it replied.

She handed the device to Ben, nodding. "He'll know how to help you. I'll be back soon, okay?"

"Be careful." He looked up at her while the phone rang, his eyes wide and plush lip quivering. For a brief moment, she felt that familiar tug in her chest, but she pushed it back down. Now was not the time to deal with all of *that.* "Please."

"I will." She leaned in and kissed his cheek right on his dimple before getting up and racing up the stairs and outside into the cold. Snow was drifting down in large flakes, slowly sinking down and covering the dark forest in ice. She waited.

She listened.

Deep in the woods out to her right, she heard the fight, snarling and snapping, snow crunching. She took off, speeding through the trees, hopping over fallen logs and ducking under hanging branches, their bristles weighed down by the heavy snow. Finally, she reached the center of the action.

Connor was pinned to the hard, cold ground, red gushing out beneath him as he barely held a snapping wolf off of his face. Elizabeth bared her fangs, tackling the monster into the snow.

The beast snapped its jaw shut, and she hissed at it, her eyes glowing red. She shoved it over onto its back, pinning its broad frame to the ground with her legs. Its eyes were golden, gleaming like bright coins in the moonlight. Snow matted its thick, brown fur. She grabbed it roughly behind the ears and forced its head down to the ground.

A deep growl rumbled through his chest. She didn't let go, her fingers digging into its skin. The snow crunched beside her, and when she looked over, she saw Connor standing there, wavering on his feet. He raised his weapon, a suped-up taser his parents had invented, and pulled the trigger, launching the silver tendrils onto the werewolf's hulking form. Elizabeth dove off of it in time, escaping the electric pulse that was zapping through it.

The wolf seized and then went limp, its golden eyes closing. Elizabeth exhaled, looking at Connor.

"Let me see the wound."

"The what?" Connor asked, he looked at both of his arms.

"Turn around," she told him, and he did. Sure enough, the back of his shirt was torn open, a giant gash dug into his skin. Blood dripped down his back. "Shit."

"Is it bad?"

"Yeah, a little. Where are your parents?"

"I don't know. There were other wolves…" Connor blinked a few times, swaying on his feet a little. "I'm dizzy…"

"Woah, okay, okay, stay with me. Sit down." Elizabeth helped him down into the snow, and he looked up at her, waiting for further instruction, his eyes glazing over. "Joelle! Jordan!"

"I'm here! What happened?" Joelle's boots crunched through the snow until she was standing beside them, her breath fogging up in puffs in the frosty winter air. "Connor, stay with us, okay?"

"Mom, I'm cold."

"Yeah, I know. It's gonna be alright. Hold my hand."

"Let's get him inside." Jordan came over next and hauled Connor off of the ground.

"How was Sage?"

"She's in the basement with Ben and the boys. They're on the phone with Jack. She didn't look that bad when I saw her, but her arm..." she told Joelle. "It didn't look good."

"We thought there were two, but there were three. We should have called in the Circle." Joelle sighed, running her fingers through her hair. "We didn't and we're gonna pay for that."

"It'll be okay." Elizabeth promised as they walked quickly back to the house, Connor hanging from Jordan's arms.

"Hang on, buddy, we're almost there," Jordan murmured.

Elizabeth ran ahead, opening the door and putting a towel on the kitchen island. As soon as Jordan crossed the threshold, he made a beeline for the spot while Joelle went to the basement to get the boys and check on Sage.

Connor squirmed once he was set down, the adrenaline wearing off in a rush and the pain hitting him all at once. Elizabeth looked to Jordan.

"Elizabeth, I hate to ask this, but..." He trailed off.

"I was about to offer." She raised her wrist to her mouth and bit into her vein, the acidic taste of her own blood scorching across her tongue. She held out her arm, putting the wound in Connor's mouth.

He grimaced, trying to turn his head away.

"I know it tastes nasty, but it'll help, I promise," she told him, stroking the sweaty, dark hair out of his face. "Just a few sips. You can do that for me, right?"

Connor sucked on her arm, his jaw moving gently against her wrist. The basement door swung open, and Ben was the first one to emerge, his eyes widening when he saw what was happening in the kitchen.

"Uh, I'll just—"

"It's fine. Come on in." She motioned him over, and he hesitantly walked into the kitchen.

Connor groaned, still suckling Elizabeth's dark blood. After a few more seconds, she pulled away. He leaned towards her until she finally cut him off.

"You did such a good job, buddy," Jordan praised him, exhaling a long relieved sigh. "It's okay. You can rest now."

"Is...that going to...*you know*...?" Ben asked quietly, watching as Connor finally closed his eyes.

"Oh! No, no, no, that's not what vampire blood does." Elizabeth shook her head. "This is all new to you, I'm sorry. Vampire blood has healing properties. It'll help close up the gash in his back."

"Looks better already," Jordan told her, turning Connor to the side so he could get a good look. "Thank you so much."

"Of course."

Joelle came up the stairs next, Sage and the boys in tow.

"How are you feeling?" Elizabeth asked.

Sage didn't look nearly as bad as she did a little bit ago. Jack knew what he was doing.

"I feel a lot better. That was scary. I didn't think...well, the werewolves I know are usually nice..."

"There are a few things that can set them off like that." Joelle pondered on it for a moment. Most of the reasons a werewolf would go rogue, lose all control, usually had magical origins. Sinister forces were at play here, that was for sure. "Or sometimes their first shift can send them into a frenzy, if they don't see it coming."

"But three of them all at once?" Jordan shook his head. "Not plausible unless there were triplets turning soon."

"The Copper Valley Pack would have told us."

"That's true... I'll have to call them and see if these are theirs." Jordan rubbed his chin before walking off into the other room, phone in hand.

"Thank you so much for coming. I really don't know what we would have done if you didn't get here when you did." Joelle pulled Elizabeth in for a tight hug, holding her for a long moment before letting her go and turning to Ben. "And thank you for coming too. The extra help was really needed tonight."

"Of course, ma'am. I'm glad I could help."

"Thank you so much, Ben, seriously," Sage said, her eyes serious and sullen as she mulled over the possibilities of the things that could have unfolded had he not been there. "You picked a good one, Elizabeth."

She looked up at him, a soft, proud smile on her face. He met her eyes, and she reached out and gave his hand a gentle squeeze. "Believe me, I know."

Chapter 23

Without a doubt, winter was Elizabeth's favorite time of year, although, she admitted that autumn was a *very* close second. Summer was too sweaty and sticky, and during the spring, Elijah had terrible allergies, but because she was unaffected by the cold, winter was perfect. She loved the snow, and she loved all of the activities that came along with it.

She spent the weeks before Christmas putting up some more decorations: a wreath, some more lights, little gel snowflakes on the windows. She'd also been baking a ridiculous amount of Christmas cookies. Ben was sitting in the kitchen while she worked, her hands gently wiggling tree-shaped cookie cutters into the dough and then transferring them to a pan. She already had six or seven tins of cookies sitting on the counter: chocolate no-bakes, snickerdoodles, chocolate chip, and gingerbread cookies to name a few.

"That's a lot of cookies."

"Oh yes. The optimal amount."

"What are you gonna do with all of them?"

"Well, I'm keeping some here for us, I'm bringing some next door for the girls and Max, I'm giving some to Jack, and some to the old ladies who own the bookstore I work at." She paused, thinking. "Oh, and some for Jay and—who's your other friend that lives with Jay?"

"Karter."

"Right, Karter." Elizabeth smiled. "Him."

Ben laughed a little, thinking about all of it.

Elizabeth raised an eyebrow. "What's so funny?"

"I never thought...well, when I was growing up, I never thought I'd ever be at a point in my life where I'd be watching a vampire bake Christmas cookies."

She laughed. "Yeah, I guess you probably didn't," she said, grabbing the pan, which was now filled with cookie cutouts, and sticking it in the oven without a mitt. That was one perk of her baking hobby: being immune to heat meant she couldn't get burned while taking things out of or putting things into the oven.

Once the oven was closed again, she walked over to one of the pans of cookies that was cooling and scraped a chocolate chip cookie off of it with a spatula.

"Want one?"

"Sure, thanks." Ben grinned.

Elizabeth set it in his large hand, and he started snacking on it while highlighting text in an article he'd printed out with his other hand. He looked so handsome while he was focused like that, his brown eyes scanning the text carefully and his eyebrows furrowed ever so gently. She wasn't sure how long she'd been staring, but at some point, she realized she'd been hyper-focusing on the crumb clinging to the corner of his stupidly plush lips.

She squeezed her eyes shut and forced herself to look away. She still hadn't brought up her discovery to Ben, nor did she plan to any time soon, but she couldn't seem to stop herself from admiring him. Her sweet, human roommate. Her *mate*.

She prayed to whatever gods were listening that maybe, someday, they'd gift her the courage to actually do something instead of silently staring at him like a weirdo.

⸮◆⸺

It was steadily approaching Christmas, and Ben was at one of his final classes before his break started. This meant finals. He'd been stressing a lot, but Elizabeth used the full extent of her knowledge from her lived experiences to help him study, and she was confident he would do well on them, given all the hard work he'd been putting in.

While he was out of the house, Elizabeth and Elijah were left on their own. She wasn't sure when it had happened, but at some point, surely, one of her two roommates had taped up mistletoe in the doorway to the kitchen.

She stared at it for a long moment, quizzically, before finally calling, "ELIJAH!"

"What, woman? Jesus, I'm right here." He walked up from behind her, brushing against her leg as he did.

"When did this get here?"

"When did what—" He looked up at said mistletoe. "Oh. Our *other* roommate put that up, uh…three days ago? Something like that."

"You watched him put it up."

"I did. Yes," he said, sitting in front of her innocently and looking up at her with those big green eyes. "He's tall, so I didn't think he'd need a footstool, but he did. Almost fell off of it too. He's clumsy, but he means well."

"He put up mistletoe," she said again.

"I thought we covered this."

"Huh." She stared at it for a while longer before she remembered that she'd been on her way to do some laundry. Maybe for her own mental wellbeing she just…wouldn't bring it up when Ben got home. She was positive she was jumping to conclusions about what that meant, but it did stir around the *pulling, pulling, pulling* feeling in her chest when she thought about it.

∼◆∼

On Christmas Eve, while she was feeling a little extra festive, Elizabeth brought her record player down from her room and got it set up in the corner of the living room. She put on one of her older Christmas records and started dancing around freely, tapping into skills she hadn't put to use in *decades*.

"Woah, I didn't know you had a record player!" Ben said excitedly. His exams were finally over, and so for the first time since they'd met, he didn't have a stack of books and homework with him. Instead, he was wearing a festive pair of pajama pants (they had snowmen on them) and a loose-fitting black T-shirt. "Cool!"

"Thought I may as well bring it down, now that my secret is out and everything." Elizabeth stopped moving and spun around to look at her roommate.

"I'm glad you did. That's really awesome." He reached up and scratched the back of his neck. "So, uh, actually, I was wondering..."

There was a long pause. Elizabeth froze, bracing for whatever words were about to come out of his mouth.

"Would it be alright if *I* cooked dinner tomorrow night?"

"Oh! Of course!" A cold wave of relief swept over her. "Got anything specific in mind?"

"Yeah, actually. My parents always made Korean food for special occasions when I was growing up, so I wanted to make some bulgogi and stuff. I've been missing it a little extra lately."

"Family traditions are *definitely* welcome here. I mean, we are kind of family, aren't we?"

He smiled, his dimples especially noticeable. "Yeah, of course we are, Liz."

The way his deep voice got all soft when he said her nickname made her heart flutter the tiniest bit.

Ben glanced down at his pajama pants and then at his watch. There wasn't time to change if he wanted to make it there on time to get everything he needed. "Okay, well in that case, I'm gonna run to the Korean market to get the stuff I need before they close. Do you want me to grab you anything?"

"If they have those little ice cream mochis, I'd *love* some of those. Otherwise, I'm all set."

"Ice cream mochi coming right up." He winked and slipped on his jacket and shoes, and then he was gone.

Elizabeth stared at the door for a lingering moment, playing his dimpled smile over and over again in her head, accompanied by "*Yeah, of course we are, Liz,*" echoing endlessly into the corners of her mind.

"Well, *you've* been extra weird lately." Elijah stalked into the living room, gracefully leaping up onto the armrest of the couch. "Care to tell the cat what's going on?"

Oh fuck. Had she forgotten to tell Elijah? It had been almost a month since she found out, and she'd somehow forgotten to tell Elijah? To be fair, she had a lot on her mind, but it wasn't really an excuse.

"It's complicated."

"How complicated?"

"Well, you remember that talk we had a few years ago about, uh, vampire mates?"

"I'm gonna stop you right there," he said. "How long have you known? Have you known since you met?" He gasped. "Is that why he lives here now?!"

"No, I didn't know. I didn't know until I tasted his blood, but it's definitely him."

Elijah was quiet for a long time, staring up at her. "Does he know?"

"Obviously not."

"Well, for the record, I'm happy for you. I hope it works out. The sooner you two face the inevitable, the better. It's getting awkward in here."

Elizabeth laughed. "Thanks for the vote of confidence."

❧◈❦

It was a few hours later that Ben got back. It was starting to get dark out, so after helping him unpack the groceries he'd bought, Elizabeth went upstairs and got changed into her special Christmas Eve nightgown, a long white vintage one with long sleeves and lace. When she got back downstairs, she started up the record player, putting on a jazzy Christmas album and letting the music fill the house.

"Can you dance?"

Ben's question caught her off guard. She turned around to look at him. He was still in his pajamas from earlier, friendly little snowmen dancing all over the pants.

"*Can* I dance?" Elizabeth scoffed. "I lived through the height of the jazz era; yes, I can dance. Get over here."

"Oh! Well, I didn't mean—"

"Now, come on Mr. Future History Professor, you're not gonna pass up on the dancing lesson of the century, are you?"

"When you put it that way..." Ben set his phone on the table and walked closer to Elizabeth. "I'm warning you now, though, I have two left feet."

"I can work with that."

"I take no responsibility for any injuries incurred."

She laughed. "I don't think you could hurt me if you tried."

"That's reassuring." He chuckled. He stopped in front of her, looking down and waiting for direction. "What now?"

"How about a little East Coast Swing?"

"That sounds complicated."

"It can be. We'll start with the basics. Give me your hand." Elizabeth raised her right hand, and he wrapped his left around it. "And then your other hand goes here." She pulled it to her waist, resting her left arm on his right. "I'm gonna lead, but we'll pretend you're leading."

"Thanks." He laughed, his heart racing. He hoped his hands weren't too sweaty. She'd definitely notice.

"Are you ready?"

"Probably not, but I'll try."

"Okay, so it's just a triple-step." Elizabeth shuffled to the side, and he followed a second or two after. "Triple-step back this way. And then you use your free foot and it goes behind like this." She put her foot down and then picked it back up. "And that's a rock step."

"Is that it?"

"For now, yes." She laughed.

They followed the music, doing it a few more times. Ben was hesitant, but he picked it up relatively easily. Once he was comfortable, Elizabeth raised his hand and spun around under it, returning to him a few steps later.

"This isn't so hard," Ben admitted. His words must have been jinxed, though, because as soon as they left his lips, his fuzzy socks betrayed him, and he slipped on the hardwood, taking Elizabeth down with him. They landed with a thud, Elizabeth on top of his chest. He grimaced and she slowly crawled off of him. They both sat up. "Ow."

"Are you okay?"

"I'm good, are you okay?"

"Yeah, I'm fine."

He laughed at himself and shook his head, cheeks reddening in embarrassment. "Typical."

"You had it there for a second."

"I did, didn't I?" he said. "Sorry."

"Don't be sorry," she told him, staring up at him through her long eyelashes.

It was quiet for a while, music playing softly in the background. Ben's heart was pounding, and he wasn't sure if it was because of the fall or her proximity to him. The longer he looked at her, the more he wondered if her lips were as soft as they looked. He watched helplessly as his hand rose to her cheek, his thumb slowly skimming her cold skin.

He started leaning closer, and so did she, until finally...

There was a knock at the door.

They both froze, staring at each other.

"Dianne and Nadia," Elizabeth whispered in realization. "I invited them over to watch movies." She stood up and brushed herself off.

"Right, yeah, of course." He stood up after her, crossing his arms. "I'll, uh, go make popcorn."

Ben retreated to the kitchen and stuck a bag of popcorn in the microwave. Elijah was up on the counter, licking his paw.

"I heard you fell on your ass."

Heat rose to his cheeks and he replied, "I didn't come here to get roasted by a cat."

"Do you know what movie we're watching?"

"Nope."

"Can I have some popcorn?"

"I mean, I can't stop you from having some, so..."

Elijah stretched and said, "I do enjoy our conversations, Benjamin."

He chuckled. "Yeah, me too."

When the popcorn was done, he poured it into a bowl, put some into a smaller bowl for Elijah, and then they both joined the girls in the living room. Elizabeth looked up at him and patted the spot next to her. He smiled and settled down, her legs curled up and resting against his thigh.

Dianne popped in *Home Alone*, and for the first time since he'd started college and gone out on his own, Ben felt like he was actually part of a family again.

Chapter 24

Approximately three weeks before Christmas, Ben went into panic mode. He'd been thinking about what to get for Elizabeth since mid-November, but he couldn't for the life of him figure out what to get for the girl who already had everything. She had all the clothes she could ever wear, and if he did go out of his way to find something vintage, she probably already had twelve of them in her closet.

He thoroughly browsed Amazon, he checked every store downtown, and every single place he went to had cool things he thought she might enjoy, but he always ended up talking himself out of it.

So, finally, exhausted and quickly running out of both options and time, he called Jack, who, of course, had a solution. And while Ben knew Jack was probably right, and felt like he'd done a good job, he still couldn't stop stressing about it the slightest bit when he woke up on Christmas morning.

"Good morning, sleepyhead," Elizabeth sing-songed when Ben walked into the kitchen in his Christmas pajamas, the set Elizabeth had bought for him a few weeks prior. Elizabeth had changed out of her nightgown from the night before and was instead wearing a set of pajamas that matched his, with candy canes all over the pants and a gingerbread man on the shirt. "Merry Christmas!"

"Merry Christmas." Ben took a look around the kitchen, which smelled heavily of pancakes and chocolate. "Something smells good."

"Christmas pancakes?" She held out a plate of her famous chocolate chip pancakes, decorated with whipped cream and red and green sprinkles.

"Thank you," he said, taking the plate from her and sitting at the table, where Elijah was playing with the puffball on top of a Santa hat. "When I was little, my mom used to make Christmas waffles, but these are definitely better."

"It's the chocolate chips, right?" Elijah looked up at him.

Ben chuckled. "And the sprinkles." He cut into the stack, smiling. This Christmas was already shaping up to be the best one that he'd had in a while.

Once Elizabeth was done cooking pancakes, she sat down at the table with him. As soon as she lifted her fork, there was a knock at the door, so she stood up, walked to the living room, and pulled it open. Jack and Jay were both standing there, a small pile of presents in each of their arms. Jay smiled nervously, but Elizabeth just motioned him inside.

"Come on in! Merry Christmas! There's Christmas pancakes in the kitchen."

"Christmas pancakes?" Jack stepped inside, stomping the snow off of his boots. "You're too good to us, Liz."

The boys set their presents under the tree with the rest of them before joining Ben and Elijah in the kitchen. Elizabeth followed them, sitting back down at her seat.

"Is this..." Jay pointed to Elijah, reaching out to pet him tentatively, "the cat that..."

"Talks? Yeah. Happy Holidays, Jay." Elijah smirked, stretching and winking up at the wide-eyed human. "Elijah Bennett. Pleasure to make your acquaintance."

"H-Happy Holidays..."

He nodded his head before accepting the pets from the stranger. Once Jay was done meeting the cat and finally sat down for breakfast with his best friend and two vampires, Elijah hopped off of the table and ran off into the living room.

"He gets the zoomies sometimes." Elizabeth chuckled, taking a bite of pancakes. "He is, for all intents and purposes, a cat."

"Mmm," Jay hummed and nodded, his eyes flicking up to Elizabeth and then over to Jack and then back down at his plate. "This is weird."

Ben shrugged. "You get used to it."

Once they were all done eating and Elizabeth had set the dishes on the counter, their little mismatched family walked out to the living room, where Elijah was already sitting in front of the fireplace, waiting for them.

Elizabeth and Jack took seats on the couch, glasses of wine (or blood?) in hand while Jay and Ben sat cross-legged on the floor.

"Alright kids, go ahead and open your presents." Jack sipped on his drink, smiling to himself as he said it.

Ben laughed, but tugged his gift from Jack out of the pile and opened it. Inside the colorful snowman-covered wrapping paper was a *giant* book of Sudoku puzzles. His face lit up. "How'd you know?!"

"A little birdie told me." Jack shrugged and scratched the back of his ear.

Jay opened his presents: a thick, knitted scarf from Elizabeth, a Captain America waffle iron from Jack, and a new set of Bluetooth headphones from Ben.

Next, Ben pulled a big box across the floor until it was in front of Elizabeth. It was really heavy, well, it was to him at least, but Jack had helped him carry it into the house without breaking a sweat. That vampire strength was seriously not something to mess with.

"For me?" She put a hand on her chest, gasping playfully. "Whatever might it be, Benjamin?"

He chuckled, looking up at her earnestly. "Why don't you open it and find out?"

So, she did, getting on the floor beside him and pulling the wrapping paper off of the large box. Inside was something she'd looked high and low to find for the past handful of decades without any luck. A functioning vintage typewriter.

"You didn't!" Her face lit up, stars in her eyes. "Oh my gods, Ben where did you find this?! I've looked all over! They always get scooped up so fast from the antique stores, especially here in the city..."

"Jack and I spent an entire day looking for that thing." He beamed proudly, his adorable dimples on full display. "Do you like it?"

"Like it? I *love* it." She dove into his arms, hugging him tightly.

When she made contact with him, he let out a soft '*oof*', processing what had happened for a moment before embracing her, his arms wrapping around her. His heart raced against her chest, pounding a hundred miles a minute.

"Thank you so much," she whispered, squeezing him one last time before letting go and fetching her present for him out from under the tree. "Now, as a disclaimer, this present isn't nearly as cool as the one you got for me."

"I'm sure it's amazing, Liz." Ben tilted his head, smiling as she handed it to him. It was a large box perfectly wrapped and tied shut with a big, red bow. He pulled the ends of it, undoing the knot holding it shut and tore through the paper, popping off the lid to find a cozy, soft, hand-knitted sweater inside of it. It was maroon and bronze, the colors of his college, the Great City Historical University. "Holy shit, did you make this?"

"Yeah, I did. All of that time you spend sleeping really adds up when you don't need sleep." She smiled, proud of her handiwork. Elizabeth shrugged. "Figured I owed you one since you let me keep your sweatshirt."

"This is so soft." He hugged it against him, feeling the soft yarn, intricately woven into the sweater that he was sure was as warm as it looked. "Thank you so much. This is seriously one of the best gifts I've ever gotten. I've never had anyone knit me anything before."

"If you're friends with her for long enough, you'll have enough to fill a closet." Jack laughed, holding out his arms so Ben could look at his sweater. "This is an Elizabeth Bloodmere original from approximately 1984."

"Oh my God. You guys are so old!" Jay's eyes went wide. "I keep forgetting how old you are."

"When you're cursed with a baby face for all of eternity, it's easy for people to forget." Jack chuckled morbidly, shaking his head.

"You think *you've* got it bad, buddy, look over here!" Elijah jumped up onto the arm of the couch. "I used to have thumbs!"

"Yeah, you do have it pretty bad. I just get carded at clubs." Jack reached up and petted Elijah's head.

Elijah leaned into Jack's hand, a purr rolling deep in his chest.

Ben looked around him. His life had gotten very weird very quickly. Never in his wildest dreams did he ever think he and his best friend would be celebrating Christmas with a couple of vampires and a talking cat, but he wouldn't trade it for anything. In fact, if he could, he would have stayed in that moment forever.

"Hey Liz?" Ben peeked around the doorway of the kitchen. "Can I borrow your apron?"

"Yeah, of course." She got up from her spot at the dining table and walked into the kitchen, taking her apron off of the hook in the back of the storage cabinet and handing it to him.

Shortly after they'd exchanged gifts, Ben had started marinating the bulgogi, and he was about ready to start frying it up. He'd also mixed together some sauce and prepared some rice cakes so he could make tteokbokki, another one of his favorite dishes. While he missed Korean food, and that was the main reason he'd decided to make Christmas dinner, he also wanted to impress Elizabeth in the same way that she endlessly impressed him.

"Jay, do you need any help with anything?"

"Nah, I'm all set." He was currently chopping up some veggies for Ben. "Thank you, though."

"Yeah, of course. Any time," Elizabeth said, opening the fridge. "If neither of you are using the oven, I'm gonna start baking the dessert."

"Have at it." Ben motioned to the oven.

"What are you making?" Jay asked.

"These are Oreo cheesecake cupcakes," she replied, pulling the bowl of batter out of the fridge. "A new favorite recipe of mine."

"That sounds *fantastic*," Jack said from the dining room table. "Where'd you find that recipe?"

"Pinterest."

"Iconic."

Elizabeth chuckled and preheated the oven before pulling out a cupcake tin. She filled it with liners and then started loading it with cupcake batter. When the oven was done preheating, she stuck them in and set a timer while the boys continued their tasks.

"What, no Cody?" Elizabeth asked Jack, who was at the table in the dining room, scrolling through his phone.

"He's got plans with his family."

"That's unfortunate," she said. "I think it's cute when you get all flustered."

Jack took a second to process what she'd said, and then he set down his phone and sat up straighter. "I do *not*—"

"You do. And it's precious," Elijah interjected. "I'm still on team 'shoot your shot,' for the record."

"Yeah, yeah, I'm working on it. It's not as easy as it looks, alright? It's been a while since I've done this."

"I feel like there's some phrase about old dogs learning new tricks that could apply here," Elijah said.

"Oh, shut up. I'm the youngest person at this table."

"That is...true."

It didn't take too much longer for Jay and Ben to finish their cooking, and while they were moving things to the table, Elizabeth pulled her cupcakes out of the oven and stuck them in the fridge to cool. Jay helped Ben set out everything he'd made and/or bought for the occasion: a big bowl of white rice, a platter of bulgogi, a few bowls of tteokbokki, and a handful of smaller dishes containing kimchi, fish cakes, and a few other pre-made sides he'd gotten at the Korean market.

"This looks amazing, you guys." Elizabeth was, in all honesty, floored. She didn't know Ben could cook at *all*, let alone an entire meal. Hell, he'd burned scrambled eggs a month before, and yet he'd pulled out all the stops, and it all looked really good. Maybe she'd have to share the kitchen with him more often.

"Thank you," said Ben, smiling shyly. "As a disclaimer, I haven't cooked anything like this in a *very* long time."

"I'm sure it's great."

"Hello, yes, the cat humbly requests someone assembles a bowl for him. Please and thank you," said Elijah, nudging an empty bowl towards Ben, who started loading it with rice and meat.

"That's still so weird, I'm sorry." Jay laughed, shaking his head. "I have a pretty high threshold for weird, but a talking cat..."

"That's the line?" Elijah turned his too-human eyes to Jay, glaring at him. "*That's* the line? Not aliens or Bigfoot or the Loch Ness Monster? Or Santa?"

"Elizabeth?" Jack whispered, looking at her. "Is...is Santa real?"

Jay, Elijah, and Ben all went quiet, their heads slowly turning in her direction, waiting for an answer.

Elizabeth mulled over her response for a few seconds. "Well, *I've* never met him."

"That did not answer the question."

"I'm gonna go with 'yes, probably,' but I have no concrete evidence to support or deny that claim."

The rest of the table was silent until Jack broke and said, "Huh. Good to know."

Ben pushed Elijah's bowl to him and then picked up his chopsticks. He looked up at the window in the front room. Snow was coming down in giant flakes, drifting down and covering Great City in a thick sheet. The lights on the Christmas tree filled the room with a warm glow. He spent a long while just sitting there, dissociating while he stared at the boughs of the tall pine, popcorn garland draped around it in a golden spiral.

His eyes wandered to Elizabeth. She'd put her silky black hair up in a bun, and a few stray hairs were framing her face. Even without her makeup, she was so beautiful. Her lips were full and red, her eyelashes long and dark.

She used her chopsticks to take a bite of bulgogi and rice and she smiled, looking at him. He smiled back, his dimples prominent. Her cold hand settled on top of his, and a chill ran up his spine. Gently, he curled his large fingers around hers and he swore something inside him clicked into place.

Ben's life had changed so much in the past few months, and although he was finally feeling comfortable with his new home and everything he'd learned about the world around him, he hoped that maybe, just maybe, it wasn't done changing yet.

Chapter 25

Once Jay and Jack left, which wasn't until later that evening, Elizabeth went to the kitchen to start doing dishes from their Christmas meals. Once she'd gotten the sponge all soaped up, she started cleaning off plates, setting them in the drying rack on the other side of the sink. The dishwasher was clean, and after such a long day, she didn't have the energy to unload it. Besides, washing dishes by hand held a certain amount of nostalgia for the simpler times, which she desperately needed. Her mind was buzzing, filled with thoughts of Ben and Dottie and Arthur Valentine. She wanted to just turn it off, flip a switch and make it all go away, but she knew that wasn't how it worked.

Her swirling thoughts must have summoned him because, after she washed a few dishes, she heard Ben's soft footsteps in the doorway.

"Hey," he said quietly, padding further into the dim kitchen. It was dark outside, the falling snow illuminated by the Christmas lights on the townhouse's exterior.

"Hey," she replied. She set a plate in the drying rack and it clacked against the one next to it. "Everything alright?"

"Yeah, yeah, I'm fine." Ben sat down at the island, kicking his legs. He stared at the back of Elizabeth's head, quiet. "I just...wanted to ask you something."

"Okay...?" She set down the sponge and dried her hand on the kitchen towel, spinning around so she could look him in the eye. "I'm all ears."

"I...well..." Ben pulled the sleeves of his pajamas down past his fingertips. This had been easier when she'd been facing the window. "Uh, never mind. Goodnight. Merry Christmas." He got up, but her reflexes were too fast, and she grabbed his wrist before he could escape. "Shit."

"Gotta be quicker than that." She pulled him back down onto the bar stool. "Spill. Obviously, something's bothering you."

"Is it *that* obvious?"

She chuckled, nodding. "I'd like to think I know you well enough by now to be able to tell when there's something on your mind. You know you can tell me if something is wrong, right?"

"Right. Of course. Yeah. It's..." he exhaled a long sigh, "it's not that anything is *wrong*, per se, but something has been bothering me for the past few weeks. I didn't want to bring it up, and believe me, this isn't coming from *nowhere*, I've thought about it a lot. Like, a *lot*."

"Okay..." Elizabeth nodded, kindness and patience sparkling in her warm eyes. But behind them, there was something nagging at the back of her mind.

Had he noticed her weird behavior? Did he know that she was keeping secrets from him? Did Elijah snitch on her?

"I love…" he paused for an uncomfortable amount of time, and Elizabeth's stomach dropped, but then he continued, "…living here with you. So much. These past few months have been some of the best in my life, and I really, well, I don't care about the risks involved. But, that said, babysitting with you opened my eyes a lot, I think. If there's a rogue werewolf loose downtown or another blood-sucking pizza guy at the front door and you're not here, I'm a sitting duck." He took a deep breath, his heart banging against his rib cage in an attempt to make an escape.

She waited for him to say something more, but he didn't, so she asked, "What are you saying?"

"I want you to turn me, Elizabeth."

She was quiet for a long time, her face unreadable. Ben's heart seized in concern. Had he crossed a line?

"Or not! It's totally fine if you don't want to or if that's something you can't do. I totally should have asked that first, but I—"

"Ben. Stop." She cut him off, her face still devoid of any discernible emotion.

He swallowed thickly, preparing for her to shoot him down.

"It's a lot to think about. You have to know that, right?" she started quietly, searching his face. "Forever…" Elizabeth sighed with the pain of someone who'd experienced it firsthand. "Forever is a very long time."

"Right." He nodded, waiting for her to continue.

"I'm not saying no. I just need you to think about the consequences. The turning process is long and drawn out, and it hurts like hell. Jack could tell you that better than anyone else, probably. It's an intimate thing, and...if I turned you...well to put it simply, you'd be sired to me. A blood bond of sorts. Does that make any sense?"

"'Blood bond' meaning...?"

"It would be *my* venom coursing through your blood. Sometimes, there are certain emotional ties that come with that. You would feel bonded to me. You'd feel like you have a responsibility to me."

Ben, who already somewhat felt that way, just nodded dumbly. "Okay..."

"You would never get any older. You'd be frozen at twenty-four forever. You'd outlive your parents, Jay, all of your high school friends, your preschool friends, your nieces and nephews and siblings and whoever else. You'd have to change your name every decade or so, jump from job to job, keep a low profile...I'm not saying it's awful, but it's not *easy* either."

He nodded but didn't say anything.

"And you'd have to drink blood. But you already knew that." Elizabeth studied his expression. She slid both of her hands into his, letting his warmth envelope her chilly fingers.

He intertwined his fingers with hers, processing everything she'd said. He was quiet for a long time before finally saying, "I still want you to turn me."

"Okay." Elizabeth nodded. "I'm not going to do it tonight." She mulled it over for a second until it clicked. "Tell you what, your birthday is coming up, so give me, say, a week of heads-up. If you still want me to turn you, tell me a week before your birthday so I can get some things in order."

"I can do that."

"And if you change your mind, that's okay too. It's a big decision. I don't want you to just jump in without giving it much thought."

"I'll think about it, I promise." He squeezed her hands, looking deep into her eyes. How easy would it be to just lean across the island and...? He straightened up, their hands separating. "Well, goodnight."

"Goodnight, Ben. Sweet dreams."

Chapter 26

Ben wasn't quite used to having so much free time. Since his classes were out for the semester and wouldn't resume until early January, he actually had time to do things for his own enjoyment, such as reading for pleasure instead of for class and dedicating unhealthy amounts of time to thinking about Elizabeth, and in turn, what it would mean to be a vampire with her for...well, forever.

So, when Ben had just about worn himself out, thinking in circles until his heart felt like it was going to carve its way out of his chest, he put on his coat, laced up his boots, and said to her, "Hey, do you wanna go ice skating with me?"

Elizabeth froze and looked up from her computer. "Sure! I haven't been in ages." She set her laptop aside and got up off of the couch. She ran upstairs and grabbed the pair of skates she had sitting in the back of her closet. She'd gotten them at a thrift shop a few years back, and they'd served her well approximately once since then.

The rink wasn't too far from the townhouse. There was one in one of the parks in the historical district that was always busy this time of year. Elizabeth used to go skating pretty frequently in the winter, and she liked to think she was pretty good at it. She wasn't sure why she had stopped, exactly. Maybe part of her was afraid of leaving Gladys alone for too long, or maybe she'd just been too busy with other tasks and hobbies.

Once they arrived, Ben rented a pair of skates, and Elizabeth found a bench to sit on so she could lace hers up. Then, when they were ready, they walked to the entrance of the rink and stepped out together.

Immediately, Ben began to wobble on his unsteady legs, but Elizabeth retained her balance, gracefully gliding across the ice.

On the opposite side of the rink, there was a *giant* Christmas tree, wrapped in lights and covered in big round ornaments, a magnificent golden star perched on the very top. Speakers suspended above the rink were playing festive music all day long. At the moment, they were playing something from the *Nutcracker Suite*. A few food trucks were parked nearby, and a cart set up in the snow was selling hot cocoa.

While he was looking around, though, Ben wasn't paying enough attention to the ice, lost his footing, and in one swift movement, slipped and fell, sliding a good few feet forward in the process.

"You okay?" Elizabeth asked, turning back towards him and coming to a clean and deliberate stop in front of him.

He gave her two thumbs-up, chuckling at himself. He didn't know why he even bothered to be surprised by this anymore. He hoped something about becoming a vampire would help him be just a little more coordinated.

Elizabeth held out her hands, and he took them, allowing her to haul him up onto his feet in one swift, strong move. Somehow, he always forgot the power she was hiding behind her small, bookstore-employee demeanor. Once he was upright again, though, she didn't release his hands. Instead, she got a better grip on them and started skating in front of him, but backwards, pulling him along with her.

"You're good at this," he said, a wonderstruck look on his face, the lights on the tree reflecting in his eyes.

"I've had practice, is all. We'll get you there," she said.

He laughed and shook his head. "I'm not so sure about that. I wouldn't put it past myself to be clumsy forever." He paused, and then added, "Like, *literally* forever."

Laughing, she pulled him along behind her. "I'd say that's pretty likely, but time will tell."

"Elizabeth?"

"Yeah?"

"How much do people…you know…*change* when they," he paused, "you know…"

"It depends," she said, thinking. "Some people make a complete one-eighty, they're completely different afterwards. Most of the time, though, they stay pretty much the same, like Jack. I didn't know him before, but from what I know, his personality was about the same before the Titanic sank as after."

"That's reassuring."

"Yeah, a complete personality change is probably the last thing you need to worry about. You'll still be my clumsy Ben when everything is said and done."

Ben didn't know why, but his heart clenched when she said 'my.'

They skated around for a few more hours before deciding to call it a day. Elizabeth sat down on the bench and switched her skates for her boots, lacing them back up with her careful fingers. When she sat back up, Ben was standing in front of her, his skates returned to the rental booth and a cup of steaming hot cocoa in each of his hands. He held one out to her.

"Thank you," she said. She stood up and took it from him, her skates dangling by their laces in her other hand.

Ben started walking back towards the apartment and expected Elizabeth to follow him, but she just stood still for a second, thinking. He looked back at her and said, "Are you coming? Home is this way."

She thought for a moment more before replying, "How about we take a little detour? I think it's about time I took you down memory lane."

As soon as she suggested it, an excited grin broke out across Ben's face. "I thought you'd never ask."

So, Elizabeth led him away from the park, away from the rink, and down to the historical district's shopping center. She led him past Turning Page, past After Hours, past Castor's Hall of Magick, and then stopped in front of a bar.

The building was made of dark brown brick, and the door had a stained glass window set into it, a large raven in the middle. The welcome mat had a moon symbol on it: a full moon in the middle, with a waning and waxing crescent on either side. From the front window, they could see several patrons inside, taking shelter from the cold weather outside.

"The Raven's Nest?" Ben asked, reading the writing on the window. "What is this place?"

"These days, it's a bar that tends to attract people like our next door neighbors, if you know what I mean." She took a sip of her cocoa.

"Yeah, it's got a witchy vibe."

"Back in the '50s, though, before the, uh, *magical* renovations, this was the busiest sock-hop in Great City."

"Woah, no kidding?" He looked up at the place in a new light. "That's awesome."

"It was called Marnie's, and it was run by one of the coolest women I've ever met," Elizabeth reminisced. "There's this diner by the hospital that's retro themed; they bought the jukebox from Marnie when she retired and the Ravenwoods took over."

Ben nodded and followed Elizabeth further down the street. They turned down an alley and walked for a few blocks until they reached a different sector, one with a bunch of big old-fashioned houses. She stopped in front of one that had distinctly gothic architecture and looked up at it.

"This is where one of my exes used to live. Her name is Iris."

Ben asked, "Vampire?"

"Yes. She is. Shortly after we broke up—we ended on good terms—she met her mate, and now they live in Italy together." Elizabeth stared up at the house, the tall windows blocked by long, red curtains. "She threw some wild parties here, though."

"I bet." He laughed. Yet, he couldn't help but wonder... "So how does that work?"

"How does what work?" Elizabeth asked as they started moving again.

"Well, you know..." He hyper-focused on the sound of his boots crunching in the snow, heat rising to his cheeks. "Vampire mates, I guess." He paused, and then added, "You don't have to answer if that's too personal."

"No, that's a valid question." She nodded.

Of course he would ask that. Why did she think it was a good idea to bring it up in the first place? She felt his eyes on her, the *pulling, pulling, pulling* feeling returning to her chest. Would it be such a disaster if he knew? Would it be so bad if she finally told him? And while part of her thought the timing was perfect, the stronger part of her was afraid.

"Mates are...well, it's not really something you choose. There have been stories and folklore about soulmates since forever. They say there's one soul out in the universe that belongs with yours; you're supposed to fit perfectly with them, like puzzle pieces. There are a lot of vampires that never find their mate. Most choose not to worry about it, but some...some get really, *really* lucky."

He was quiet for a long time, processing. Then he asked, "Did you ever find yours?"

She stopped walking, and he turned to face her, his tall frame looming over hers. Snowflakes caught in his thick, brown hair, his warm breath fogging up his glasses ever so slightly. She looked up at him.

Yes.

She couldn't bring herself to say it, though. So instead, she shrugged. "It's hard to tell. Some meet theirs, and...they never realize it until they're already gone."

"That's really sad," he whispered.

She nodded. "It is."

"Do you think you'll find them?"

She paused, her breath hitching for a second before she nodded again. "I have a good feeling I will."

At some point as they walked on further through the snowy town, Elizabeth finished her cocoa, and Ben finished his, so they threw out the cups in the next trash can they passed. With both of their hands freely swinging at their sides, it was only inevitable that every few minutes, Ben's large, warm hand brushed against hers. Elizabeth supposed it was also inevitable that gently, slowly, *cautiously*, Ben reached out and slipped his hand into hers. She gripped it tight, her fingers slotting into the spaces between his.

They walked in silence for a long while, neither of them acknowledging the warmth they were fostering between their palms. Then, without warning, Elizabeth stopped and pulled her hand out of Ben's. Her arms wrapped around herself instead as she stared up at the big brick building in front of them.

The Bloodborne Bar.

Ben gasped. His foggy breath rose into the freezing air. "Woah."

"They remodeled the place. A few times, actually." She pointed up to the window on the second floor. There was a single candle lit, flickering. "That's where I lived, just a cute little apartment. It wasn't much, but it was better than living on the streets. The bartender and his wife took pity on me, pregnant and alone in a new world. I was terrified that Arthur was on my heels, coming for Katherine and I."

He was quiet, staring at the building. He'd read so many accounts of the tale of Elizabeth Bloodborne, but he had chills. This was the real deal. He'd been writing a thesis on his roommate, and he'd known that for some time, but it was decidedly *different*, standing in front of the bar with her, hearing her talk about it.

"When the battle in the field outside of town— there's a suburb there now—took a turn for the worse, a lot of the rebels retreated and took shelter in town. The bar was one of those places. But the Red Coats followed them. There was fighting in the streets, gunshots taking out windows and leaving holes and dents in the bricks of a lot of the buildings. Some of them are still there, if you look closely. I think it was probably because of the stress of it all, but during the battle, I went into labor. I got really lucky. There were medics and a midwife, and because of it, the fighting stopped. I gave birth to Katherine without complications. Over the next few days, a carpenter in town helped build a crib. Before I knew it, I was a new woman, I had a new name, a new daughter, a new life. I wasn't as afraid anymore. When Katherine was a little older, I picked up work as a seamstress, eventually moved into the townhouse as a tenant. And the rest is," she laughed, "well, the rest is history."

"Woah…" It was incomprehensible to him just how many lifetimes she'd lived. She'd been through more than he could fathom. So, he just stood there in shock for a while, staring up at the building in awe.

"I can answer any questions you have."

"I do have one, but it might be too personal."

"Go ahead."

"Why...why did you run from Arthur?"

Elizabeth let out a long sigh, her thoughts yanked centuries back. "We were in an arranged marriage. Just before our wedding night, he..." she stopped, flinching.

"You don't have to."

She closed her eyes and nodded. "I didn't realize I was pregnant until I'd already escaped and was on the boat to the new world. His family is extremely powerful. The vampires from his bloodline can convince anyone to do anything. *Anything.* My bloodline is powerful too. We have what's called 'Siren's Venom,' which causes our victims to actually *enjoy* having their blood drained. That's why I stopped."

"That...explains a lot, actually."

She laughed. "I thought it might." Elizabeth glanced down at her watch. "We should head back."

"Yeah." He nodded and followed her back in the direction of their townhouse. "Thank you. For the tour. It really put a lot into perspective."

"Anything for my favorite future history professor." Elizabeth's red lips curled into a smile, and once again, she slipped her cold hand into his much larger one. And maybe it was just in her head, but she was

pretty sure his hand was exactly where hers belonged.

Chapter 27

The day before New Year's Eve, Elizabeth wasn't really expecting anyone to wander into Turning Page Bookstore. They didn't really put on any big sales after Christmas, so the post-holiday shoppers tended to flock to other places that did. Jean and Barb weren't in, so she was alone, running the empty store, dusting the shelves and balancing the checkbook in silence.

The snow was coming down outside, snowflakes the size of quarters sticking to every surface they could find. The busy streets were filled with slush and speeding cars. There were still string lights wrapped around every telephone pole, the shop windows still as festive as ever.

Unexpectedly, the bell above the door chimed, ripping her out of whatever daydream had been stirring around in her head. And when she looked up, her stomach dropped, numbness spreading through her chest.

Arthur Valentine.

His black hair was slicked to one side, his eyes sharp, flakes of gold flickering in his amber irises. He looked over her, licking his lips as he approached the register. His nice loafers clicked against the wooden floors, and a blood red tie was fastened around his neck, the finishing touch on his pristine black suit.

"Elizabeth Bloodmere. It's been a while, hasn't it?" His voice was smooth, a siren's call.

She glared. "Arthur."

"Oh come on, don't be so short with me, darling." He grinned in a way that made her feel sick to her stomach. "It's been centuries, and you can't even get my name out of those perfect lips of yours?"

"I have nothing to say to you, is all." Her expression remained hardened, stance guarded. He was a man of many tricks, and she didn't doubt that he had one up his sleeve. "I assume you're not here to get the latest John Green novel."

"Unfortunately not. I was actually hoping to have a conversation with you. A conversation concerning our daughter perhaps."

"You get out of here right now." She harshly pointed to the door, fire in her eyes.

"A sore subject? There must be some reason you neglected to tell me she existed. She *is* my blood after all. Maybe I've come to finally repay you two-hundred years of child support."

"She is nothing like you and she never will be."

"What, I don't even get a name? No pictures? Surely you must have saved some from her youth. Or, I suppose given the time, some sketches or a painting would suffice. Is she in town?"

"And just why the fuck would I tell you that?"

"Things have been happening, have they not?" He raised an eyebrow, resting his arms on the counter.

"Things might *keep* happening if you don't tell me what I want to know."

"And I might put a stake through your heart before you can so much as snap your fingers." Her irises flashed red, fangs sliding into place. "Get out of my shop. Now."

"I'm on my way out right now, my love." He leaned against the counter.

The bell over the door rang out again, this time welcoming none other than Dottie Edwards, her short blonde hair arranged in neat waves and a red and white polka-dotted dress adorning her slender frame. As soon as Elizabeth made eye contact, Dottie's eyes flashed red and she couldn't look away no matter how hard she tried.

"Don't worry about it too much, Ella." Dottie grinned, her red lips curling into a perfect crescent. "You won't remember any of this..."

❧ ◈ ❧

"Hey, are you okay?" Ben waved a large hand in front of her face, and she blinked a few times, looking around the apartment. "Liz? You're scaring me."

"What happened? How did I...Fuck."

"What? Did something happen?" Ben's expression melted.

"I don't remember. I don't remember how I got home." She shook her head, brewing for a moment before shouting, "Fuck!"

"Hey, it's okay. It's gonna be okay, alright?" Ben reached out for her, and she sighed, letting him pull her into his broad chest. He rested his chin on top of her head. "Nothing happened, right?"

"I don't know." Her voice was quiet, scared.

"We'll figure it out, alright? I promise."

"Okay..." She nodded, embracing him tightly to ground herself in the moment. She felt a familiar dizziness lingering in her head, one she hadn't felt in a *long* time. "It had to be Dottie. She's the only reason I've ever felt like this."

"Maybe." Ben hummed, combing his fingers through her silky black hair. "Do you think Dianne would have anything to...I don't know, protect you from that?"

"Probably. She's always got tricks up her sleeve. Maybe a protection talisman or something I can wear. I don't know..." She looked up at him, and his gaze was gentle and warm. "I'm sorry, I'm just shaken up is all."

"You don't have to apologize. Running into an ex-girlfriend is never fun."

"Understatement of the century." She chuckled and pulled out of his embrace, finally calmed down enough to think clearly. Elizabeth took a deep breath. "I'm going next door. I'll be back in a few minutes."

Elizabeth walked back out the front door and up the steps of the neighbors' house. She raised her fist to knock, but before her knuckles even made contact with the wood, the door swung open, Dianne standing there with her eyes fogged over and purple. The fog dissipated and her irises returned to normal.

"I thought you might come." Dianne motioned her in, and Elizabeth stepped over the threshold, still not quite accustomed to seeing Dianne in that state. "You feeling alright?"

"Kind of." Elizabeth shrugged. "I had a recent run-in with—"

"Arthur, yeah, I know."

Elizabeth froze. She turned and looked back at Dianne, shaking her head slowly. "I...I thought..."

"It wasn't just Dottie."

She ran her fingers through her hair, exhaling a shaking sigh. It was worse than she feared. "How much did you see?"

"Most of it." She motioned Elizabeth over to her couch, and the two of them sat down. She had two steaming mugs of tea sitting on the coffee table. With a flick of her wrist, one of them slid closer to Elizabeth, inviting her to drink. "My intuition was giving me some weird vibes, so I tapped in. He didn't get anything out of you, don't worry."

"Okay, good." A silver lining. If she remembered her ex as well as she'd like to think she did, he'd probably just been there to watch her squirm, toy with her while she couldn't do anything about it. Of course, Elizabeth didn't actually know *where* Katherine was, or even what surname she was going by these days, so her limited information wouldn't have been much help to him anyway. Elizabeth took a sip of the warm, earthy tea, letting the tension roll out of her. "I was worried…"

"I know." Dianne smiled and reached over, putting a comforting hand on Elizabeth's knee. "He's a scary guy. But Nadia and I have been working on something for that very reason."

"All done." The witch in question emerged from their casting closet, a small room where they kept their brooms and cauldron and other mystical trinkets and knick-knacks. It was where they did the majority of their magic while they weren't working their storefront. In Nadia's hand dangled two necklaces. She walked closer and handed them to Elizabeth.

From the simple black cords hung round metal disks, each of them littered in various sigils, a round tumbled amethyst the size of a dime embedded in the centers of them. While she held them, Elizabeth felt the familiar buzzing that only magic could bring, warm and tingling as it tried to integrate with her energy.

"For you and Ben. Arthur and Dottie won't be able to mess with your heads as long as you're wearing these. We're working on more, but for now, we have these two," Nadia explained.

Elizabeth nodded and slipped one necklace over her head, tucking it into her shirt. She stood up and pulled Dianne and Nadia into a hug, which they gladly reciprocated.

"Thank you so much. I can't tell you how much I appreciate it."

"Elizabeth, after everything you've done for us, this is the least we can do."

And though she knew it was true and that they would do anything for her in the same way she would do anything for them, she was still grateful to have her witchy neighbors looking after her, especially with both of her worst exes back in town. She had a feeling she and her mate would need all the help they could get.

Chapter 28

What more than a mere flicker in an eternal candle is a new year? Ben wondered. When you were well over four hundred years old, did a new year mean anything, really? Or was it just a number on the calendar, one that would go away in the blink of an eye, only to be replaced again and again for all of eternity?

These were the thoughts he'd had since he'd asked Elizabeth to turn him.

Ben figured he'd had more existential crises in the past week than he'd had in all of his college years combined, but he couldn't help it. Everything in his meager existence had been filtered through an immortal lens, and there was no way to put things back to the way they had been before.

Would he even want to be a history professor if he'd be teaching college students *forever*? Would he and Elizabeth have to move when he'd been at one university for too long? Would Elizabeth even want to stick with him if he *did* have to move?

Those were the only two things he could think about these days: Elizabeth and immortality.

"Elijah?" Ben asked, fiddling with the necklace around his neck. Elizabeth and Jack had gone to the store to get things for the impromptu New Year's Eve party they had decided to throw, which meant he and the cat were, once again, alone for a little while.

"Yes, Benjamin?"

"Can I ask you something?"

"Aren't you *already* asking me something?"

Ben huffed, an annoyed smile on his face. "You know what I meant."

Elijah stretched, grinning that mischievous feline grin. "What's on your mind?"

"Is being immortal...scary?"

The gray cat thought for a bit. He sat up straight, his little paws planted firmly in front of him. "It is at first, I won't lie to you. It takes some getting used to. It doesn't even feel real, at first, you know? Everything feels normal until your friends start getting older. Your family starts getting older. And you're just...trapped in a cat's body." He paused and then added, "I mean, *you* won't be trapped as a cat, that's just my point of reference."

"Right. Yeah." Ben caught his bottom lip between his teeth, thinking.

"It's okay if you back out, you know. She wouldn't be mad."

He nodded and chuckled a bit to himself. "There's this little rational voice in my head telling me not to do it, but...part of me feels like it's a decision I was always supposed to make. I don't know if that makes any sense..."

"It makes sense. Just know that if you need more time to think about it, there's no expiration date for that kind of thing. She'll still be here when you're thirty or fifty or seventy-eight."

Ben thought about it for a moment. He did. He imagined wrinkles forming on his smooth cheeks, gray streaking through his dark brown hair. Would Elizabeth want to live with him if he aged into a grumpy old man or if his memory started fading? What if he got dementia and he slowly forgot everything, and she was stuck taking care of him until the very end?

He shuddered at the thought.

No, he wanted this. He wanted to be a vampire, even if it meant drinking blood and outliving his friends. He wanted to stand by Elizabeth's side through the conflict with Arthur and Dottie and whatever conflicts came after, and he wouldn't be able to do that if he was still a fragile human. He knew, somewhere deep down, that he and Elizabeth were meant to meet. For what purpose, he wasn't sure, but he couldn't wait to find out.

✺◈✺

About an hour later, Jack and Elizabeth returned with bags of noisemakers, confetti, cheesy novelty 2020 glasses, cardboard top hats and tiaras, and several bottles of champagne.

"Guess who didn't get carded at the grocery store!" Jack announced victoriously, holding a bottle of champagne high. "I bought alcohol, and they didn't even question me!"

"You probably wouldn't get carded in Canada, you know." Ben chuckled at the triumphant look on his hundred-year-old friend's face.

"Don't even remind me. That's bullshit. The drinking age is bullshit. The whole system is bullshit." Jack shook his head as he walked into the kitchen to deposit the champagne onto the counter.

Elizabeth grinned, tossing Ben a pair of ridiculously large glasses. "Happy New Year. Well, almost."

"Thanks." Ben chuckled and took the glasses, resting them on top of his head.

He helped the others get everything set up, taping some decorations and streamers to the walls, blowing up balloons, helping them make some finger foods. He wasn't sure what kinds of guests were going to walk through the door, but he knew Jay and Karter were coming, so at the very least, he wouldn't be the only human in attendance.

Speaking of humans, though, around eight o'clock, there was a knock on the door, and Elizabeth walked to go answer it, dressed in her glittering silver New Year's Eve gown. She'd had it for well over a decade, but only ever wore it one night a year, on one of her favorite holidays of all. There was something so special about celebrating a new year, reflecting on the old one, and she loved doing it surrounded by those she loved.

"Cody! Come on in!" She opened the door, grinning at the sight of the pink-haired barista in his Christmas sweater.

A glass shattered against the floor in the kitchen, and Elizabeth could hear Ben laughing from the other side of the house.

"Sorry I'm early. I brought cupcakes from that place downtown. Sugar & Spice?" Cody opened the lid of the box so she could see the cupcakes, marble cake with white frosting and edible glitter.

"Thanks so much! You can set them on the island in the kitchen."

"Watch your step," Ben warned, still chuckling, "Jack dropped a glass."

"I'll take them in there, then," Elizabeth offered, and Cody handed her the box.

"Aww, you have a cat?" Cody cooed, looking down at Elijah, who, based on the look he shot Elizabeth, was less than enthused about the whole situation. "What's his name?"

"This is Elijah," Elizabeth said, Elijah scurrying behind her leg to evade Cody's outstretched fingers. "He's a little shy, but I'm sure he'll warm up to you."

Cody smiled, and Elizabeth walked into the kitchen to find Jack standing there with a broom, sweeping up broken pieces of a champagne glass.

"What happened in here, butterfingers?" She laughed and set the cupcakes on the island, opening the lid of the white bakery box they were in.

"I got nervous, okay?" Jack snapped through clenched teeth. He sighed and shook his head at himself, chuckling pitifully. "What's happening? I never get nervous around boys."

Elizabeth's heart jolted, and she looked at him, smiling softly.

Jack met her gaze, smiling back with the same energy before saying, "Well, I guess that makes two of us then, huh?"

"Oh, hush." Elizabeth shook her head. "I mean, yeah, but it's not *confirmed*. Yet."

"Well, it's soon, at least." Jack glanced at the clock. "I mean, midnight is, *technically*, a week before his birthday, right?"

"Don't remind me."

"Do you need any help in here?" Ben walked into the kitchen. He looked at the dustpan filled with glass shards.

"I've got it handled, thanks," Jack grumbled, getting rid of the sharp pieces carefully.

It was then that the pink-haired barista, finally done petting the cat, came back into the kitchen to see what was going on. He ruffled through his fluffy tufts of hair, smiling at Jack. "Thanks for inviting me. I wasn't sure I'd have anywhere to celebrate this year. My roommate and I don't even have cable…"

"No problem, Cody. Elizabeth always goes all out for New Year's. The more the merrier."

"We need someone to eat all of this food." She motioned around the kitchen to the shrimp platters, the meat trays, the veggies and dip, the bags and bags of chips, and bottles of champagne. "Leftovers are great and all, but…"

"Elizabeth! We're here!" Max announced, running through the house. "Ooh, cupcakes!"

"Happy New Year." Dianne hugged Elizabeth with one arm, her other hand in Nadia's. "Thanks for inviting us over."

"We're the neighbors," Nadia explained, looking at Cody. She offered her hand. "And you are…?"

"Oh! I'm Cody. Nice to meet you."

"Ohhhhh, *Cody*, alright." Dianne nodded, a knowing smile spreading across her face. "Nice to meet you."

"I'm Nadia. This is my girlfriend Dianne, and our little trouble-maker over there is Max."

Max was already running around the townhouse chasing Elijah, who scurried away from him to go get one of his toys.

After Nadia, Dianne, and Max, their next guest was someone Elizabeth had invited but hadn't expected to show up.

"Will! You came!" She embraced him tightly.

"I did!" He smiled warmly before stepping aside. "And I brought a friend."

Waiting behind his broad frame was a face she had not seen in the longest time. Her fair features were framed by her curly red hair, freckles dotting her pale cheeks. She had Elizabeth's eyes, warm and brown with speckles of amber, but her cheekbones she had definitely inherited from her father.

"Katherine," Elizabeth whispered, pulling her in and hugging her tight. "I missed you *so much*, how have you been? How is everything going? Spill."

They walked into the house and went to the kitchen, where Ben was standing beside the veggie tray. He dipped a piece of broccoli in the French onion dip and popped it in his mouth. "Hi, I'm Ben."

"Katherine. Pleasure." She batted her eyelashes at him.

Ben's eyes widened, and he almost choked. "K-Katherine...as in...?" He looked to Elizabeth, mindful of Cody, who was standing over by the cupcakes with Jack.

Jack looked up, spotted Katherine, smiled warmly, and then grabbed two glasses of champagne and motioned for Cody to follow him out into the other room to watch the New Year's broadcast.

"Yes, this is my daughter, *that* Katherine." Elizabeth laughed. "Kate, this is my roommate Ben."

"Oh, *Ben!*" Katherine looked at William and smirked. "I hope you're not giving Mom too much trouble."

"Oh, never." Ben's cheeks were flushed scarlet. He reached up and scratched the back of his neck, chuckling. "Well, maybe sometimes..."

"He's good to me. Keeps me on my toes, for sure." Elizabeth gave him a gentle nudge in the ribs, and he laughed. "Life is boring without a happy little accident here and there." Her smile faded when she remembered what she had yet to tell her children, though. "I ran into your father."

"My—" The color drained from Katherine's face, her perfect red lips drawn into a frown. "When?"

"Yesterday. I don't remember any of it, but Dianne said nothing happened. I think he just showed up to scare me. He still doesn't even know your name."

"Let's keep it that way." Katherine nodded. She bit her lip and twirled a red curl around her finger. "I'm skipping town tomorrow, so he won't have a chance to run into me."

"And you're welcome to spend the night tonight, just in case." Elizabeth took Katherine's hand in one of hers and grabbed William's in the other. "That goes for you, too."

William grinned, squeezing his mother's hand. "We were already planning on it."

"Good. I'm sure we have a lot to catch up on." Elizabeth brought each of her kids into her arms. "But until then, let's eat, drink, and be merry. We have time to worry later."

And so, be merry, they did. Jay wandered into the house a little while later, accompanied by his roommate, a doe-eyed undergrad named Karter, who didn't have anywhere to be and had therefore been dragged along. He shook the shaggy, black hair out of his face, grinning when he saw Ben.

"Hey! Glad you could make it!" Ben hugged Jay and Karter, his face lit up in a bright smile. He led them further into the house, which was slowly but steadily filling with people as midnight approached. "This is the place."

"It's so nice…" Karter murmured, looking around as he admired the place. "How'd you get this lucky?"

"I ran into an angel at a coffee shop." Ben shrugged, grinning. He caught Elizabeth's gaze across the room and motioned her over.

She smiled, crossing through the growing sea of people to see who he'd found in the crowd. "Jay! Good to see you again. And you are…?"

"Karter. I'm one of Jay's roommates."

"We've all been pals since high school," Ben explained. "Karter here is the baby of the friend group."

"But we love him." Jay laughed, pinching Karter's reddening cheek.

"Someone always has to be the baby," Elizabeth reassured him. "That's just how it is."

"Yeah, I guess so. But the cheek-pinching can stop anytime." Karter rubbed the spot Jay had pinched.

"Never in your wildest dreams." Jay ruffled his roommate's hair so it fell in front of his eyes.

"There's *tons* of food in the kitchen, so please, help yourselves." Elizabeth smiled, tucking a piece of hair behind her ear before disappearing back into the other room to mingle some more.

"*That's* your roommate?" Karter watched as she walked off, her silver gown sparkling with every step. "Holy shit, dude."

"I told you she was something," Jay agreed, staring.

Something bristled in Ben's chest, and he crossed his arms, hiding the pang of protectiveness welling up inside of him behind a dimpled grin. "Yeah, she's gorgeous."

"Woah!" Jay marveled, studying the look on his friend's face. "You *like*—"

"No! No. Never—n-not like that," Ben stammered, his face an even deeper red than Karter's had been moments before. He felt Elijah rubbing against his leg, tail tickling the back of his knee. Oh great. Now he'd never hear the end of it.

"Oh come on, we've seen you with crushes, Ben. This is that." Jay crossed his arms and nudged Ben, grinning. "I mean, you don't have to *tell* her, but it must be so awkward..."

"I'm already awkward, believe me, I don't need any help in that department." Ben took a sip of his champagne. Maybe a few more glasses wouldn't hurt...No, he remembered, he had a decision to make later that evening, and he doubted Elizabeth would let him make it drunk. "She's nice and sweet and so kind it hurts, but we're roommates first and foremost, and I don't want to ruin that."

"Shoot your shot, dude." Karter gave Ben a slap on the back. "You only live once."

If only you knew the half of it.

"Ben!" Elizabeth called from deeper in the crowd.

Perfect timing, Ben thought. He saluted his friends, saying "Well, duty calls," before maneuvering through the people until he finally found his roommate, whose dress was as glittery as a disco ball in the dimly lit room.

"Ben, this is my sister, Victoria. She's just in town for the night."

The vampire standing beside Elizabeth was tall, at least 5'10". She had long, wavy blonde hair and was wearing a gold dress, which was similar to Elizabeth's, and a fur coat. Large black sunglasses sat on top of her head. She offered Ben a gloved hand, and he shook it.

"Nice to meet you."

"Aww, Eliza, you're right! He's so cute!" Victoria giggled.

Ben scratched the back of his neck, his cheeks especially warm all of a sudden. "Well, I don't know about *that*—"

"Ooh and dimples! Precious," Victoria cooed and then turned back to Elizabeth. "*Anyway*, as I was saying, I'm headed back home tomorrow. Are you *sure* you don't want to come? Mother and Father—"

"Not this time." Elizabeth shook her head. "I have...other responsibilities here that I need to take care of first."

Ben sensed that the casual conversation had transitioned into more personal territory, so he looked to Elizabeth before motioning back to the kitchen. She nodded, and he walked back towards the food, pulled right back to the veggie tray.

"Well, I'll pass along my regards, then." Victoria nodded. "But don't hesitate to call."

"I'll be in touch," Elizabeth promised, hugging her sister. Once her sister had moved on to chatting with Katherine, Elizabeth mingled with the other party guests, flitting from group to group and showcasing her skills as a competent entertainer.

Ben admired her from afar. She was way more outgoing than he was. His social anxiety could *never*.

A while later, most of the party had congregated in the living room in front of the TV. The countdown started, everyone holding a glass of champagne in their hand. Ben, quite literally, bumped into Elizabeth.

She stumbled at the contact, but looked up at him, laughing. "We really have to stop meeting like this."

...49, 48, 47...

"At least I didn't ruin your shirt this time." He chuckled, reaching up to scratch his ear with his free hand, dimples digging into his cheeks.

"And I told you, that shirt isn't ruined. But I *did* get a cozy new sweatshirt out of it, so I'm not complaining." Elizabeth laughed. "I'm glad your friends came. It looks like they're having fun."

...33, 32, 31...

"I'm glad they came too." He looked around for them and spotted Jay and Karter standing over on the other side of the room next to Dianne and Nadia, who were holding hands and looking at each other like they were the only people on earth. "And I'm glad that...everything that's happened led me here."

"Me too." Elizabeth set her champagne glass on the table, and Ben followed suit. She looked up at him, tucking a strand of soft, black hair behind her ear. "Our neighbors always say that everything happens for a reason."

...19, 18, 17...

"I can't help but agree with them." For a long time, he just admired her porcelain skin, the little flecks of amber in her eyes, the little freckle on the tip of her nose. "Thank you, for choosing me. I promise you won't regret it."

Elizabeth smiled softly, taking a step closer. She let one of her dainty hands rest on his chest, approaching his shoulder. The countdown was getting dangerously low, the numbers mushing into one another, until finally...

...10, 9, 8...

"Do you mind if I...?" Elizabeth inched closer and closer to his face, the pull in her chest tugging her until she was right in front of him.

Ben's breath hitched. He swallowed, his pulse pounding in her ears. His response came out as a faint whisper that she doubted she would have heard, had it not been for her enhanced hearing. *"P-please..."*

"*3, 2, 1, HAPPY NEW YEAR!*"

Elizabeth pressed up on her toes, connecting her lips with Ben's. He gasped, arms wrapping tight around her waist and pulling her against him. He melted, letting her lead and willingly following wherever she decided to take him.

Kissing Elizabeth Bloodmere was worth waiting centuries for.

When she pulled back, he rested his forehead against hers. "Happy New Year," Elizabeth whispered, smiling.

He smiled back, replying softly, "Happy New Year."

Ben picked yet another empty champagne glass off of the table, carrying it back to the kitchen where Elizabeth was getting a head start on the dishes. The vacuum was whirring in the other room as William cleaned up the confetti on the carpet, and Katherine was upstairs, changing into her pajamas.

"Hey," he said quietly as he set down the glass next to the growing collection on the marble counter-top.

"Hey," she replied, turning her face so she could see him and his sheepish smile, his adorable dimples coming out of hiding.

"So, you said to tell you my choice a week from my birthday, and since it's past midnight...I fig-ured...*technically*..."

"Sure you didn't have too much champagne, Ben-jamin?" she teased, her eyebrow quirking upward, but her playful demeanor quickly faded. "It's a big deci-sion to make. Are you sure you don't want more time?"

"I don't need any more time. I want you to turn me." He was certain, his brown eyes set on hers, his plush lip unquivering and his words deliberate. "I've never been more sure about anything."

Elizabeth was quiet for a long time, watching him. She nodded slowly, her expression unreadable. Fi-nally, she said, "Okay. Give me a week."

Chapter 29

Ben noticed he hadn't been sleeping very well since New Year's Eve. It had been a few days since his kiss with Elizabeth, since he finalized his decision and Elizabeth had started making calls and ordering things online. He wasn't sure what all he'd need to undergo such a transformation, but he was both excited and terrified to find out.

So, on one of his sleepless mornings, he wandered down to the living room and clicked on the news, his hair a disheveled mess and his glasses slightly crooked on his nose. The glow of the TV filled the dark room, and the week's stories started playing.

"This week in Great City, four more reported missing are tied to a suspected human trafficking scheme, and a break-in at a local blood bank leads to a blood shortage. More information on how and where to donate at five."

Ben stared at the screen, his mouth hanging open. Kidnappings, *blood bags* being stolen? If that didn't scream vampire activity, he didn't know what did.

"Well, that's not good." Elijah rose from his spot in the corner of the room. His sudden statement made Ben, who had been under the impression that he was alone, jump.

"Do you think…"

"That Arthur and Dottie are involved? Without a doubt. The missing people mean they're strengthening their numbers, and the blood...well, that's pretty obvious."

"Should I go get Liz?"

"She probably already knows. She's awake upstairs and gets alerts for this sort of thing."

As soon as she was mentioned, Ben heard her footsteps coming down the stairs. She emerged wearing an old, oversized concert shirt and a pair of worn sweatpants and made a beeline for the landline in the kitchen. A few seconds later, he heard her talking on the phone for a few minutes before hanging up and walking out to the living room.

"You're up early," she noted, her head tilting as she admired Ben's adorable bedhead.

He pointed to the screen. "The news—"

"I know, I saw. The Hunters are handling it. There's not much we can do about it anyway. Well, without some serious reinforcements, that is."

"We could move," Elijah suggested.

Elizabeth let out a long sigh, shaking her head and perching on the armrest of the couch. "I'm tired of running." She crossed her arms. Her expression hardened. "No, I'm not running anymore. He can come for me, but he's gonna learn the hard way that I'm a lot stronger than I look."

Later in the afternoon, the mail arrived, so Ben walked out to the mailbox to get it. There wasn't a lot. A few bills, some coupons, and a letter for Elizabeth. It had looping cursive handwriting on it, but there was no return address, and a large, red, wax seal was holding it shut. He stared at the seal for a long moment, admiring the rose stamped into it.

Being a history major that lived with a vampire did have its perks from time to time.

"Liz, mail." Ben walked over to where she'd settled on the couch, typing away on her manuscript.

"Anything fun or just bills?" she asked, taking the small stack of envelopes from him. She flipped through them and stopped, freezing when she saw the wax seal stamped with an innocent red rose.

"Are you...okay?"

Elizabeth didn't respond, instead breaking the seal and opening the envelope. The paper inside was yellowed, blank aside from three words in handwriting that was all too familiar:

Soon, my love.

She stared at it for a long while, tracing the letters with her eyes. Chills spread down her arms. There was only one person a note like that could have come from. So, without saying anything, Elizabeth stood, walked to the fireplace, and dropped the note in the flames, watching as it was reduced to ash.

"Oh." Ben stared into the flames.

"Best not to take chances with things like that. I don't know if he has a witch on his side. Sometimes letters like that can have tracking spells on them," Elizabeth explained, using the fire poker to nudge the remains further into the hearth.

"I just think wax seals are cool. That's why I was staring at it for so long."

"They *are* cool. I have a whole wax seal set upstairs if you want to play around with it."

Ben's jaw dropped. "You're kidding."

"I'm not. It's the second drawer on the left side of the desk in the office."

He gasped and raced up the stairs, followed by Elizabeth, who helped him get out all of the pieces of the kit. She set up the tealight, lit it with a match, and then set the metal spoon and its stand overtop of the little flickering flame.

In a large wooden box, she had a few handles and a few dozen metal stamps. Ben watched attentively as she took out one of the handles, an ornate bronze one, and picked out a stamp with her initials, EB, in curling script on it.

"Lots of Es," Ben noted, studying them. She had a good variety of Serif and Sans Serif, as well as Script. There were a few that didn't have letters on them and instead had stars or flowers or leaves, but there were only a few with her actual initials on them.

"They come in handy." She chuckled, screwing the stamp onto the handle. She pushed a tackle box full of little wax beads towards him. "Pick four."

"Any colors?"

"Anything you want."

He thought carefully before picking two wine red ones, one that was white, and one that was black. "Do I just…?" He motioned to the heated metal spoon, and Elizabeth nodded, so he carefully set them in and watched as they melted down.

Elizabeth got out some stationary and folded an envelope into shape with her expert fingers. She slid it to Ben and then asked, "Do you know how to do this?"

"Kind of. I've seen a lot of videos online."

"Alright, go ahead." She motioned to the spoon full of melted wax and set the stamp next to him.

Focused, his clumsy hands moving slowly and carefully, he lifted the spoon off of its stand and poured the melted wax onto the envelope. He admired the way the colors swirled and bled together, and then pressed the stamp down into it.

"Try not to move it until it dries," she advised him and he nodded, his brown eyes staring at the wax intensely. After a long few moments, Elizabeth helped him gently wiggle the stamp out, revealing the beautiful design, EB. Elizabeth Bloodmere.

Or, Ben's brain provided unhelpfully, *E and B.* Elizabeth and Benjamin.

❧◆❧

It was the night before Ben's twenty-fifth birthday. He was sitting on the couch in the living room, watching TV and scrolling through his phone. He'd finished his homework for the next few days, trying to get a jump on things before his life got flipped on its head. Elizabeth had warned him it might get hard for him to be productive at the end of the process, so it would be wise to get as much as he could done until then.

The doorbell rang, pulling him from his thoughts. He stared at the door for a few seconds, still a little traumatized by the fanged pizza guy that had started his descent to vampirism in the first place.

To his surprise, Elizabeth rushed to the door from the kitchen.

"Are you expecting someone?"

"Yep," she said, pulling open the door. She grabbed a few bags from whoever was standing on the porch. "Thank you!"

"What's all that?"

"Why don't you come out to the kitchen and find out?" She winked and then walked back in the direction she'd come from.

He sat on the couch for a second, confused, before he clicked his phone off and stood up, walking towards the kitchen, where Elizabeth was rapidly unpacking take-out from what looked like three different places.

"What...?"

"Surprise!" She beamed, proud of what she'd accomplished. "I got all your favorite foods!"

Ben swore his heart melted at the look on her face. He smiled and went in for a hug, which she gladly reciprocated. "Liz, this is so sweet! Is there an occasion?"

"Well, your birthday is tomorrow, and I know we're celebrating with the guys tomorrow night, but I wanted to make sure you got to have all of this stuff at least one more time while you're...well, you know, still *fully* human."

"What did I do to deserve you?" he murmured, finally releasing her from his hold.

She shrugged, laughing softly. "Just got lucky, I guess." She continued to set everything out. "May I present: Olive Garden breadsticks."

"The superior restaurant bread, yes," he said, nodding approvingly.

"Sushi from that place you like downtown." She set the little plastic boxes on the counter, a few different varieties for each of them to try. "Ice cream from Lucky's for dessert; I'll stick that in the freezer real quick." She opened the freezer and set the cups of ice cream inside, and then once the freezer door was closed again, she pulled the fridge open. "And finally, last but not least, honeydew milk tea with boba from a place Jay told me you like."

Ben's eyes widened. "You really pulled out all the stops, huh?"

"Only the best for my—" *Mate*, the voice inside her asserted. "—roommate," she amended. She knew she had to tell him. Wouldn't it be better to get it out of the way now? If they went through with their plan for tomorrow, he'd find out anyway. Would he be mad she hadn't told him when she'd known for so long? Probably not; she couldn't imagine Ben getting mad at her. She could, however, imagine him being disappointed. She didn't want that either.

"Thank you. For everything." Ben sat down on one of the stools at the island and patted the one next to him.

"Of course." She sat down. "I just...A lot is going to change tomorrow. I want to make sure not *too* much changes."

"Yeah, I get that." He nodded, letting his warm hand rest atop hers. "I'm not going anywhere. You're stuck with me."

She laughed. "Good. I'd like to keep you around for quite a while."

His cheeks reddening and his deep voice getting softer, he asked, "How does forever sound?"

Elizabeth was quiet for a second until she felt that familiar tug in her chest, pulling her closer to him. She reached up and gently turned his face towards her, leaning in to press the softest kiss to his plush lips. And then, looking up at him through her thick eyelashes, she whispered, "Forever sounds great."

Chapter 30

Elizabeth pulled the warm cake out of the oven, admiring the way the vanilla and chocolate swirled together into one cohesive flavor. A marble cake, just as requested. She dipped a toothpick into the fresh pastry, smiling when the wood came out clean.

"All done?" Elijah asked, sniffing the air as he entered the kitchen.

"I just have to let it cool and decorate it. Glad to have that out of the way. What time is it?"

"Three," Jack replied, coming into the kitchen from the living room. He had a bag of party balloons in his hand. "All decorated in there. What's next?"

"Are the boys back with the drinks yet?"

"No, not yet," he reported.

"Alright, well, the pizzas are getting here at six thirty, so that's taken care of..." Elizabeth tapped her finger against the corner of her lip. "I'm pretty sure that's everything. All that's left is the icing on the cake."

"Perfect. Great. Wonderful." Jack pulled Elizabeth in for a tight hug that she gladly reciprocated. "He's going to love it. I'm so happy for you."

"Thank you." She smiled. "I just...I don't know. I'm nervous. It's been a while since I've done this."

"It'll be fine," Jack reassured her, looking down at Elijah. "Right?"

"Of course. You already kissed him. You already drank his blood. Turning him shouldn't be that much more difficult, all things considered..."

"Hey, we're not sure how *that'll* go yet."

"We will be soon, though." Jack smirked suggestively. "But I've had a feeling since day one."

"Me too." Elizabeth chuckled and shook her head at herself. "Well, obviously *I* have. I don't know, it's just nerve-wracking. In all of my years..."

"You deserve it. You deserve to be happy after all of this time." Jack's comforting hand rubbed against her back, and she nodded, exhaling a deep sigh. He was right, and she knew it. After all, she'd been waiting four hundred years. It was about time. It felt exactly like her mother said it would.

"We're here!" Jay called, carrying two large reusable grocery bags full of drinks. "Ran into a little traffic on the way. Everything ready?"

"Yep. Just waiting for the cake to cool. Thank you so much for helping out."

"Of course. We'd never miss Ben's birthday. I mean, you only turn twenty-five once, right?" Karter grinned innocently. If only he knew how false the sentence he'd just said was...

"You're right. It is indeed a big day." Elizabeth smiled, pulling her hair out of her face and putting it up into a ponytail. "It's his first quarter of a century. That's definitely a big deal."

"Wow, when you put it like that..." Jay shook his head. "He really is getting old, huh?"

"Ouch." Jack put a hand over his heart, chuckling.

"Woah, dude, you're twenty-five?" Karter looked at Jack, his big, innocent, brown eyes wide.

"Somewhere around there, yeah." Jack chuckled, shaking his head. "Cursed with a baby face forever."

"I'm sure you'll grow into it, dude. No worries." Karter laughed and gave Jack a friendly pat on the back.

"I have to at some point, right?"

The four of them stood around the kitchen chatting until Elizabeth finally deemed the cake cool enough to decorate. She took it out of the pan, expertly covering it in the sweet cream cheese frosting the birthday boy had requested. Once it was covered thoroughly, she took out the tubes of colored decorative frosting and started delicately crafting the sugary words across the top of the cake.

Happy Birthday, Ben!

"I picked these up. Didn't know if you'd have any or not," Jay told her, setting a few packs of birthday candles on the table. He had plain candles as well as a big 2 and 5 to put right at the top of the cake.

"Running low. Good call. Thanks, Jay." She smiled. Once she was satisfied with the words, she let the boys put the candles in place. She looked down at her messy T-shirt, which was covered in flour and chocolate. "I'm gonna go upstairs and get changed. Let me know if you need anything."

"Will do."

Elizabeth retreated up the stairs and slipped off the old concert shirt, searching through her closet for something nicer to wear. This would be Ben's last day fully human; she wanted to make it special. After thinking it over for a few minutes, she ended up settling on a nice red sweater, the talisman Dianne had given her, some pretty dangly earrings, and a black pencil skirt. She walked back down the stairs to find the cake finished and Jack and Jay standing beside a slack-jawed Karter.

"Is everything okay?"

"The cat talks," Karter blurted, staring at Elijah, who was up on the island.

He turned his gaze to Elizabeth. "Sorry. Force of habit."

"Yeah, so, uh, the cat talks." Elizabeth looked to Jack, who only shrugged. She looked back at Karter. "Surprise?"

"How does the cat talk? *Why* does the cat talk?"

"*The cat's* name is Elijah," he snapped. "And I'm *sure* he'd love to explain it to you if you ask nicely."

"Does Ben know?" Karter looked at Jay, who nodded wordlessly. "Wild."

Jay put a hand on Karter's shoulders, chuckling to himself. "You don't know the half of it, buddy."

While Jack and Jay explained the situation to Karter, who listened wide-eyed with a glass of fruit punch, Elizabeth made sure everything was *perfect*. She organized the stack of presents on the coffee table, biggest on the bottom, smallest on the top, and then vacuumed up some more cat hair and taped up a few more pieces of streamers. Next, she got out a box of candles and went around the house, setting them up on the various surfaces for later. As she reached for the broom to sweep up the kitchen a little, Jack stopped her.

"Quit stressing," he told her, freezing her in her tracks. "He'll love it no matter what."

"Well, I know, but I want it to be perfect."

"It already is. Look around. Not a present out of place." Jack tilted his head, trying to get a reaction out of her. He couldn't remember the last time he'd seen her so worked up over something. He understood why, but it was still concerning. Jack patted the seat next to him. "Come sit down. We're teaching Karter about vampirism. It's fun!"

She looked over at Karter, who looked back at her with eyes like saucers. She pointed at him and looked at Jack accusingly. "Look what you did, you're traumatizing him!"

"He'll be *fine*." Jay batted a hand in her direction, taking a large sip from his glass, which she was pretty sure was *not* filled with fruit punch. "I'm fine, aren't I?"

"*Are* you, though?" She raised an eyebrow, laughing. After standing there for a few more seconds, she sighed. "I'm gonna go set this down and then I'll be back out here."

She walked back to the closet and put the broom away, and then gave the house a final once-over. It looked good. Jack was right. She was just nervous. Proud of her handiwork, Elizabeth walked back into the living room and sat next to Jack, his arm wrapping around her shoulders and giving her an affectionate squeeze.

"So are you two, like, vampire mates or some shit?" Karter motioned between Jack and Elizabeth, who both erupted with laughter.

"Kid, I'm so gay." Jack looked at him and then to Elizabeth and then back at Karter, still laughing. "Like, *so* gay."

"The gayest," Elizabeth added, agreeing. "I, myself, am a bisexual, as you kids say."

"She was bi before it was cool."

"It's always been cool," she interjected. "He means I've been bi since before 'bi' was a thing."

"Yes. That. Perfectly articulated as always." Jack nodded. "That said, we don't have mates. Yet."

"Well…" Everyone turned to look at the talking cat.

"Not officially," Elizabeth interrupted him. If looks could kill, Elijah would be down to eight lives.

"Do you choose that, or…?" Jay piped up. "I've always been curious. Is it like a werewolf thing? Like from *Twilight?*"

"Similar?" Elizabeth, the resident *Twilight* expert, thought about it. "From my experience, it's something you just sort of…*feel.* There's this pulling in your chest. But you can't tell for *sure* until, well, if you turn your mate, I've heard the mark from your venom is supposed to turn gold instead of silver, and if you're both already vampires, then you're just…supposed to be able to tell? I don't know. It's hard to describe."

"So you don't have a mate?" Karter's big doe eyes fell on her, and he pouted. "That's so sad."

"I'm not in a rush. If I meet them, I meet them. I've got all of eternity to figure it out." If there was anything her years and years of life had taught her, it was patience. But all of this recent talk of mates was making her a little antsy, if she was being honest. Or maybe she was antsy for other reasons…

For a long time, Jack and Elizabeth and Elijah sat there, answering their curious human friends' questions until, finally, the doorbell rang. Elizabeth sprang off of the couch, pulled her stake out of its hiding place, and tossed it to Jack, who got up and stood by the door, just out of sight of whoever was there. Since their last incident with a pizza guy, they weren't taking any chances.

"Three mushroom and green pepper pizzas for Elizabeth Simon," the pizza guy said once she pulled the door open.

"Eww, mushroom?" Karter gagged.

"Birthday boy's favorite." Elizabeth shrugged. She looked over the pizza guy. He couldn't be any older than seventeen, a constellation of acne scattered across his cheeks. And he was definitely human. She handed him the money in exchange for the pizzas. "Keep the change."

"Gee, thanks!" he said, taking the money from her and hopping back down the stairs into his car.

Jack relaxed, letting his stake arm go limp as Elizabeth shut the door with her foot. She carried the pizzas back into the kitchen and set them on the counter, pulling out a stack of paper plates. No reason to break out the good ceramic plates for pizza. She'd asked Ben if he wanted her to cook anything special, but he had said no. He'd rather just have pizza and his friends and some good times. She knew he'd only said that so she didn't have another thing to stress about, but the idea of it was still nice.

"All set?"

"All set," Elizabeth confirmed.

And it was a good thing, too, because only a second later, the front door opened and in came Ben, his bag slung over his shoulder and a tired look in his eyes. It took him a second to realize what was going on, but he snapped out of his exhaustion very quickly when his friends all yelled, "Happy Birthday!"

"Aww, you guys! You didn't have to do all this!" He grinned brightly, looking around the room at the balloons and the streamers and everything else. The scent of pizza wafted out of the kitchen.

"Of course we did!" Elizabeth walked over to Ben, wrapping her arms around him. "It's your birthday! You only turn twenty-five once, you know."

"Right, right." He laughed, hugging her back. He pressed a quick kiss to her forehead, so quick it could almost be mistaken as friendly. Almost. "Thank you so much."

Once she was out of his arms, he hugged each of his other friends while Elizabeth snuck off to get the cake. She lit the candles quickly and then carried it out to the other room, where the boys were assembled.

"Oh my God, you guys." Ben admired the cake in all of its glory. "Thank you so much."

"Quit thanking us and blow out your candles, grandpa." Karter laughed.

So he did, extinguishing all of them in one breath.

"What did you wish for?" Jack asked.

"He can't tell you, or it won't come true," Jay interjected, winking at Ben, who blushed red.

"Right," Ben agreed. "Everyone knows that."

"Alright, keep your secrets." Jack smirked. "I'll go get some plates."

❧ ◈ ❧

It didn't take them long to wear down the supply of pizza and cake, and before they knew it, Elizabeth and Ben were cleaning up after yet another party. Given that they were paper plates and Solo cups, though, it didn't take all that long. When they were just about finished, Elizabeth sent Ben out to the living room to wait for her.

When she walked into the living room, he was sitting there with a timid look on his face, awkwardly fiddling with his hands. He looked up at her, waiting for her to say something, but she didn't, just walked into the room with a lighter. She went around the room and lit all of the candles she'd set up on the side and coffee tables, and once they were flickering, she turned off the lamp, striding over to where Ben was. His big, brown, innocent eyes were filled with curiosity, with anxiety. He swallowed thickly, taking off his glasses with shaky hands.

"S-so, how do you want to, uh, do this?"

"First of all, calm down. Take a breath, alright?" She mimicked inhaling a breath and letting it out.

"Right, you're right." He nodded and took a deep breath. Ben let his eyes shift to the candles on the table. "Is there...a reason for the candles?"

Elizabeth shrugged, gently taking his wrists and uncrossing his arms, using the opportunity to climb onto his lap. She guided his hands to her waist. "Sets the mood better."

"Is it...gonna hurt?"

"Yeah, it is." Elizabeth nodded. She was quiet for a second, and then she asked, "Are you sure this is what you want? Because...once I do this...there's no going back. You know that, right?"

"Right." Ben nodded. He tugged her a little closer. "Can I ask you something first?"

"Anything."

"Is it me? Am..." His eyes locked on hers, and he whispered, goosebumps trailing up his arms, "*Am I your mate?*"

Elizabeth was quiet for a long time, her eyes wide and red, frozen in place by the question that had just slipped from his stupid, perfect, plump lips. Tears pricked her eyes, and when she blinked, one slipped down her cheek.

"I-I'm sorry, I didn't m-mean to—"

"Shut up," she mumbled, laughing through her tears as she pressed a finger to his lips. She took a shaky breath. "Ben, I...I've only been *sure* since...since the last time I bit into your neck, but...I've been suspecting it since the moment we met."

A tentative smile tugged at his lips. "I knew it." He laughed softly, his chest all fuzzy and warm, "I *knew* it!"

"I...didn't want to tell you because—"

"You wanted me to make the choice on my own."
Ben nodded. "I get that. And thank you for letting it
be my choice..." He reached up and tucked a piece of
black hair behind her ear so he could get a better look
at her face. With a careful thumb, he wiped her tears
away. "But I think part of me has always known it'd
be you."

"You have no idea how long..." Elizabeth sighed
and tucked her face into the crook of his neck, arms
embracing him tightly. She murmured into his ear,
"I've been waiting centuries for you. So, so long.
Months and years and decades, and just when I'd
given up hope, you bumped into me and got coffee all
over my nice white blouse."

His arms wrapped around her and pulled her
against his chest, his laughter rumbling deep and
warm. "Hey, I apologized for that."

"And if the stain didn't come out, I might not have
forgiven you," she teased, pulling away from him to
admire his handsome face, for once unhidden, free of
the glasses that always blocked her view. Her hands
settled on his cheeks, thumbs nestling into his dimples. She tilted his head up to hers and fit his lips into
the slot of her own, kissing him softly.

Ben's large, warm hands settled around her waist,
lips dancing against hers. His kisses became rushed
and greedy, desperate to take it all in before his world
changed forever. In all twenty-five of his years, this
was the first moment he'd felt really, truly alive.

"You have no idea how long I've wanted to do this," Ben murmured against her, his words swallowed up by her loving kisses. "If I'd known you felt like this…"

"If you'd known I felt like this, you wouldn't be human right now," she answered, pulling away to look at him, the thin layer of sweat glistening on his forehead. His breaths were heavy, broad shoulders heaving. This was the first time she'd really gotten to admire his body, his strong arms, his broad, toned chest, his *warmth*. "You would have begged me to turn you months ago. That's why I didn't…you know."

"Then turn me. We've waited long enough," he rasped, something *pulling* in his chest. "I'm yours. Forever."

"Are you sure?"

"Yes."

"Are you *positive*?" she asked one last time, searching his blown-out irises, afraid that something had changed, but he didn't waver, not even for a second.

"I've never been more positive about anything in my life."

"Do you want a countdown, or…?" She repositioned, shifting her hips and taking his head in her gentle hands, carefully tilting his neck just so.

"Just go for it." His heart thudded against her chest, quick and strong.

"I'll be gentle," she promised.

"O-okay." He shivered, trembling slightly while he tried not to move too much.

Elizabeth slowly approached his racing pulse, the vein protruding perfectly from his neck. She licked her lips and then attached them to his skin in a slow kiss. He inhaled sharply, and then as quickly as she could, she plunged her sharp fangs into his jugular.

Immediately, the sweet taste of his blood flooded across her tongue, and her body went slack in bliss as an ever-familiar *zing* rushed through her limbs.

Mate! Her brain reminded her. *That's our mate!*

She'd almost forgotten just how good his O Positive tasted. It was addictive for sure, her own personal brand of nicotine, and this was the last time she'd ever get to taste it. In that moment, she did something she hadn't done in decades: she injected him with her venom.

As soon as the chemical hit his system, Ben gasped, the sting harsh and sharp. He flinched and squirmed a bit in her grasp, but she held tight, one arm wrapped around his shoulders and the other hooked under his arm on the side where she was latched on. She squeezed him tighter, holding herself in place as he writhed. As much as she wanted to tell him it was okay, her mouth was occupied with other things.

He tried not to be too vocal. As much as it hurt, and as loudly as the rational voice in his head was screaming for her to stop, he wanted this. He wanted *her*, no matter how much pain it caused him.

Ben's face contorted. He let out one tortured "AaaaAAAhh!" and then bit down on his lip, pushing through the acid sting. His breaths became ragged and uneven, and his eyes squeezed shut. He clenched his jaw, his muscles tensed, and he grabbed onto Elizabeth, desperate for anything to ground him in the moment.

The pain was excruciating until it wasn't. At some point, his arms went limp around her, hands sliding slowly down her back. His groans of agony stopped, and his body gave up its fight with the poison she'd pumped into his veins. She released, retracting her fangs and pressing the tip of her tongue to each of the two fang marks.

Elizabeth broke her hold on him and sat up in his lap to get a better look at him.

He looked up at her with his half-lidded eyes, his arms sitting heavily at his sides.

"Did it work?" he mumbled, trying to give her a smile, even with her venom weighing him down. It was so hard to move.

"I think so." She nodded, leaning closer and pressing a soft kiss against his lips. His lips twitched in response as he attempted to kiss her back. "You did *so* well."

"Okay…"

"I'm gonna take you up to bed now, alright?" she asked, tilting her head as she looked down on his pathetic form, absolutely drained even though she hadn't taken any blood.

"Mmhmm…" He nodded slightly and tried his best to sit up on his own, straining against his invisible bonds, but he slumped right back against the couch.

She stood and took his hands, pulling his dead weight upright. He fell into her, but she held him steady. In his drowsy state, he managed to wrap his arms around her, humming at her touch, her scent.

"…Love you…"

"I love you too, buddy." She hugged him to her body, chuckling softly before readjusting him to a more efficient position for carrying up the stairs. Her enhanced strength allowed her to easily lug him up to the second floor and into her room onto her plush bed. She turned to leave, but his large hand lingered loosely around her wrist, radiating warmth from his long fingers.

"Stay," he pleaded, and then, when she didn't react, he added quietly, "*please*."

"I can stay," she nodded, climbing onto her king-size mattress beside him.

He used what was left of his rapidly depleting strength to roll on top of her, an arm thrown across her waist and his face buried in the crook of her neck. He didn't even get time to say goodnight before the first snore rumbled out of his plush lips.

She laid there, trapped under his weight, and stared up at the ceiling. From her position, with his neck right beneath her face, even in the darkness, she could make out the marks she'd left permanently on his soft skin, both of them flushed golden.

Chapter 31

"*Am I your mate...?*"

"*...I've been suspecting it since the moment we met...*"

The words echoed in his head over and over, memories floating through his mind until finally, he opened his eyes. It had been such a wonderful dream. Or...not?

Ben looked around the bedroom and realized very quickly based on the red painted walls and the rows upon rows of scrapbooks and photo albums, the walls covered in posters, and the violin mounted on the wall that this was not his room.

"Elizabeth?" he asked, looking around. The bed was empty, and when he sat up, his head spun. Oh God, he was dizzy.

The door opened, and she walked in, wearing his sweatshirt and a pair of plaid pajama pants. She was carrying a plate of eggs and bacon. She laughed softly when he looked at her, a bewildered look in his eyes.

"Was last night a dream?" he blurted.

"Nope." She sat on the bed and handed him the plate with a fork. She poked his fang marks with the tip of her finger, and he winced. It hurt slightly more than poking a bruise. "You've got the marks to prove it."

"Oh. So, am I...?"

"No, not yet." She brushed the hair off of his sweaty forehead and pressed her hand to it. "Mmm, you're warm. Might have a little fever."

"Fever...?"

"Your body is trying to fight it off. It's gonna take about a week." She lifted his chin and looked into his eyes. "Today, you'll feel mostly fine, but it's all down-hill from here. Vampire venom is basically poison. It'll slowly shut your body down, and then at the end, it'll change you completely."

"Oh, okay." He nodded, setting the plate in his lap and sitting in front of her awkwardly. He was pretty sure their make-out session the night before had been a dream too, and he didn't want to overstep any boundaries. "Thanks for breakfast."

"Of course. You feeling alright otherwise?"

"I'm a little dizzy."

"Okay. If you get a bad headache or if you're in a lot of pain, let me know, and I'll let you have some of my blood. That helps out a lot." She ran her fingers through his hair, organizing the messy strands, her perfect red lips curling into a pout. "I have to take care of my mate, after all."

He gasped softly, a smile causing his dimples to emerge once more. "I thought that part was a dream, too."

"Not in the slightest." Elizabeth scooted closer and cupped his cheeks in her hands. She nuzzled her nose against his. "I'm sure you were pretty far gone by the time you said this, but you kind of confessed last night."

"Oh, I did?" His cheeks flushed, and he wished he could blame it on the fever. "Sorry. Was it...too soon?"

"No! Well, I mean, maybe? I just...even though we're *mates*, I don't want you to think that we have to rush into anything. We can take it as slow as you want to. I just want you to be comfortable and happy and safe. That's all I've ever wanted."

"Thank you. So much. I really appreciate you letting me set my boundaries. I...I wouldn't mind if we kept, uh, kissing, though." He chuckled, staring at the plate in his lap, suddenly too embarrassed to make eye contact. "I really like kissing you."

She used one slender finger to tilt his chin up towards her and gently kissed him, drawing a blissful hum from the depths of his chest. "I really like kissing you too."

"Sweet." He leaned in for another kiss, smiling. "Because I plan to keep kissing you."

"Good." She smirked and then motioned to his plate. "Now, eat up. You're going to need it."

"Will do," he nodded, lifting the fork to his mouth to start eating his breakfast as she commanded.

Elizabeth was right. He didn't feel too bad. In fact, he felt well enough to go to the coffee shop with Elizabeth and Jack later that afternoon to get some more work done on his thesis. He had a bit of a headache, but not enough to prevent him from accomplishing *anything*. In fact, he wrote a few pages he was really proud of, meanwhile, Elizabeth was tap-tap-tapping away on her keyboard next to him.

"Got your marks?" Jack asked, a dark smirk on his face.

Ben nodded and tugged the collar of his shirt down, showing off the shiny golden bite mark.

Jack's jaw dropped, and he leaned across the table to get a closer look. "Woah, holy shit!" he laughed excitedly. "Elijah owes me twenty bucks." He looked between Elizabeth and Jack. "Congrats, you two. That's...wow..."

"Took me long enough, huh?" Elizabeth grinned. She grabbed her empty coffee cup, shook it, and then started sliding out of the booth seat. Leaning back over, she kissed Ben's cheek and grabbed his cup too. "I'll go get us some refills."

"Thank you." Ben smiled, watching as she walked off towards the counter to order more coffee for the two of them.

Jack turned to Ben as soon as Elizabeth was out of earshot. "Hurts, right?"

"It did, yeah." Ben grimaced. "She was gentle with me, though."

"Be thankful for that." Jack lowered the collar of his shirt, showing off his own battle scars. He had three sloppy silver bite marks spread down his neck and onto his shoulder.

Ben stared, looking at each one while they were exposed. "Why...?"

"I got this one because a vampire thought I was cute." Jack pointed to the first mark, closest to his neck. He slid his finger down to the next one. "This one is because I tried to run away, and *this* one," he pointed to the third, furthest down his shoulder, "is because I fought back." He shook his head. "Well, *tried* to, anyway. Didn't get very far."

"*Who* turned you?"

"Don't know her name. All I remember is her curly red hair and her blue silken dress." Jack shrugged, taking a sip of his coffee. "And then a week later I woke up in freezing ice water. And *then*, I met your mate."

"My mate," Ben murmured, grinning and resting his head against his hand. "That's still so weird to me..."

"I mean, we both knew." Jack chuckled. "Day one in this very booth, I teased her because I thought you two would make a cute couple, and here we are."

"Really?" He laughed, his cheeks flushed red.

That day seemed so far back now, so buried under his months of living with her that the first day they ever met felt like a distant dream. And yet, he could so vividly remember the sharp panic that had hit him when he spilled his coffee on her. Things could have gone so much worse, but luckily for him, he'd dumped the scalding drink on the one girl in the coffee shop who couldn't get burned by it.

"Really," Elizabeth chimed in, slipping back into the booth with the two drinks. "And I teased *you* about someone else, if I recall, Mr. Ellis."

"Oh *yeah*!" Jack laughed, scratching his ear. "Forgot."

Elizabeth turned her attention on her mate, looking him over. He looked pretty normal, all things considered. "How are you feeling?"

"A little dizzy, but it's not bad," he replied, his arm rising to rest on the seat behind her. "I feel pretty okay."

"Alright." She nodded and leaned in to peck the corner of his lips. "Let me know when that changes. I can help."

"Okay." Though he didn't say anything else, he did look a little uneasy about what that entailed. He'd already seen Connor Hunter choke down some of her blood, and it didn't look all that fun...

"Trust me. Take the blood." Jack put his hand on the table in front of Ben, a serious look in his eyes. "As someone who couldn't, take the blood. Hindsight is 20/20, as they say."

"Noted."

Ben knew Jack was right, he really did, so he wasn't sure why a day and a half later, when his headache evolved from faint and annoying to acute and painful, he was still hesitant to say anything to her.

Elizabeth, the angel that she was, had taken work off for the week to take care of him, as she knew that the worse he got, the harder it would be for him to do things without help.

"How are you doing, bud?" She popped into his room, her hair up in a messy bun. She'd been doing laundry, but as she had been doing since she'd bitten him, she checked in on him frequently to make sure everything was okay.

"I...I, well, I uh, have a bit of a headache..." he admitted. The volume of his own voice made him flinch. So, he added softly, "It hurts."

She pouted and pushed past his door, walking into the room. She sat on the side of the bed and pressed her hand to his forehead. He was hot to the touch. "Definitely a fever. Feeling achy?"

"Yeah..." He lifted his heavy arms. "Sore."

"That's what I thought." She tilted her head before asking, "Do you want some blood?"

Exhaling a sigh, he nodded. "Yeah, I think that would help."

He didn't want to make her do this for him, but before he so much as looked up at her, she was already biting into her own wrist. She offered it to him, and he slowly brought it to his lips, reluctantly drinking the thick, bitter substance. It tasted way worse than he imagined it would. He coughed, but forced himself to swallow it down until the pain in his head dulled. When he pulled away, he had a guilty look in his eyes and dark vampire blood smeared on his cheeks.

She laughed. "I know it tastes icky. I'm sorry."

"Did I do it right?" he asked, finally meeting her gaze.

Elizabeth chuckled, plucking a napkin off of the nightstand and using it to clean him up. "The first try is always messy. It comes with practice."

"Yeah…" He supposed he hadn't given all that much thought to the process of drinking blood, but this was what his future looked like. His long, long, fang-filled future.

"Feel any better?"

He lifted his arms and bent them, pinching his upper arms to see if they still felt like they were filled with acid. The soreness had indeed left them, as had the throbbing in his head. "A lot better. Thank you."

"Do you need anything else? I know this isn't gonna be easy on you." The most empathetic expression he'd ever seen was etched across her face.

"Could you just…" He shrugged. "Could you just stay with me for a little while?"

"Of course. Scoot over." Once he had moved over some, she repositioned herself, sitting beside him in the bed.

Elizabeth laid down on her side, and Ben rolled over to look at her. She stared at him for a long time, admiring his messy hair, his flushed cheeks, his glistening skin. This would be the way he looked forever, every mole and freckle frozen in time. His thick hair would never gray, his smooth face would never wrinkle, he'd be perfectly preserved like this for all of eternity.

"You would have been a cute old man, you know." She reached up to smooth a strand of hair off of his sweat-coated forehead.

He laughed, an amused smile overtaking his handsome features. "Too late for that, I'm afraid. I'm stuck like this."

"Unfortunately, I'll never get the pleasure of witnessing silver fox Benjamin Kim, and neither will any of your future history students." She faked a frown.

"Real shame that is," he said. "Promise me you'll still tease me about getting older even though I'm not actually getting older."

"Of course. You can expect prune juice and a ridiculously large TV remote as birthday presents when you turn forty."

"I look forward to it."

They were both quiet for a moment. "It'll get better, I promise," she reassured him, tilting her head up towards his. "It'll get worse first, but it'll get better eventually."

"I know." He nodded and tugged her against him, arms tightening around her frame. Then, drowsily, he added, "You're worth it."

Chapter 32

Turning into a vampire was not fun, Ben decided. In fact, it was quite the opposite. He wasn't so sure why Bella Swan had ever wanted it so badly in the first place, and as he slipped further into the abyss between life and death, he wasn't sure why *he'd* wanted it either. Well, until Elizabeth checked on him. And then he remembered.

Maybe it was the fever melting his brain or her venom ravaging his body, but she called to him like a siren's song. Her long, black hair looked silky and soft, her skin smooth and vanilla-scented, and her voice lifted his spirits. And then there was her blood. The first taste he'd had wasn't great, but now, he swore he was addicted. Every time she offered, he accepted without hesitation. It chased his pain away, and deep down, he knew that every sip was connecting him further to his mate.

His mate. He smiled drowsily. His *mate*.

He hadn't entirely understood it before being bitten, but he sure as hell got it now. Elizabeth was his mate. She'd been his mate centuries before he was even born, and she'd be his mate centuries into the future. He knew in his soul that he'd do anything for her, and he wasn't even fully turned yet. He couldn't imagine what it would be like when he was a vampire too, but according to Elizabeth, his urge to protect and please her would only get stronger.

Things were changing, that was for sure. He wasn't sure exactly when, but at some point, food had started, slowly tasting...wrong. He didn't know why, but Elizabeth's cooking, even his favorite dishes, didn't taste good any more.

He took a few bites and stopped, a sour look on his face.

"Oh, so that's where we are," she noted, nodding. "It's okay, this is normal. It just means that things are changing. You're, well, *you're* changing."

"You look awful," Elijah added. "Just so you know."

"Thanks." Ben turned his gaze from the cat to Elizabeth. "How much longer?"

"A few more days. Almost there, Ben. You're taking it like a champ."

"Mmm," he hummed, dead in the eyes. "I'm going upstairs."

"Alright. I'll be up there in a bit." She watched him struggle up the stairs and looked at Elijah.

"So I take it the roommate agreement isn't temporary, then?"

"It's actually the opposite of that, sorry to tell you." Elizabeth chuckled. "You love him and you know it."

"I'll admit, he *has* grown on me." Elijah stretched before hopping down from the table and walking towards the other room. "But that doesn't mean that once he moves into your room I want us to get *another* one. His friends are too loud to live here."

The doorbell rang.

"Well, I hope they don't have enhanced hearing, because they're on the front porch." She laughed, walking towards the door.

She'd invited Jay and Karter over to see Ben before he got too sick, but she wasn't sure if he'd told them what was happening. They just knew that he'd been under the weather and needed a pick-me-up. She was sure that seeing them would make him feel better, even if it was only a little bit.

"Hey guys, come on in."

"Where's our sick little monster?" Jay asked, a Thermos of soup in his hands. Karter stood behind him, peering into the townhouse.

"Upstairs in his room. Follow me." Elizabeth led the way through the house and up the stairs into Ben's room, where he was sitting in bed, a book propped open in his lap. He flipped through it sluggishly, turning the pages with his heavy arms.

"Dude, you look like shit." Karter laughed, walking into the room. "What do you even have?"

"I don't know." Ben closed his book, shrugging. He was leaned back against the heap of pillows on the bed, tucked under the blankets. "I don't think it's contagious, though."

"Good. We brought you soup from that place you like on campus." Jay walked over and set it on the nightstand, smiling. "How are you feeling?"

"I'm alright." He smiled sleepily. "Kind of. Mostly. I will be in a few days, I'm sure."

"I brought these from your professors." Jay rested his backpack on the bed and pulled out a thick folder. "The rest should have been emailed to you."

"They were, yeah. Thanks." Ben flashed him a lazy thumbs-up.

"Wow, you are *out* of it. What kind of pain meds are you *on?*" Karter waved a hand in front of his friend's face, and his eyes wouldn't focus. "Follow-up question: can I have some?"

"Whatever Elizabeth gave me," he replied, shrugging as he laid back, retreating further into the pillows. "It worked, though."

"That's good." Jay smiled. He roughed up Ben's hair, making it even messier than it already was. He looked back at Karter. "Well, we don't want to bother you too much. We'll see you soon, alright? Call us when you're better, and we'll all go roller skating or something."

"Sounds fun." Ben smiled. He crossed his arms. "Thanks for coming. I...missed you guys."

"Of course, dude. We missed you too. Get better soon, alright?"

"I'll try."

Jay and Karter didn't say too much more, leaving a few minutes later. Elizabeth put the soup they'd brought for him in the kitchen and let it cool before sticking it in the fridge. Maybe he'd want it once food actually tasted good again. Ben napped for a good few hours, tired beyond belief, and when he woke up, Elizabeth brought him the very few things to eat that didn't absolutely disgust him, which was toast with the teeniest bit of butter, some plain white rice, and every once in a while, a banana.

He propped himself up against the pillows, his arms shaking as he hoisted his body upright. He groaned, leaning back and exhaling a long breath.

"When did moving get so hard?" he joked, staring up at Elizabeth with half-lidded eyes. He looked pitiful and he knew it, but at the moment, he didn't care. He had bigger problems, such as the searing pain in his head and the rumbling in his seemingly endless stomach. No matter how much food he consumed, he never felt full. In fact, he doubted he'd ever feel full again. He knew he didn't have much time left, he just didn't know quite how long it would take.

Dying was a lot harder than he'd thought it would be.

"Did you hear what I just said?" Elizabeth asked, waving a hand in front of his face.

He shook his head, chuckling. "No, I didn't, sorry. I'm pretty sure my brain is melting."

"I said you should probably go to the bathroom before you go back to sleep."

"Yeah, that's a good idea." Ben nodded and slowly swung one leg over the edge of the bed, and then the other. It felt like his limbs were filled with lead, almost impossible to move.

"Can you stand?" Elizabeth asked, her lip pulled between her teeth, worry tugging her eyebrows together.

"I hate that that's even a valid question..." Ben murmured, shaking his head. He planted his feet on the floor and slowly pushed himself into an upright position. He wobbled a little, but managed to take a few steps forward before collapsing altogether, his knees buckling.

Elizabeth's quick reflexes helped her catch him before he hit the floor, gently lowering him down the rest of the way. She tilted his head up so she could see his face and was surprised to find tears rolling down his cheeks.

"I'm sorry."

Her expression softened. "Why are you sorry? There's nothing to be sorry for."

"I'm...I can't do anything anymore..." he whispered, another tear slipping from one of his tired brown eyes.

"Ben," she sat down with him, her hand resting against his warm cheek, "there is literally poison in your body. It's killing you. It's a miracle you're even still talking, honestly."

He sniffled, his shoulders shaking. "Yeah?"

"You are so strong. You always have been. But it's okay to let me be strong for you right now." Her thumb stroked his scalding skin soothingly. "I'm gonna give you some of my blood, and we're gonna get you to the bathroom, and then we're gonna get you back to bed, okay?"

"Okay," he nodded, his eyes wandering to her wrist. As soon as she'd mentioned it, he could almost taste her blood on his tongue. Now, his body was screaming for it, one final jolt of energy, enough strength to walk again, even if he was pretty sure it would be for the last time.

Elizabeth raised her wrist to her mouth and sank her teeth into her vein, piercing a clean hole to her bloodline. She pressed the wound to his chapped lips, and he eagerly drank, chasing after the feeling he knew it would give him. He was beyond the bitter taste. In fact, he was pretty sure he'd acquired it in a similar fashion to his coffee addiction.

He finally released his hold on her wrist, tingles running all through his body. He shifted from his position sitting on his feet to a kneeling one, and then, slowly, he stood up again. Elizabeth wrapped one of his arms around her shoulders and helped him to the bathroom. When he was done, she helped him back to bed so he could eat what he was pretty sure would be his last meal. And then, when he was finished, he leaned back against the pillows, staring at her in a feverish daze.

"You okay?" she asked.

He only nodded in response, reaching for her hand weakly. She slipped hers into both of his large, very, very warm hands. He thought about Jack for a second. He couldn't imagine going through all of this on his own, confused about what was happening and alone on a cruise ship doomed to sink.

"I'm glad I'm not alone."

Elizabeth sat on the edge of the bed and cupped both of his burning cheeks in her hands. She pulled him in for a soft, drowsy kiss. "I'd never let you go through this alone."

～◆～

A few hours passed. Ben tried to do some reading, but he couldn't get his eyes to focus. He thought about going to sleep, but he knew if he did, he wouldn't wake up again. So, he texted Elizabeth.

He heard footsteps coming up the stairs, and then, finally, Elizabeth walked into Ben's room and pressed her hand against his forehead.

"Not feeling so hot, huh?"

"Mmmm..." he nodded, barely looking up at her from under his droopy eyelids. When he pressed his lips together, his dimple was especially visible, one perfect little indent in his smooth cheek. His forehead was coated in sweat, and his skin was so hot to the touch that she was surprised it wasn't sizzling off of him.

"You want some water?"

"Please."

She was down to the kitchen and back before he could say "Dracula." Elizabeth pressed the cold glass against his dry lips, helping tilt his head so he could drink it properly. He lifted a hand to support the glass, sipping it greedily until, only a few seconds later, the glass was empty.

"Thirsty," he rasped, shivering and tugging the blankets higher around him. "S-so thirsty."

Elizabeth was quiet for a second, pouting. She sighed. "Yeah, I don't think water is gonna cut it..."

Ben didn't even bother to ask what she meant because a few seconds later she was gone again, this time returning with a tall glass of something that was red and swirling. He stiffened. "Is that...?"

"No, no it's not. It's something called 'fledgling juice.' Had Dianne whip this up a few days ago. Should help with the thirst at least a little bit." She handed it to him, and he looked at it skeptically, sniffing it before taking a tentative sip. Once it hit his tongue, however, he downed the whole thing in a few greedy gulps, exhaling once it was gone and tilting the glass back for more.

"Oh, that hit the spot." He hummed and fell back against the pillows again. "Thank you."

"Of course. I'll be downstairs doing—"

"Can..." Ben started, but stopped when she turned to look at him. "Never mind..."

"What do you need, Ben?" she asked, her eyes attentive and warm.

"Can I have a kiss?"

She rushed over to him in the blink of an eye and sat on the bed, leaning in. She cradled his weak body gently and dipped down to press her lips to his. He kissed her, slow and sloppy, his plump lips chapped and sticky with fledgling juice. "You can have as many kisses as you want."

"Elizabeth?" he whispered, looking up at her, his eyes glazed over and his hands shaking.

"Yeah?"

His voice came out small and trembling. "*I-I'm scared.*"

"It's okay. It'll be okay, I promise." She laid down beside him and wrapped her arms around him. A pale hand reached up to turn his face towards hers. He was so overheated, warmth radiating off of him in waves. "You'll barely even feel it."

"Are you sure?"

"Positive." She took both of his hands in hers, intertwining his large, warm fingers with her smaller, colder ones. "Do you want me to stay with you until you fall asleep?"

He nodded, using what was left of his strength to roll onto his back, pulling her on top of him. Her weight was comforting, he decided. "I'm so...tired..." He yawned, his eyes drooping and his arms fastened loosely around her. "But...I don't...want to go yet..."

"Don't fight it," she told him, resting her head against his chest as it rose and fell. She listened to his slowing heartbeat. "Just let it happen. I'll be here in the morning."

"Okay," he nodded, nuzzling his nose into the crook of her neck and letting out one last, long breath. "Love you..." he slurred, finally slipping away.

"I love you too, Ben..."

Chapter 33

Elizabeth had made a promise to Ben, and it was a promise she intended to keep. No one deserved to wake up alone when everything about them had changed. It was scary, and he needed someone there to guide him once he finally opened his eyes again. So, once she moved him from his room to hers, she grabbed her knitting bag and set up on the unoccupied side of the bed, casting the yarn onto her small circular needles. She started up a rib stitch, knitting and purling alternatively until she'd made a nice rim for a hat.

Once she'd switched colors and started to knit the body of the hat, she heard a knock on the door. So, sticking the ends of her needles into the yarn, she swung her feet off of the bed and padded down the stairs in her fuzzy socks.

It was Jack that was standing on the front porch, lugging a slightly larger cooler than he normally had.

"How's he doing?"

"He's out."

"Is he…?"

Elizabeth nodded. "I'm pretty sure he's *out* out.

"Well, in that case, I got here just in time." He walked into the house, setting the cooler on the dining room table. He popped the lid and after closing the door, Elizabeth looked at all of the blood bags crammed into it, more than double her usual supply. From here on out, this would *have* to be the normal amount.

"Holy shit."

"Packed a little extra. Wanted to make sure he had enough for his first few days. You know how it is."

"Right, right. Thank you, Jack. I owe you." She hugged him, and he chuckled, shaking his head.

"I think we're about even, Liz. If we kept track, we'd just be owing each other for all of eternity."

"As it should be." She laughed. After looking through the cooler, she picked it up and carried it up the stairs into her room.

Jack followed her, not really expecting to see Ben there, dead asleep. He walked over to the side of the bed and lifted Ben's wrist, only for it to drop heavily back onto the mattress. His skin was cold to the touch, his chest barely moving. "Yeah, I think you're right."

"Promised I'd be with him when it happens." Elizabeth motioned to her sleeping mate. "He was really scared last night."

"Hence the knitting stuff." Jack chuckled. "Well, it definitely beats waking up alone. Believe me, it's not fun. You fall asleep feeling like you're dying, and when you wake up, the Titanic is sinking. And you're dead."

"That might not be a universal experience, but yeah, I get what you're saying." Elizabeth laughed, unloading the blood bags into her mini fridge. It would be good to have some on hand whenever Ben finally woke up. She knew he'd be thirsty.

"If either of you needs anything, let me know."

"Got any plans today?" she asked, hoping for some company for the long day or so while Ben was out.

"I do, sorry. Cody and I are—"

"Ooh, *Cody*!" Elizabeth teased.

"Shut up."

"You find your mate too?"

Jack shrugged grinning a little. "Maybe. I don't know. How do you know?"

"I didn't *know* for a long time. You just..." She put a hand over her chest. "*Feel* it. You'll know. Or maybe you already do."

"Maybe. I really don't know. But we're going ice skating, so I'll keep you posted if I figure it out."

"Cute. Have fun."

"Will do." Jack shot her a thumbs-up, taking his cooler from her and heading out, leaving Elizabeth alone once again with her Ben.

At some point, Elijah wandered up the stairs and in through Elizabeth's opened door, hopping up onto the bed while she knitted. He looked down at Ben's limp body and then up at his vampire roommate. "He looks dead."

"Yeah, he probably will for a while." Elizabeth shrugged. "He'll be up soon enough."

"Are you gonna be in here all day?"

"Yeah, probably."

"Do you want company?" Elijah took a few steps closer to Elizabeth, looking up at her with curious green eyes.

"I'd love some company." She patted the spot beside her and he stalked over, sitting down and leaning on her thigh. Her knitting needles clicked against each other, her hat getting longer by the minute as she looped more and more yarn together, alternating colors to make new stripes every four rows or so. She looked over at Ben, sighing. He looked so peaceful, but Elijah was right. He did look dead. He was barely moving, and if she looked closely, she swore he...wasn't moving at all, not even his chest.

Would things be different once he woke up? She'd been thinking about it a lot recently. Maybe, once he was a vampire too, he'd decide he didn't need her and move across the country. It wasn't unheard of for people to get close to vampires only for their immortality. She'd certainly met people like that, had a few close calls with cultists and people obsessed with the idea of living forever without ever realizing what a lonely and dangerous existence it could be.

But then she saw the golden mark bitten into his neck, *her* mark, the place where her venom had entered his bloodstream. They were mates, and once he woke up, that would only be further solidified. He'd feel it too, just as strongly as she did.

Her room was a mess, she lamented, looking around. Papers were scattered across every surface, books sitting in stacks on the floor, the stray blood stain here or there. She set to work, putting the books back on her shelf in whatever space she could find, she organized the papers and set them in neat stacks on her desk, scrubbed at the blood stains on the hardwood until they were gone.

She wandered over to her shelf of photo albums, her finger tracing each book's spine until she settled on one from the 1700s. She was mostly looking for things she could show Ben: remnants of old letters, flowers she'd pressed between the scrapbook pages, paintings she'd had scanned. When she pulled the cover open, she stopped and stared at the page for a long time. It was a very familiar image, one of her in her wedding dress from when she was supposed to spend the rest of her life stuck with none other than Arthur Valentine.

The dress was gorgeous, made of silk with big, ruffled sleeves, hundreds of pearls and gemstones sewn into it, as well as seemingly endless lace worked into the sleeves and the train, which trailed behind her a few good feet. Her black hair had been arranged in delicate curls, her veil hanging in front of her eyes.

She'd posed for hours to have that painting done, and the only reason she had a tangible copy was because Victoria had snapped a picture of it, still hanging in the grand hall of Bloodmere Manor. Elizabeth studied her stern features. She looked so unhappy. She *was* so unhappy. Getting married to a Valentine vampire was the last thing she wanted, but as an heiress to the Bloodmere Coven, she had no choice. Her parents had been convinced it was the only way to make peace between their families.

For a while, Elizabeth's mother had her convinced that she could learn to love Arthur in time, but then he'd done the unspeakable to her mere nights before their wedding, and she couldn't bear the thought of being bound to him for the rest of eternity. So she ran away, and the rest was, literally, history.

She let out a long sigh. It had been a while since she'd thought about that dress, about that day. It didn't hurt as much as it once had, but there was still pain there, pain that was all because of Arthur.

And now he was back.

She closed the book and put it back on the shelf, choosing to pull out something else, something with better memories inside of it. This led her to her photo album from 1945. She sat on the edge of the bed and started flipping through pages. There were pictures with her friend Betsy and all of their other lady friends who were not necessarily only attracted to men, sitting in a diner together and laughing and smiling.

This version of herself was a little more recognizable, even though the pictures were in black and white. Her hair was done up in victory rolls, and she could tell she was wearing her signature bright red lipstick in almost every photo. She'd been so happy then. With all the men at war, she and the rest of her friends weren't as constricted by the rigid rules of society. Namely, they could kiss each other more often, and there wasn't anyone to stop them.

She flipped through a few more pages, and then stopped, staring intensely at a picture that had been taken in a ballroom on VE day. Standing beside her, looking *very* handsome in a Navy uniform, was Ben. Her Ben.

Her hands were shaking as she held the book, staring at him. She remembered that day.

She'd been flitting from party to party all day, and when she'd gotten to that particular party, it wasn't much different than the others. She chatted with her friends, whichever ones she could find, and got hit on by just about every soldier in the room. But there was one who was different. And it was him.

A slow song swept over the hall, and after some encouragement from his slightly drunk friends, he made his way across the room to her. "Can I have this dance, ma'am?"

While she'd said no to every other soldier who'd asked thus far, she only laughed and said something like, "I could be convinced." Her hand slipped into his, and they went out onto the floor, dancing away well into the evening. She knew there was something different about him: his kind brown eyes, his smile, his charming dimples, and yet, she didn't know how to put the feeling into words.

"Where are you from, soldier?" she'd asked.

"Richardson, Michigan, ma'am. I'm headed out first thing tomorrow."

"I bet you miss home."

"I do."

"Got a sweetheart waiting for you?"

He'd laughed, his broad shoulders shaking. "No, ma'am. Just my mom." His eyes had softened, and he studied her features. "I don't suppose you're waiting for a special someone to come home?"

"You're the only soldier I've had the pleasure of speaking with...I didn't catch your name."

"I'm John Park. You are?"

"Elizabeth Rogers."

"Well, Elizabeth Rogers, with permission of course, it's been four years since I've kissed anyone. Would you mind if I...?"

She'd been bolder back then and had grabbed him by the collar and pulled him in. And that was when the camera flash went off.

She hadn't ever seen him again after that, but she remembered his face as plain as day. In fact, it was the very face of the man laying on her bed, trapped in a deep, dead sleep.

She set the photo album aside and slid closer to Ben, staring at his face, his thick eyelashes, his plush lips set into a straight line. She let one of her hands wander to his smooth cheek and gently stroked his skin with a cold thumb, admiring him silently.

*So much wasted time...*she thought, shaking her head. She'd met him in a past life, a whole seventy-five years before. She'd held him in her arms, kissed his sweet lips, and never even knew what she'd lost until he was already gone. She was lucky he'd been reborn so close to her, and even luckier that the fates had been much more forward in their efforts to bring the two of them together this time around.

Done with her brief trip down memory lane, she picked up the hat she was knitting and finished it off, and then, seeing as there was nothing better to do, she popped in *Twilight* and started knitting a blue and bronze scarf. She'd picked up the yarn after a conversation with Ben. Apparently, it was *impossible* for him to find any Ravenclaw merch that was the right color, thanks to the movies using the house's wrong ones. She intended to fix that for him. If she had to make it herself, then so be it. She hoped he'd like it.

About a third of the way through the scarf, *Twilight* ended, so she put in *New Moon*. She looked at Ben. She hoped being a vampire was everything he wanted it to be. If it wasn't, then he really was screwed. Vampirism was kind of a forever thing, after all. He was stuck with her; roomies for life.

It was so weird that he was lying there silently. By now, she was more than used to the sound of his snores, thanks to her superior hearing. It was endearing, really. It made him so...well, so *human*. That was gone now. Her sweet, dorky human Ben was changing before her very eyes, transforming, being molded in the hands of her venom. There was no guarantee that the Ben that awoke would be anything like the one she'd lulled to sleep.

Just after Elizabeth put in *Eclipse*, there was another knock on the door. So, she walked down the stairs and opened it to find Dianne and Nadia standing there, holding a pot covered in tinfoil.

"Hey Liz, we knew you had a lot going on here, so we brought you some gumbo," Dianne explained, handing the pot over to their vampire neighbor.

"Old Broux family recipe." Nadia winked. She looked to Dianne, who nodded, a giddy smile on her face. "And we...well, we cooked up another Castor-Broux family recipes of sorts." She peered around Elizabeth into the house. "Is Elijah here?"

"Elijah!" Elizabeth called behind her, motioning the girls inside. They stomped their snow-covered boots on the welcome mat and discarded them, setting them next to the wall while they took off their coats. Elizabeth took the soup into the kitchen and set it in the fridge, returning just as Elijah was slinking down the stairs, the tags on his collar jingling with every step.

"Hello, witches, what brings you to our humble abode?" he asked, looking up at them from his spot on the floor.

"We have a little surprise." Dianne took Nadia's hand, and when she did, the Castor family amulet hanging around her neck glowed.

They both raised their casting hands, glittering, glistening power dancing around their fingertips. They drew sigils in the air, causing the symbols to take shape, suspended around them, and once they had a handful of them cast, they started murmuring something in Latin. The sigils began to swirl, and the lights in the house flickered. A supernatural wind picked up, causing the chandelier to rock, papers to rustle, and Elizabeth's silky, raven hair to blow around uncontrollably.

Elijah squirmed, looking around for some sort of explanation as to what was going on. Just as he was about to speak, his words were drawn out into a pain-filled groan. His body stretched and grew, his back legs elongating exponentially as his tail shrank back into his spine. Fingers stretched out of his paws, the pads of them melting into human palms. He held his hands in front of his face, his gray fur melting away and replaced instead with pink flesh. He stared at them with wide, green, *human* eyes. Jolting, he brought them up to his cheeks, coming in contact with soft human skin. Fingers trembling, he traced his nose, his chin, his forehead, and he reached back to touch his fur-free human ears, which were settled on the sides of his head, as opposed to the top of it.

"Holy shit!" His legs gave out and he fell onto the floor, stark naked. Wide eyed, he covered himself. "Holy SHIT!"

"Here." Elizabeth zipped across the room and grabbed a blanket, tossing it to him.

Elijah caught it, spreading it across his lap as he sat there in shock, wiggling his toes. It had been so long since he'd had toes. He laughed in disbelief. This wasn't happening. This simply wasn't happening.

"*How*?!" he asked incredulously. He looked up at Dianne and Nadia, who were giggling with pride, beaming brightly. "This is insane!" He reached up to push the shaggy silver *human* hair out of his face. "Is it temporary?"

"Shouldn't be."

"This is *permanent*?!" Elijah's jaw hung wide open, and he stared at his body in disbelief. "If I wasn't naked, I'd hug you both. I...holy shit!"

"You're welcome."

Elijah looked up at Elizabeth, staring at her. He had such a youthful face, his smooth skin dotted in freckles. When he smiled, she noticed his front teeth were slightly crooked. Tufts of shaggy silver hair hung in his eyes, and he had a long, narrow nose dominating his face. "A picture might last longer, Bloodmere."

"You look so young."

"I was only seventeen when I was cursed." He shrugged. "Seventeen seemed a lot older back then, I guess."

"Yeah, you're telling me." She blinked a few times before she realized that she should go get him some actual clothes. She was sure Ben wouldn't mind if she borrowed some of his stuff. "I'll, uh, go get you something to wear."

She turned and ran up the stairs into Ben's room. She plucked a black sweater out of his closet and pulled a pair of jeans out of his drawer. Before she went back down the stairs, she peeked into her own room, looking at Ben. Nope. Still asleep. She chuckled. Boy, was he in for a surprise when he woke up.

Elizabeth went back down the stairs and tossed the clothes at Elijah, who caught them with a grateful smile.

"Thank you."

"Well, we'll leave you to it, then. We're taking Max out to the mall, and you know how impatient he is." Dianne jabbed a thumb behind towards the doorway. "Once everything is...settled, we should get together for tea."

"I'd love to." Elijah carefully stood up, wrapping the blanket swiftly around his waist before walking back towards the bathroom to change.

"See you later." Elizabeth said her goodbyes to the neighbors and closed the door behind them, turning to face the empty living room. It seemed *everything* was changing today, her cat included. They'd either have to get rid of all of their pet supplies or...well, or they could adopt another cat. She laughed at the thought.

The bathroom door creaked open, and Elijah emerged, his hands covered up by the ends of the sleeves. It seemed Ben had longer arms than he did. Elijah jammed his thumbs in his pockets, arms shrugging outwards. He spun around for her.

"Well, how do I look?"

"Human," she blurted, laughing as he crossed the room to her. "You look human, Eli."

"I *feel* human, Liz." He wrapped his arms around her, and she embraced him tightly. "Thank you so much. For everything."

"Of course," she nodded. She wanted to be happy for Elijah and celebrate with him, she did, but her mind was elsewhere. Namely, upstairs. "I'm gonna..."

"Yeah, go check on our boy. If you need me, I'll be down here figuring out how to use this fucking microwave now that I've got thumbs."

"Knock yourself out." She laughed. "Holler if you need any help."

"Oh believe me, I will."

Elizabeth walked back up the stairs and into her room, reclaiming her spot and resuming her knitting project. It didn't take her long to finish her scarf, casting it off and weaving in her ends. And then, when that was done, she dug through her knitting bag for something else to make. There had to be one unfinished WIP that needed some work. She settled on a pair of socks she'd been toiling away at for a few years and started knitting.

She looked over at Ben, who was still motionless. She grabbed his wrist and lifted it, as Jack had done earlier, dropping it heavily back down at his side. Yep. Still out. It was almost scary to look at him like that. He looked dead. And technically, he probably was, or pretty close to it. In terms of butterflies, he was still pretty liquid-y in his cocoon.

She missed him.

Just when she settled in, there was yet another knock at the door. She set her project aside, cast one more longing look at Ben, kissed his cold forehead, and then walked back down the stairs one last time. When she got to the living room, Elijah was standing there next to William, who stared at the gray-haired boy in disbelief.

"So this *just* happened."

"Yeah, like twenty minutes ago," Elijah nodded, plucking a pizza roll off of the paper plate he was holding and popped it into his mouth. He looked up at William's towering form. "You're, like, taller than I expected you to be."

"I get that a lot, yeah." He chuckled and then looked up at Elizabeth, the smile fading from his stoic features. He tucked a piece of long, raven hair behind his ear. "Hey, Mom."

"Hey, kid. What are you doing here?" She walked closer to him and wrapped her arms around him. He hugged her tightly, holding on for just a little longer than she expected him to.

"I'm headed out. I, uh, got a lead, so I'm following it."

"Oh." She nodded, serious. "Be smart. Be safe."

"Always," he agreed. "Just wanted to check in and let you know. And, you know, visit. I never visit enough."

"Once we get everything around here figured out, I'm gonna need you and your sister here a whole lot more, alright?"

"I think that could probably be arranged."

She took a long moment, just staring at him. Although he didn't share her genes like his sister, he looked more like Elizabeth than Katherine did. His nose was very similar to hers and his hair was the same color and texture. She pulled him to her again, wrapping her arms around him and whispering, "I love you. Come back to me, okay?"

"I promise." He looked down at her. "I love you too."

And then he was gone, just as fast as he'd come, out into the dangerous world of hunting down monsters and bringing supernatural creeps to justice.

"They grow up so fast…" Elijah said, staring at the front door after him. "It feels like only yesterday he was yanking on my tail and trying to pull my whiskers off."

"He's everything I dreamed he'd become," Elizabeth said, pride welling up in her chest. "He's making his ancestors proud."

"He's making his mom's cat proud too." Elijah paused. "Wait, can I even make those jokes anymore? I'm gonna have to rework my entire sense of humor."

"Yeah, you are definitely...not a cat anymore."

"What does that make us, then?"

Elijah's question made Elizabeth's eyes widen as she stared at him. "If you're seventeen, does that mean I have to adopt you? Like, legally? Am I your mom now? Oh God."

"Weird," he agreed. "Whatever you do, though, there is no way you're sending me to public high school. I don't care if I don't know how to read."

Elizabeth was quiet for a moment, processing. "You don't know how to read?"

He shrugged. "I've gotten this far."

"We're gonna fix that soon. That's not gonna fly. But right now..."

"Right now, we've got bigger fish to fry." Elijah tilted his head back towards the stairs. "Go be with him."

"Thank you." She gave him a grateful smile and then raced back up the stairs. She knew it was almost time for her Ben to come back to her, and she didn't want to miss it. She promised him she wouldn't.

She climbed back onto her bed and looked down at him, her sleeping mate. Something akin to electricity *zinged* through her when she thought about it. Her *mate*. The guilt that had been eating at the back of her mind for missing him in his last lifetime and however many lifetimes of his she'd missed before faded. She could have had John Park from the ballroom in 1945, that was true, but everything that had happened to him in this lifetime made him unique, different from all of the other versions of him he'd been in the past. He was her mate, her Ben, and finally, after four centuries, he'd found his way back to her.

Her thoughts were cut short by the abrupt motion to her side. Ben sat straight up, breathing heavily. He stared at her with wide, red eyes, his fangs long and white and sharp. When his gaze met hers, his expression softened and he grinned.

"Good morning."

Chapter 34

Black.

Everything was black.

Everything was black, and he was on fire. His veins were filled with lava, his brain was melting, and his muscles were filled with acid. His ears were stuffed with cotton, and every thought that passed through his head was fuzzy and muffled. He wanted to call out, wanted to scream into the abyss that enveloped him, but his jaw was bolted shut, his vocal chords scorched beyond use.

A piercing pain tore through his gums, and his eyes were burning. He couldn't recall a time he'd ever felt worse. Not even in the sixth grade when he'd broken his arm falling off of the roundabout at the playground.

I think I'm dead, he thought. *I think I died and now I'm dead.*

It hurt more than he'd expected it to, but he guessed that was only fair. He was changing species, after all. His lungs cried for air, but he couldn't breathe. He couldn't move. All he could do was sit there and wonder what would be awaiting him on the other side.

And then, all at once, his head broke the waves of the surging sea.

He took a desperate breath, bolting upright as he did. Everything was blurry, the room smeared red, but eventually the image sharpened into vivid detail, the edges crisp and the colors saturated.

That was the first weird thing. He could see without his glasses. Really well, in fact.

The second weird thing was: ouch! He poked his tongue against his tooth. Fang? Yeah, it was definitely a fang. Long and sharp.

His eyes wide, he turned his head and spotted her there. Elizabeth. Her thick, raven hair was hanging down her shoulder, her eyes focused on him. He inhaled sharply as he felt something tingle deep in his brain as the voice inside him whispered, "*Mate*."

He grinned. "Good morning."

"Good morning." She smiled, scooting closer to him and cupping his cheeks with her hands. She peered into his red eyes, looking for some indication that her Ben was still in there. "How do you feel?"

Ben thought for a long moment, searching all of the strange new feelings inside him. His throat felt raw and seared, like someone had stuck a hot branding iron down it. Was this what it felt like? Bloodlust? After a moment, he answered her. "Thirsty."

She zipped to the mini fridge and back, holding a blood bag out to him. He took it from her, holding it carefully in his large hand.

"How do I...?"

She zipped there and back again, holding another bag, this one for herself. "There's a straw." She laughed, waving the little blood-filled tube at him. "But, if you're well-versed like me, you can just..." In a quick, efficient movement, she bit into the side of the bag and drained it quickly.

Ben slipped the plastic tube into his mouth and tilted the bag slowly. Somehow, he still managed to make a mess. As soon as the sweet drink hit his tongue, he knew he was a goner. She was right. It *did* taste different now. It tasted...good.

"It takes practice," she reassured him, laughing. Her careful hands wiped the blood stains from around his lips, and she smirked. "You're a messy drinker."

"Sorry." He smiled sheepishly.

"Don't be. I guarantee I was worse." She flashed back to a time where she was a much younger Elizabeth, about half of her current height and much, much, much younger. "My baby fangs were hard to use."

"Aww, baby fangs? That's so cute," Ben cooed. "I bet you were such a cute little vampire."

"To other vampires? Yes. To humans? I was their worst nightmare. It was a different time for everyone involved. We didn't have easy ways to derive blood like this without drawing attention. Things were... messy."

Ben's gaze was focused on her, his expression soft and warm. He leaned in closer to her, pulled by the longing in his chest.

She chuckled, amused, one of her eyebrows quirking up as his face got closer to hers. "What's that look for?"

"It's so different now," he murmured, one large hand settling on her waist, his eyelids lowering to hide his red irises, which were gradually beginning to return to their normal brown hue since his thirst had been quenched. "Everything is so different now."

"Different how?"

"I've always had a crush on you, Liz." Ben pulled her closer, tugging her into his lap with strength he didn't know he had, his nose almost touching hers. "But this...this *feeling*." He poked a finger to the center of his chest, right at the heart of the sweltering *pulling* sensation that was taking control of him. "This is something else. I don't think I've ever been more attracted to you."

"Yeah?" she asked, touching her nose against his, her hands coming up to cup his cheeks. "What does it feel like?"

"I..." He tugged her even closer so that their chests were flush against each other. "I can't even look at you without thinking about how...much I wanna kiss you. It feels like there's a string tied around my heart and it's always *pulling* me towards you. It's inescapable, inevitable, no matter what I do, I know I'll end up in your arms."

"Poetic." She kissed him, smiling against his lips. "Who knew dying would make you such an intellectual?"

"Well, when you're dead, you have a lot of time to think about things." Ben's lips caught hers, kissing her softly. "Speaking from experience. I spent most of it thinking about you."

"There are much more important things to think about than me."

"That's not true. I could spend eternity kissing you and never be tired of the taste of your lips." He pressed three more gentle kisses to her soft lips, smiling.

"Well, that's good, because you're looking at an eternity stuck with me." She giggled and pecked his cheeks and his nose, covering them in dozens of little kisses.

He chased her lips until he finally caught them again, kissing her long and deep. He hummed, kissing her a few more times as his strong arm fastened tight around her, pulling her against him. He flipped her onto her back and she yelped in surprise, her laughter swallowed up by his plush, warm lips. Ben pinned her in place, strong hands grabbing her wrists and holding them against the headboard. He was stronger now, he realized, faster.

"Ben..." she murmured, surrendering in his strong grasp, leaning up to kiss him. "Where did all of this confidence come from?"

"I don't know," he admitted, laughing. He released her wrists and wrapped her up in his arms instead, leaning down to match his lips to hers. "But I like it. Do...do you like it?" He was quiet, his eyes filled with stars, but also with doubt. "Is it okay? That I'm...that I'm different now?"

Elizabeth nodded, pecking the tip of his nose. "My awkward little Benjamin is in there, I'm sure. Right there." She poked him in the chest. "You're not a *different* Ben, you're just...Ben 2.0. You've been upgraded, is all."

Smiling, Ben kissed her again, electricity sparking in his chest. "This is why I love you so much."

She brushed the stray hairs off of his forehead, taking a good long look at him. He was still in there, her Ben, swirled around with a good amount of her venom. "I love you too."

Just as he leaned in to resume, there was a knock on the door downstairs. He sat at attention, shocked he could hear the faint noise so clearly from all the way up there. It was like all of his senses were dialed up to eleven, not that he was complaining.

Elizabeth stood, taking Ben's hand and leading him down the stairs. By the time they finally got there, they found Elijah, who was holding a plate of Pizza Rolls, standing beside Katherine. As soon as

Katherine spotted her mother, she rushed to her, hugging her tightly.

"Mom, I fucked up."

"What happened? Are you alright?"

"I...I think Arthur found me. I wasn't careful enough, and I..." She cried, shaking in her mother's arms. "I'm so sorry."

"We'll figure it out." Elizabeth shook her head, squeezing her daughter tightly. "It's going to be okay, I promise. I've outsmarted him before, I'll outsmart him again."

"O-okay," she nodded, sniffling as she pulled away. "You're right. You're probably right. Can I...can I stay here for a little while? Just until I know it's safe?"

"You can stay here as long as you like. You're *always* welcome here. I love you so much."

"I love you too." Katherine reached up and wiped the tear from her cheek.

They were all quiet for a second, standing there. And then, Ben looked up at Elijah, his eyebrows furrowing. He motioned to the gray-haired guy with half of a Pizza Roll in his mouth. "Wait, who are *you?*"

He laughed, scarfing down the rest of the Pizza Roll and then scoffed, pretending to be offended. "What, you don't recognize me, Benjamin?" His hand rose to his chest. "I'm hurt, honestly."

"Elijah?!"

"Surprise." He held out his arms, turning around so Ben could see him in all of his human glory. "Like it?"

"Dude, congratulations! I'm so happy for you!" Ben hugged him, chuckling. "Wait, is this my sweater?"

"Yeah, uh, I don't have any clothes." Elijah laughed, shrugging. "Elizabeth figured you wouldn't mind if I borrowed some of yours."

Ben gave him a thumbs-up. "Knock yourself out."

"Wait, speaking of changes..." Katherine narrowed her eyes and turned Ben towards her, looking over him. A smirk grew on her sharp features. "*He's* human now, but *you're* not."

"Surprise..."

"Let me see the mark," she said, watching as Ben tugged down the collar of his shirt. Her eyes widened when she spotted the shiny gold bite. "Holy shit!" she squeaked, her hands covering her mouth as she looked at him and then back at Elizabeth. "You're...?"

"Yeah," Elizabeth nodded, stepping closer to Ben and pulling his arm around her waist. "We are."

"Congratulations, you two! Aaaah!" Katherine rushed at the pair of them, pulling them both into a strong hug. "Oh, but Ben, I'm not calling you 'Dad.' Sorry."

Ben chuckled. "Yeah, that would be weird, all things considered..."

Once they were settled, Elizabeth wandered out to the kitchen and started making dinner. Ben followed her, once he'd talked to Elijah for a bit longer. He wasn't quite sure if he could get used to their cat...not being a cat anymore.

"Hey, Liz?"

"Yes?"

"I don't want to be annoying, but I'm...*really* thirsty..." His hand wandered up to his neck and rubbed over it, as though it would solve the problem.

When Elizabeth glanced back at him, his irises flashed red, his fangs slowly sliding into place, like he was resisting it. "That's normal. There's more blood bags in the mini-fridge up—" he zipped up the stairs and back in easily under two seconds, his hair tousled in the wind once he returned, blood bag in hand, "—stairs..."

"Holy shit..." He glanced behind him, up the stairs. He didn't realize he could move that fast. He knew Elizabeth had some superhuman speed, but she barely used it. "*Woah.*"

"You okay?"

"That was *awesome!*" Ben's red eyes were wide, and he looked around, still absorbing what had just happened. "Why don't you do that all the time?"

"When you're older, you won't be in such a rush." Katherine laughed, walking into the kitchen and sitting at one of the stools pulled up to the island.

"What's for dinner," Elijah looked to Elizabeth, an evil grin on his face before he added, "*Mom.*"

"Chicken alfredo with red and green peppers," she paused, "*Son*."

"Wait, what?" Ben asked, looking between the two of them in confusion. "*What?*"

"Elijah's only seventeen, so I might have to legally adopt him," Elizabeth explained. "I'm still looking into the details…"

"I can start calling you Dad, if you want, Benjamin."

"Please don't."

Once Elizabeth finished up dinner and Elijah had his first, proper, home-cooked meal as a human, the four of them went out to the living room to chat. Remembering her earlier discovery, Elizabeth went up to her room to pull out her photo album to show Ben.

She walked back out and found Ben sitting on the couch. Without hesitation, she planted herself on his thigh and one of his long arms wrapped around her waist, pulling her closer to him.

"I found this earlier," she explained, flipping through the pages until she found what she was looking for: VE day.

At first, when his eyes landed on the picture, jealousy bristled in his chest. Why was his mate showing him a picture of some other guy kissing her decades before he was even born? He looked to her for some sort of explanation.

"Does he look familiar?" She pointed to the man. There was another picture of the two of them together next to the first, but this time, they weren't kissing, just standing next to each other, his arm around her shoulders. She pointed to the man's dimples and then leaned up to kiss Ben's cheek. "Is that perfect handsome face ringing any bells?"

"Is that...me?" he asked slowly, putting the pieces together. "...He looks like me."

"Let me see." Katherine walked over and looked down at the book, her eyes widening. "Woah, oh my God."

"What does it mean?" Ben asked, resting his chin on Elizabeth's shoulder, staring at the other version of himself, this one more muscled and dressed in a vintage Navy uniform.

"I think we met in one of your past lives."

"Were we...in love? Did we go out? What was I like? Was I—"

"We only met once. These pictures were taken on VE day. You and I were both at the same party and you were a little tipsy, but your friends encouraged you to come over and ask me to dance. And that was the last time I ever saw you." She reached up to stroke his cheek, his skin finally the same temperature as hers. "Remember that thing I said about meeting your mate and never even knowing it's them?"

"Mmm..." Ben hummed, holding her just a little tighter. "I remember."

"When you moved in…you said I was your second chance. I didn't realize it until now, but I think you're mine too."

❧ ◈ ❧

Later in the evening, the four of them started playing a game of Monopoly, something Elizabeth hadn't done in a very long time. Ben rolled the dice and then moved the thimble three spots forward, right onto Boardwalk.

He groaned. "Noooo!!"

"Pay the piper, Benjamin." Elijah held out his hand, beckoning him to hand over the colorful bills.

"Ugh, goddammit…" Ben flipped through his stash of cash and then reluctantly handed them over. "I'm gonna go broke if I keep landing on your stupid properties."

"That's the plan."

"Elizabeth, your turn." Elijah nudged her. "If you roll a six, you owe me big bucks."

"We'll see about that…" Elizabeth reached for the dice, but stopped when her phone started ringing. She picked it up off of the table and answered. "Hello?"

"Elizabeth, darling, how good to hear that beautiful voice again." A chill ran up her spine, and the phone slipped out of her hand, clattering against the game board. Thanks to her impeccable hearing, though, she could still make out Arthur's words loud and clear. "You see, I did run into some trouble finding our daughter, but I didn't have any difficulty in locating your son..."

Chapter 35

"I'm gonna kill him," Elizabeth decided, pacing back and forth across the living room floor. "I am going to *kill* him."

"You kill him, I'll kill him, let's all kill him," Katherine agreed, pacing right alongside her mother. "Elijah, you wanna kill him too?"

"I'm down."

"Are we sure we have to...*kill* him?" Ben asked from his spot on the couch. His plush lip was pinched between his teeth.

Both of the girls spun around to look at him. "Yes!"

"No, no, I get it. Right. Bad guy. Awful guy. But like, murder?" Ben backtracked, waving his hands back and forth. "*Murder?*"

"If we've gotta..." Katherine bit her lip in the way he'd seen Elizabeth do so many times. "He's evil."

"So evil..." Elizabeth whispered, wrapping her arms around herself and hanging her head.

Katherine saw her mom lost in thought and walked over to wrap her arms around her, resting her head against Elizabeth's. "We won't let him hurt anyone else. I promise you."

"He has Will, Kate. He has my boy. He has *our* boy." Elizabeth let a tear trickle down her cheek. "I can't lose him."

"And you won't. We won't." Katherine shook her head. "It's me he wants, right? We'll let him have me and—"

"Absolutely not. No. Never. He's not getting either of you." Elizabeth was stern, shaking her head. "I'm not trading one kid for the other. I...hell, I don't even know what he wants with you. And I'm never going to find out."

The front door opened and in came the witches and Max.

"We're here. Where are they? Where are we going?" Nadia asked while Dianne walked to the dining room table and began to rapidly unpack the supplies she'd put together. Max walked over and flopped onto the couch next to Ben, looking up at him.

"You're a vampire now, huh?"

"Yep," Ben nodded, his arm crossed and his jaw tensed. He wanted to help out, but even as a vampire, this entire topic was about as far from his area of expertise as one could possibly get. But he softened when Max came over, smiling at him. "I've got the fangs and everything."

"Sweet." Max grinned, his legs swinging.

Elijah settled into the spot beside the young spellcaster, ruffling the boy's brown hair beneath a large human hand. "Don't get any ideas, trouble."

"It's weird that you're human now."

"Yeah?" Elijah chuckled. "Things change, and that's okay sometimes. It would be boring if nothing ever changed."

"Yeah, I guess you're right," he agreed, pulling his legs up onto the couch. He looked up at Dianne and Nadia, who were standing at the table with Elizabeth and Katherine, hashing out plans.

Jack pushed open the front door next, walking to Elizabeth immediately and taking her in his arms, stroking her hair. Behind him trailed the pink-haired Cody, looking awfully cozy in his wintry scarf, his nose red from the cold.

"We're gonna get him back, don't you even worry."

"I'm so sorry I cut your date short."

"Family comes first," Cody piped up, not entirely in the loop, but still supportive nonetheless. "We have all the time in the world for dates."

"Thank you for being so understanding." Elizabeth pulled him in for a hug too, which he gladly reciprocated.

"Of course," Cody nodded, stepping off to the side once Elizabeth let go of him. He sat on the couch next to Elijah. "Hi, I'm Cody."

"Elijah. Welcome to crazy town."

"Yeah, seems like there's a lot going on..." Cody murmured.

Sick of listening and watching, Ben got up and walked to his mate, slipping his large hand into hers. She was upset, and it was killing him. Every ounce of his soul was screaming at him to make it better, but he couldn't. He felt completely and utterly useless.

"So it's settled then. Is everyone good with the plan?" Katherine looked to the others.

"What plan?" Ben asked.

Elizabeth squeezed his hand and looked up at him. "You're staying here with—"

"What? Staying here?" Ben shook his head. "There's no way you're going without me." Then, softer, he said, "*I just* got *you.*"

"Precisely. I just got you. I'm not risking losing you over some drama with my ex. It's not happening." Elizabeth looked up, right into his eyes, which were gradually growing redder from his stress. "You're going to stay here where it's safe. Please, *please* listen to me."

"Liz..."

"Ben, you are a newborn vampire. You've been a vampire for a few *hours*. Arthur has been a vampire for a few *centuries*. He has a way of getting information. He knows what you mean to me. You step foot near him and he'll kill you. Dottie's already tried to, remember?"

"That was *different*."

"No. Ben, it's not happening. Please don't fight me on this." Her eyes flashed red, irritation and fear making themselves known. "The Hunters are on the way. We have enough help. We'll be fine."

Ben bit his lip, wincing as his fang poked into the soft flesh. "I'm just worried."

"I know you are. So am I, but I need you here. Max is here. Elijah is here. Cody too. They need to be protected." She took both of his hands and squeezed them. "I need you to protect them, okay? Can you do that for me?"

Something defensive bubbled up in his chest, and he stood a little straighter. His mate had just given him a job, and he was determined not to fail her. Then, softening, he let go of one of her hands and raised his hand to cup her cheek, gently tilting her head up towards his.

He kissed her slowly and then murmured against her lips, "I would do anything for you. But please be careful."

"If you think I'm going to let Arthur of all people be the person who gets to kill me, you don't know anything about me," Elizabeth tried to reassure him, straightening out the wrinkles in his shirt with her careful hands. "I've survived four centuries of his bullshit. I fully intend to outlive him."

"Good." Ben tilted his head, studying her, his brave, beautiful mate. He kissed her one last time. "And when you get back, we can get started on our forever."

Dianne, ever the clever and powerful young witch, was able to track William using one of his childhood toys that Elizabeth had tucked away in a box upstairs. And when she told the others where they were headed, an uneasy feeling settled deep in the pit of Elizabeth's stomach. Of course that was the place Arthur had chosen. The Bloodborne Bar. He'd been looking for Katherine for all of that time after all, it only made sense to travel right back to the place she had been born.

Each of them equipped with an enchanted stake, the girls and Jack parked in front of a coffee shop a little ways down the street, safely out of sight, where they could regroup and make a better plan.

"I'm coming in with you," Katherine insisted.

"Absolutely not."

"Mom—"

"If he gets you, it's all over. You get that, right? Everything I've done to protect you…"

"He has Will. And besides, he won't be alive for much longer anyway." Katherine held up her stake and flashed her fangs. "I'm about to be fatherless."

Elizabeth looked at Katherine for a long moment, studying her face that was so much like her own, but also so much like Arthur's. Katherine wasn't born yesterday. She was strong, just the way Elizabeth had raised her. In all their years together, she had more than proven herself.

Elizabeth sighed deeply before agreeing. "Fine. Alright. But be careful. Your father...he's one of the most dangerous vampires I've ever met. We need to be on our toes at all times. I don't know how many vampires he's recruited, and I don't know what he's got up his sleeve." She paused to think. "Dianne, you and Katherine will go in the back door. I'll take Jack and get in through the front. Nadia, you stay here and put a ward on the getaway vehicle."

"Sounds good to me," the witch nodded.

"I'm going with you. Jack, you go with Dianne," Katherine interjected. She took her mom's hand. "We're doing this together."

After staring at Katherine for a long moment, Elizabeth squeezed her hand and agreed. "We're doing this together."

Someone knocked on the window and both of the witches turned to the source of the noise, hands raised and spells swirling around their fingertips. It was only Joelle, standing there beside her husband. Elizabeth rolled down the window.

"Ready?"

"This might be out of the ordinary for you, but we call clearing out a vampire den a Thursday night." Joelle laughed.

Elizabeth and the others got out of the car, all geared up and ready to go. The necklace Dianne and Nadia had given her was hidden beneath the fabric of Ben's sweatshirt, the metal cold against her skin.

Katherine had hers, too, a choker, the silver pendant resting between her collarbones. They were well-protected against whatever mind games awaited them inside.

"Where do you want us?"

"Can you take the back with Jack and Dianne?"

"We can do whatever you need us to," Jordan nodded. "Let's go get your son back."

Elizabeth and Katherine split off from the others, walking through the quiet, snowy night to the Bloodborne Bar. There was a candle lit in the apartment above the bar, flickering. Elizabeth had spent so many lonely, pregnant nights up there, crying, worried that Arthur would find her, and here she was, walking into the very same building, right back to him. She'd be lying if she said the irony didn't scare her a little bit.

Katherine stepped in front of her mother and pulled the front door open for the two of them. Elizabeth walked in first.

She wasn't sure what she was expecting to find, but a little blonde-haired girl sitting at the bar sipping blood out of a milkshake glass through a striped straw was not one of them. As soon as the door creaked open and the bell above it jingled, the girl spun around.

Her silky, honey hair was arranged in elegant waves that reached her shoulders, and the dangling pearl earrings in her ears matched the string of them around her neck. Her nails were long and as red as her bloodthirsty irises. A dead body wearing an apron was slumped against the bar, a pool of red dripping from his neck. That would be where the bartender went, then.

"Dottie," Katherine stated through gritted teeth. "Of course *you're* here."

"It's smart business management is all it is, dear. Combining assets, making partnerships, eliminating threats to sales." Dottie tilted her head and slipped the straw into her mouth, taking a long sip of the thick, red liquid, her eyes locked on her ex-girlfriend. "You were a liability. Well, *are* a liability. And besides," her eyes fell on Katherine, "you have something Artie wants. And Artie *always* gets what he wants."

The red curtains dividing the bar from the kitchens parted, and Arthur stepped through, his loafers clicking against the hardwood floors. He, as always, was dressed in a sharp black suit, not a hair out of place from his pristine, blood red tie to his bat-shaped cufflinks. Two large vampires dressed in black followed him, each of them holding one of William's arms. He was gagged with a garlic-soaked rag, the stench wafting over to where the girls were standing, and his arms were bound in thick, silver chains. He looked up at his mother and sister, his eyes falling.

"I see you've come to make the trade, darling. Good choice." Arthur grinned, strolling around the bar and standing beside Dottie, who he put his arm around, retracting it once he finally looked at Katherine, his eyes wide. He gasped softly and offered her his hand. "And you, my dear, must be my daughter, Katherine. It is so nice to finally meet you."

Katherine looked at him, dead in the eyes. "Hand over Will, and *maybe* I won't kill you."

"You get that from your mother," Arthur scoffed, stepping closer to Katherine, who took a step further back. "Don't worry too much, my child. I'm sure you have some of me in you too. I can tell already."

"I'm nothing like you."

"Well, you'll learn to be." He shrugged with confidence, his eyes flashing a fiery, glowing red as he locked onto hers. "*Come here.*"

Unaffected by his compulsions, Katherine didn't waver, her hand rising to the holster on her belt. "Make me." She whipped out her stake, and Elizabeth followed her lead, pulling out her own.

"I wouldn't do that." Dottie snapped her perfect little fingers and four more vampires stood up from behind the bar, murder in their eyes. "We're well-staffed tonight."

"So are we." Jack parted the curtains and staked both of the guards that were holding William, who used his newfound freedom to hop over the bar and stand behind Katherine and Elizabeth. Elizabeth looked to him with concern, but nodded once she saw that he was alright. Then she turned her attention back to the foes in front of them. Things were about to get messy.

❧◆❦

"I'm hungry," Max complained, his arms crossed over his chest.

"My cooking skills are limited, but I can make you some pizza rolls," Elijah offered.

"I can make spaghetti," Ben added.

"I'm good with pizza rolls." Max gave a thumbs-up. Elijah got up off of the couch and walked towards the kitchen.

Meanwhile, Cody was scanning the shelf of DVDs Elizabeth had been collecting, searching for something for the four of them to watch while they waited for the others to return. Something kid-friendly, preferably, for Max's sake. "Are we in the mood for *Aladdin* or *Mulan*?"

"Either is fine with me." Ben turned to look at the young spellcaster seated beside him on the couch. "Max, do you have a preference?"

"*Aladdin*, please!"

"Can do." Cody opened the DVD case and stuck the disk into the Blu-Ray player. He handed Max the remote, and then he turned to sit down, but before he could, a red brick came sailing through the window and landed with a thud in the middle of the rug. Glass rained into the room, sharp shards covering the carpet.

Ben stood up at lightning speed, rushing to look for the source and finding a cluster of vampires dressed in black three-piece suits. One of them had another brick and threw it at the other front window, but Ben caught it with a quick hand and threw it back at them.

"What's going on?" Elijah ran back towards the living room, his green eyes wide. "Oh, fuck."

"Elijah, take Max and Cody." Ben picked Max up and carried him over the broken glass, handing him off to Elijah. "Go upstairs and lock yourselves in the bathroom."

"I'm with you." Cody shook his head and stood up next to Ben.

"Cody, these guys are—"

"Vampires, I know." Cody rolled up his sleeves, revealing a plethora of sigils tattooed into his forearms. His fingers were covered in shining gold rings with various stones set into them. Golden swirls of magic floated around his hands, and his eyes glowed. "I'm with you."

"Y-you're with me," Ben nodded, wide-eyed. He gulped and looked out the window. There were two vampires coming up the steps to the porch, and he wondered how they planned to get past the protection spell around the townhouse, but then he spotted the woman standing at the foot of the tree outside, her eyes glowing like Cody's, dressed in all black. "They have a witch."

"I can take her. You get the vamps." He snapped his ringed fingers and then disappeared in a puff of golden glitter.

Ben looked around for something to fight off the intruders that were banging against the door. A few more hits, and it would come in. Unable to locate a stake or anything similar, he walked over to the dining room, prayed to Elizabeth for forgiveness, and then tore one of the armrests off of the dining chair with ease. He was shocked by his raw strength for a few seconds, but it didn't last long because as soon as he had his new weapon in his hand, the front door came down, knocked off of its hinges.

Immediately, Ben shifted into fight mode, his irises turning bright red and his fangs sliding into place. It was an unfamiliar feeling, but one he suspected he would soon get used to.

The first vampire lunged at him, but he rolled into a dodge, his eyes wide. "Woah." He stood back up and ducked in time to avoid a dining chair being swung at him. Looking at the makeshift stake in his hand, Ben's only thought was, *I hope this is sharp enough.* So, to see if it was, he stabbed the nearest vampire, the sharp wooden edge burying itself in his chest. The vampire disintegrated.

One down, three to go.

The next vampire's expression hardened, and he tackled Ben to the ground, wrestling the stake out of his hand. Ben rolled out from under his attacker and tried to get back up, but he was pinned down by his broad shoulders.

"Think you're tough, Bloodmere's bitch?" the vampire above him hissed.

"I'm not anyone's bitch." Ben shoved the vampire off of him in a single push, hurling him across the room and into the wall in front of the door. He was pretty sure that would leave a dent. Ben scooped his stake up off of the floor. He heard footsteps travelling up the stairs, and his eyes widened. He zipped up them after, only to find the bathroom door broken off of its hinges.

"Get away from them. It's me you want." Ben pulled the vampire's shoulder, and he turned quickly, backhanding Ben over the railing of the stairs and down to the first floor.

Oh. That one hurt. He was pretty sure he had a cracked rib or something. There was a lot of pain concentrated in his abdomen. But, groaning, he pushed himself off of the floor as quickly as he could.

He struggled up the stairs, moving a little faster when he heard Max scream, and by the time he cleared the top, The vampire flew out the window, the bathroom lights flickering and Max's hand outstretched, Elijah standing behind him.

"Woah." Ben looked at the little spellcaster in awe. "Good job, buddy."

"You okay, Benjamin?" Elijah asked, taking stock of Ben's pained stance.

"I just fell down a flight of stairs, no biggie. You guys okay?"

"We're fine." Elijah gave him a thumbs-up and then pulled Max back into the bathtub, where he was taking shelter.

Ben picked up the bathroom door off of the floor and set it against the doorframe. It wasn't perfect, but it would have to do.

Next, he went back down the stairs, limping with every step. The pain started to subside. He pulled up his T-shirt and watched as the bruise on his smooth skin faded before his very eyes. That was a neat perk. Cody came back inside, panting. He had a cut over his eye, but besides that, he appeared to be unharmed.

"Are we all good in here?"

"Just about." Ben staked the vampire that was still slumped against the wall and watched as he turned into a pile of ash. Hmm, he might need to vacuum before Elizabeth got back.

"Good." Cody raised his hands and cast a wave of magic into the middle of the room with one fluid movement, all of the broken glass and wood patching back together until they were like new.

"How long have you...been a...what's the word, warlock?"

"Nope. Warlock means 'oath-breaker.' Most of us prefer 'sorcerer,' or even 'witch' is fine." Cody chuckled, rubbing the back of his neck. He was right back to being the sweet, pink-haired barista from Ben's favorite café. He tugged his sleeves down over his sigils. "I've been a witch since forever, basically. Just got done with magical boarding school a few years ago, actually."

"Woah. Cool. So I take it you know…"

"That Jack is a vampire? Yeah. I know. I don't think he knows I know, but I know."

"Oh, okay. Cool."

"We good down here, fellas?" Elijah asked, carrying Max back down the stairs, despite his protests.

"We're good," Ben replied. He only hoped Elizabeth and the others were doing just as well as they were, wherever it was they had ended up.

❧◈❧

At the Bloodborne Bar, 241 years and a few months after the infamous battle that had marked the building down in history in the first place, another battle unfolded.

Dianne disintegrated the chains binding William's arms with a flick of her wrist. He pulled the gag out of his mouth and caught the stake that Joelle tossed to him as soon as she and Jordan came in through the back. They eliminated the four other guards with ease, but as soon as they were reduced to ash, a pack of at least twenty vampires walked in through the front door.

Dottie tackled Elizabeth to the floor, straddling her hips and choking her against the hardwood. She leaned in close, her perfect red lips right in front of Elizabeth's face. "We could have had everything, Liz. I could have made you the happiest vampire in the world. But I wasn't good enough for little Countess Bloodmere."

Elizabeth bucked her hips, forcing Dottie off of her. She used her momentum to deck her in the face, and while Dottie scraped herself back together, Elizabeth snatched her stake off of the floor. She raised it to drive it through Dottie's heart, but Arthur grabbed her wrist and wrenched the wooden weapon from her grip.

"Nice try, darling," Arthur scolded, throwing it across the room. He took hold of her and passed her off to Dottie, who grabbed her by the hair and pulled. Hard. She stumbled backwards.

Elizabeth grabbed Dottie's wrist with both hands and forced her elbow over Dottie's arm, bending it back up to her ear and effectively forcing Dottie to the floor. "Didn't your mother ever tell you not to pull hair?"

While Elizabeth had Dottie on her knees, Arthur walked behind her and put her in a headlock. She let go of Dottie and forced Arthur's arm off of her head.

She grabbed him and threw him over the bar, resulting in a resounding crash as bottles of alcohol shattered all over the floor.

Dottie charged and pushed Elizabeth back into the brick wall, her fist speeding towards Elizabeth's nose, but she ducked out of the way, and Dottie's fist busted through the brick, leaving a large crater in the wall where Elizabeth's head should have been.

While she was crouched down, she grabbed Dottie's high heels, forcing her feet out from under her. With Dottie collapsed, it was all too easy to grab her by the ankles and whip her out the front window of the bar. Glass shattered, raining down and scattering across the sidewalk in front of the building. Jack kicked Elizabeth a stake, and she bent down and picked it up once it reached her foot.

Arthur came at her while she was doubled over, and when she straightened up, she stabbed it directly into his heart, twisting the sharpened end deeper into his chest. Thick, black blood seeped from the wound, and he looked down at the spot before looking back up at her with wide, red eyes. Slowly, he began to crack at the center, ash breaking off of his skin until he fully disintegrated, the dust piling at Elizabeth's feet.

"That's it. My turn." Dottie's expression turned dark and determined. She dove back through the broken front window and zipped right up to Elizabeth. Before she could react, Dottie snatched her by the wrist and twisted until Elizabeth was forced to let go of the stake. Dottie's perfect, slender little hand fastened itself around Elizabeth's neck, and she pushed her back into the wall. "You're gonna regret that." Dottie smiled and positioned the stake above Elizabeth's heart. "Tell him goodbye for me."

"Tell him yourself." Katherine drove her own stake into Dottie's heart from behind.

The wooden stake clattered to the floor as Dottie's hand went limp. Her red eyes widened, and a tear slipped down her cheek, splattering against the floorboards before she joined Arthur's ashes there.

Elizabeth exhaled. She looked around the bar. The fighting had all ceased, and thick piles of dust covered the hardwood floors. She ran a headcount, double-counting to make sure. Everyone was accounted for.

Her fingers wandered up to her neck, now free from Dottie's suffocating grasp. In relief, she fell to her knees, millions of pounds of stress rolling off of her shoulders. For the first time in centuries, she felt like she could finally breathe. She didn't have to hide anymore. She didn't have anyone to run from. Both of them were piles of ashes on the floor.

Dianne knelt beside Elizabeth, sweeping the dust into a stein from the bar. "I'll destroy these. I don't know if they have any witch friends that would try to bring them back, but I'm not willing to take any chances."

"Thank you," Elizabeth nodded. "They're finally dead. I think we'd all like to keep it that way."

Will walked over to her and reached out for her hands with both of his, pulling her to her feet again. He hugged her tightly, resting his head against hers. "Thanks, Mom."

"Of course. No one left behind." She extended one arm to Katherine, pulling her into the hug too. "It's over. It's finally over."

"Breathe, Mom." Katherine brushed the hair out of her mother's face. "You can just breathe now."

They stood there in the quiet peace that followed the battle, arms around each other. Over behind the bar was the spot where she'd given birth to Katherine on the floor and her life had changed forever. And now, she had the choice to start over. She could be anyone she wanted to be, but most importantly, there was nothing and no one stopping her from being Elizabeth Bloodmere.

Elizabeth took Katherine's hand in one of hers and Will's in the other, and she led them up the stairs to the tiny little apartment on the second floor. The door was unlocked, so she walked in. It had been redecorated. It was chic and modern, the bed was pristine and white with a few pillows on it. Three of the walls were painted, and one was exposed brick. A few paintings hung on the walls.

"This is..." Katherine whispered, walking forward and putting her hand on the comforter. "Wow."

"It's different than it was when I raised you." Elizabeth laughed. "Well, obviously. The bed was pushed against the wall, just a twin bed. There was a desk right there, a fireplace against that wall, with a little bench in front of it where I used to sew your clothes."

The three of them were quiet for a moment, admiring the place that had once been Elizabeth's home, her shelter from a cold, cruel new world. The silence was interrupted by a muffled, high-pitched wail. Elizabeth stood stiff. She was all too familiar with that noise.

Will pulled open the closet door, the source of the wailing, and stopped, frozen.

There, tucked into a basket of blankets, was a screaming, red-eyed baby, writhing its little fists as it sobbed big, beautiful tears. On one of the blankets, the name Nicholas was embroidered in red thread.

"Oh no." Elizabeth covered her mouth. "Oh God."

Thin tufts of angel-soft blond hair stuck up off of his round, little head. There was no doubt in her mind as to who this child belonged to. She was currently a pile of ash in a stein downstairs.

"What do we...?" Katherine looked to Elizabeth for an answer, but her mind was already made up.

She stepped into the closet and carefully picked up the baby, swaddling him with expert hands and cradling him against her chest. Immediately, he calmed down, lulled by her gentle rocking motions.

"He's a baby," Elizabeth whispered, her heart torn. "I don't care who his mother was, he's...he's a *baby.*"

"You have my permission to turn my old room into a nursery," Will told her, an unsure look on his face. He was a bit unsettled by the whole situation, but had it not been for Elizabeth's caring nature when he was in the same boat, he very seriously doubted he'd be standing there that day.

"I might just have to." She thought about it, still bouncing the child gently. "I...well, I don't think I have any choice..."

Epilogue

"I'll take him." Eli stretched his arms out, making grabby fingers.

It had been a week since they'd found Nicholas hidden away in the closet, and since then, Ben had moved into Elizabeth's room, Elijah had moved into Ben's room, and Nicholas was in the process of moving into the guest room, which was slowly but surely turning into a fitting nursery for the little fledgling. Ben was in there at the moment, making a noble attempt to assemble a crib.

Elizabeth transferred the baby to Elijah's waiting arms and handed him the little bottle filled with blood. Nicholas fussed, squirming, his little face twisting into a scowl as he wailed. "He's thirsty."

"Aww, our little angel is thirsty?" Elijah popped the bottle into Nick's waiting mouth, effectively quieting the crying baby. "Uncle Eli will take care of that."

"You're enjoying this, huh?"

"Do you know how badly I wanted to hold William when he was growing up?" Elijah asked, bouncing Nicholas gently in his arms. "This is everything."

"Glad you like it because that's going to be our lives for the next several years." Elizabeth grinned, her chest warm at the thought.

"Good."

Elizabeth laughed and walked up the stairs to where Ben was sitting on the floor of the guest room, squinting at the directions for the crib, mumbling to himself.

"Screw Blue 1 into A2...Now where the fuck is Blue 1?" He looked around the scattered pieces, moving things aside to try and find it. He looked up at Elizabeth, smiling softly. "Oh, hey."

"Hey." She plucked the blue piece off of the ground and handed it to him.

"Thanks."

"Mmhmm." She sat down next to him on the floor. "And you're alright with all of this? It all just kind of...happened."

"I have my mate." He reached out and took Elizabeth's hand. "And we have all the time in the world to figure out what that means for us."

She leaned in and kissed him, her lips slow and sweet. "In fact, we have forever..."

Acknowledgements

O Positive would not have been possible without some very key people, the first of whom was my sophomore year roommate. Daly, if you're reading this, I would not have been in the right headspace to write a vampire rom-com without you. Your love of *Twilight* (and endless marathons) fueled my love for Elizabeth, Ben, Elijah, and Jack more than I ever thought was possible, and because of you, I wrote something that I'm truly proud of.

A giant thank you to Rachel Slomba, an *amazing* photographer and a dear friend of mine. Without you, I would not have my spectacular author portrait. Thanks for such a fun day and an awesome photo shoot. To see more of Rachel's awesome photos, be sure to check out her Instagram @rachelslomba!

To my amazing beta readers and spectacular proofreader, thank you so much for helping my story sparkle and shine and thank you for lending your eyes and ears to me when I needed you.

Mom, thank you for everything. Thank you for being there through the worst moments of my life. Thank you for supporting my wildest dreams and standing by my side until they came to fruition. Even when the world was crumbling around us, you held me together.

To my Tumblr followers, thank you for everything. You guys have been with me for so long and I honestly don't know what I would do without you. Your kind words never fail to make my day, so I hope this book could bring you some happiness, too.

And finally, the biggest thank you to *you*! Yes, you! You lovely reader, you. Thank you for giving this book—and in turn, me—a chance.

About the Author

Morgan Marie Steele is an author from Michigan. She recently graduated from Grand Valley State University with a degree in Film and Video Production and minors in Writing and Women, Gender, and Sexuality Studies.

Morgan started writing she was eight and has been in love with storytelling ever since. Her other published works include *Doing Just Fine*, *Recensere: The Lost Queen*, and *L.O.S.T. and F.O.U.N.D.*. When she's not writing, she spends the majority of her time playing *Skyrim* and watching cheesy rom-coms.

To keep up to date on Morgan's upcoming works, you can follow her on her social media accounts:

Instagram, Twitter, and TikTok: @msteele1212

Facebook: Morgan M. Steele Books

All author-related inquiries should be sent to her email, morganmariesteele@gmail.com. She enjoys doing school visits, both in-person as well as virtually on Zoom.

Support the

Author!

Leave a Review